THE MOURNING SHOW

DICK BELSKY

BERKLEY PRIME CRIME, NEW YORK

If you purchased this book without a cover, you should be aware that this book is stolen property. It was reported as "unsold and destroyed" to the publisher, and neither the author nor the publisher has received any payment for this "stripped book."

This book is a Berkley Prime Crime original edition,
and has never been previously published.

THE MOURNING SHOW

A Berkley Prime Crime Book / published by arrangement with
the author

PRINTING HISTORY
Berkley Prime Crime edition / June 1994

All rights reserved.
Copyright © 1994 by Dick Belsky.
This book may not be reproduced in whole or in part,
by mimeograph or any other means, without permission.
For information address: The Berkley Publishing Group,
200 Madison Avenue, New York, NY 10016.

ISBN: 0-425-14246-9

Berkley Prime Crime Books are published by
The Berkley Publishing Group,
200 Madison Avenue, New York, NY 10016.
The name BERKLEY PRIME CRIME and the BERKLEY PRIME CRIME
design are trademarks belonging to Berkley Publishing Corporation.

PRINTED IN THE UNITED STATES OF AMERICA

10 9 8 7 6 5 4 3 2 1

The world of TV news is totally glamorous. Yeah, right.

Just ask Jenny McKay... She's a TV news reporter in search of a break, a boyfriend, and a reason to feel good about turning forty. The high sleaze and low ratings of New York's WTBK aren't exactly what she aspired to—but hey, it's a living. And when broadcasting turns to crime-solving, she uncovers the city's deadliest secrets.

It's a dirty job—but someone's gotta do it.

READ ALL OF THE JENNY McKAY MYSTERIES by DICK BELSKY

BROADCAST CLUES
A missing heiress. A shocking scandal.
It's the biggest story of Jenny's career.
And it may be her last...

"BELSKY HITS HIS STRIDE WITH THIS FAST-PACED, CYNICALLY WITTY, EXCITING MYSTERY!"
—*Publishers Weekly*

"SEX, MAYHEM, GOSSIP, HEADLINES, EXCLUSIVES, TV DIRT AND SOCIETY JUICE... A FLAVORFUL READ!"
—*New York Post*

"NOT ONLY IS THIS BOOK TOUGH TO PUT DOWN, YOU END UP HOPING BELSKY IS WORKING ON A SEQUEL."
—*Associated Press*

"VIVIDLY RE-CREATES THE GRITTY, DOG-EAT-DOG WORLD OF TV NEWS... A RIVETING THRILLER PENNED BY A NEWS PRO."
—*Star Magazine*

LIVE FROM NEW YORK
Taking a tip from a call girl can only lead to trouble—
as Jenny investigates the rotten core
of the Big Apple: City Hall...

THE MOURNING SHOW
When America's most popular TV talk-show host
is accused of murder, Jenny wonders if the man
she once loved could really be a killer...

MORE MYSTERIES FROM THE
BERKLEY PUBLISHING GROUP...

THE INSPECTOR AND MRS. JEFFRIES: He's with Scotland Yard. She's his housekeeper. Sometimes, her job can be murder...

by Emily Brightwell
THE INSPECTOR AND MRS. JEFFRIES
MRS. JEFFRIES DUSTS FOR CLUES
THE GHOST AND MRS. JEFFRIES
MRS. JEFFRIES TAKES STOCK

JENNY McKAY MYSTERIES: This TV reporter finds out where, when, why... *and* whodunit. "A more streetwise version of television's 'Murphy Brown.'" —*Booklist*

by Dick Belsky
BROADCAST CLUES
LIVE FROM NEW YORK
THE MOURNING SHOW

CAT CALIBAN MYSTERIES: She was married for 38 years. Raised three kids. Compared to that, tracking down killers is easy...

by D. B. Borton
ONE FOR THE MONEY
TWO POINTS FOR MURDER

KATE JASPER MYSTERIES: Even in sunny California, there are cold-blooded killers... "This series is a treasure!" —*Carolyn G. Hart*

by Jaqueline Girdner
ADJUSTED TO DEATH
THE LAST RESORT
MURDER MOST MELLOW
FAT-FREE AND FATAL
TEA-TOTALLY DEAD

RENAISSANCE MYSTERIES: Sigismondo the sleuth courts danger—and sheds light on the darkest of deeds... "Most entertaining!" —*Chicago Tribune*

by Elizabeth Eyre
DEATH OF A DUCHESS

PENNYFOOT HOTEL MYSTERIES: In Edwardian England, death takes a seaside holiday...

by Kate Kingsbury
ROOM WITH A CLUE
DO NOT DISTURB
SERVICE FOR TWO

CHARLOTTE GRAHAM MYSTERIES: She's an actress with a flair for dramatics—and an eye for detection. "You'll get hooked on Charlotte Graham!" —*Rave Reviews*

by Stefanie Matteson
MURDER AT THE SPA
MURDER AT TEATIME
MURDER ON THE CLIFF
MURDER ON THE SILK ROAD
MURDER AT THE FALLS

For Laura

Prologue
Murphy, Mary, and Me

My favorite moment in TV history comes in the very first episode of "The Mary Tyler Moore Show." It's when Mary goes to station WJM to apply for a secretary's job and meets news producer Lou Grant. He asks her religion, and she tells him that's too personal to answer. Then he asks why she's not married, and she blurts out that she's Presbyterian. The next question is even more personal, so she answers the one about marriage. Mary finally gets mad and says he's asking about a lot of things that are none of his business. Lou tells her she's got spunk—but he hates spunk. Finally he offers her a job as associate producer. She's ecstatic until she finds out it pays ten dollars a week less than the secretary's job.

That's basically a microcosm of my entire life.

I mean I've got a lot of answers, but they're not always for the right questions. Even my good qualities tend to annoy people. And when I do get something I want, it's never as good as it seemed.

My name is Jenny McKay, and I'm forty-one years old, single, and a TV reporter. I used to work at a newspaper called the *New York Tribune*. But then people stopped reading or something, and newspapers started disappearing off the face of the earth faster than the ozone layer. Now I work at Channel Six News in New York City, which means I get to say neat stuff like: "Over to you, Liz," and "More details at eleven," and the ever-popular "We're having technical difficulties. Please stand by."

I'm a child of TV.

I grew up watching "Superman," "American Bandstand," and "Leave It to Beaver." I was eleven years old before I knew Superman couldn't really fly. Fifteen before I figured out you couldn't just twitch your nose like Samantha on "Bewitched" and make people disappear. And somewhere around thirty before I accepted the fact that Jim Rockford didn't actually live in a trailer in Malibu, with Rocky and Dennis and Angel dropping by to watch a ball game or go out for tacos. Actually, I'm still not one hundred percent sure about the Rockford thing.

Sometimes people actually tell me they think I'm living in a fantasy world, confusing television with real life. Maybe they're right.

I mean, I do daydream about jumping on the shuttle, flying down to Washington, and hanging out with Murphy Brown. Me, Murphy, Corky, Miles, Jim, and Frank could all have some laughs at Phil's Place. Then we'd go back to Murphy's house and dance to some Temptations music with Eldin.

Maybe Mary could fly in from Minneapolis to join us. And Lois Lane from Metropolis, too.

Sometimes I think Lois was the best of them. Better even than Mary or Murphy. I mean, there was Lois breaking big news stories back in the goddamned 1950s. Hardly any women were allowed to be real reporters in those days. Women covered cooking, fashion, and society news. But not Lois—she beat out Clark, Jimmy, and Perry for scoops on front-page crime stories.

She was journalism's first feminist is what she was.

I was expounding on this and other great thoughts to my friend Clare Lefferts. Clare is a Legal Aid lawyer, who's a full-time friend and a part-time pain in the ass. She's always trying to get me to help her save the world, get married, and clean my apartment. So far, I haven't made a great deal of progress on any front.

"I think I'm going to be to the nineties what Lois Lane was to the fifties, Mary Richards to the seventies, and Murphy Brown to the eighties," I announced.

"Murphy Brown is the nineties," she pointed out.

"Okay, she's the early nineties. I'll take the rest of the decade."

Clare gave me a disgusted look.

"Why are you wasting time working on television?" she asked. "You're a talented writer. You should be writing a great novel, or trying to win a Pulitzer or something important."

"You know what my problem is?" I said. "I just don't care anymore."

"That's not your problem," she told me. "Your problem is you care too much."

I didn't have any answer for that.

We sat there for a while in silence. The way good friends do when there's no need for words. Both of us sensed we were thinking about the same thing.

"Listen, Jen," Clare said finally, a note of concern in her voice, "are you okay now about that business with Meredith and Rivera?"

Meredith and Rivera. Linked together forever for me. Just like Martin and Lewis, Lennon and McCartney, Abbott and Costello. I'd never be able to say one's name without thinking of the other.

"Sure." I smiled. "No problem."

But I was lying, and we both knew it.

I wasn't okay about Meredith and Rivera.

Not at all.

1
Love the Hair, Lose the Hat

I was in the Times Square subway station when I found out Jerry Meredith's wife had been murdered.

It was a hot afternoon in late August, and I was all tuckered out from a tough day of reporting. I'd covered a three-alarm fire in the Bronx that turned out to be a non-story because it was an empty warehouse, a hearing by the city council on municipal waste, and a press conference by a guy in Washington Heights who claimed there was an image of the weeping Jesus on a tree in front of his house. People were flocking there to pray—so the office wanted to check it out. To me, it just looked like a tree.

None of this was exactly making me feel like Diane Sawyer or Barbara Walters. No one cried for me during an interview. No one told me any secrets. No one revealed any scandals. I never ran into John F. Kennedy, Jr., Marla Maples, or anyone who claimed to be one of Bill Clinton's old girlfriends. There might be eight million stories in New York City, but I couldn't seem to find any of them.

I had a plan though. My plan was to go home early, turn on the air conditioner, open an Amstel Light, and cook an intimate, candlelight dinner for the man in my life. It was a good plan, and I was very proud of myself for thinking of it.

There were a couple of snags. First, the air-conditioning in my apartment was broken. Second, I had no food in my refrigerator. Third—and perhaps most problematic—there was no man in my life right now. But I did have the Amstel Light. This could still work for me.

I bought a snow cone from a vendor in the station to try to beat the sweltering heat and made my way to a bank of pay phones on the wall. There was someone asleep in front of one of them. I gingerly stepped over him to get to another phone, dropped a quarter in the slot, and dialed the number for Channel Six.

"McKay here," I said to the switchboard operator who answered. "Get me Kaiser."

Barry Kaiser was the assignment editor who'd sent me up to Washington Heights with a camera crew. After we were finished, he put the crew on another job. So I had to take the Seventh Avenue IRT back into midtown by myself. This did not fill me with love for mankind.

"Who's calling?" the operator asked.

"McKay."

"Ray?"

"McKay. Jenny McKay. I work there."

"Sorry, Miss McKay. I'm new here."

"No problem. I'm in a hurry though, huh . . ."

"Hold on please. I'll get Mr. Kaiser."

While I waited, I amused myself by counting the number of potential mass murderers I could see in the station. There was a kid hassling riders for change on the subway platform; a wild-eyed, bearded man involved in a loud political argument—with himself; and Rip van Winkle snoring peacefully on the ground a few feet away from me. I was up to either sixteen or seventeen, depending on whether or not you counted the guy who sold me the snow cone, when Kaiser came on the line.

"Jesus, Barry, what took you so long? I'm standing here watching a casting call for 'America's Most Wanted.' "

"I'm glad you called in, Jenny. I've got an idea."

"Me too."

I started to tell him about my Amstel plan, but he cut me off.

"Eileen Clayton is dead," Kaiser said.

"The one with all the money?"

"She was found bludgeoned to death in her penthouse apartment on Park Avenue, near Sixty-first Street. The word is they're about to arrest her husband. The guy on TV in the morning. Jerry . . ."

"Meredith." I tried to make my voice sound calm.

"You know him, right?"

I knew Jerry Meredith. He hosted "The Morning Show"—one of those talk programs that people go on to tell how they cheat on their spouses, hate their father, or like to dress up like Little Bo Peep before having sex. *People* magazine called him the new Donahue. He was also married to one of the richest women in the world, worth an estimated $800 million to $1 billion. And ten years ago, I'd had a love affair with him that ended badly. These facts were not necessarily listed in their order of significance.

Kaiser cleared his throat nervously. "People say that you and he had a thing together . . ."

"That was a long time ago."

"Well, Pesin thinks it's good for us. He wants you on this story. He figures it might give us an advantage over the competition." Kaiser paused, then added with a snicker, "Just don't wear a hat."

I sighed. I was going to have to live with the hat jokes for a long time.

Donald Pesin was our new news director. He was a hotshot who'd been brought in to try to turn the station's ratings around. He'd only started a few days ago, and I barely knew him. But he'd already buried us under a blizzard of memos.

Pesin was very big on memos. And slogans. He was the kind of guy who posted stuff on the bulletin board like: "If you anticipate success, you will find success. If you anticipate failure, you will only find failure."

My only direct contact with him so far was a memo he had sent me. I'd decided to try out a new look for the camera. So I splurged for a two-hundred-dollar perm at one of those fancy places on Madison Avenue that promises to make you look like Cindy Crawford. Then I went out and bought a hat. A nifty white one with a wide brim. I wanted to make a fashion statement. I figured the hat could maybe become my trademark. Sort of like Hedda Hopper, Bella Abzug, or Garth Brooks.

I only got to wear it once, during a live remote we did from outside the Manhattan Criminal Court building. It was a windy day, and my new hat kept threatening to blow away. First I tried to pull it down tighter on my head. Then I put one hand up to it. By the end of the newscast, they tell me I was pretty much holding on with both hands for dear life.

The next day when I got to work there was a brief memo from Pesin on my desk: "Love the hair. Lose the hat."

I changed the subject back to Jerry Meredith. "This is a little uncomfortable for me," I said. "It's kind of personal. Maybe you should get somebody else."

"Pesin wants you."

"Yeah, but . . ."

"Jenny, the cops are up talking to Meredith at the apartment now. The word is they're going to walk him out soon, take him down to the station house to book him for murder. That could be our chance for a . . ."

"Video opportunity," I said.

"Exactly. I've got a crew on the way, you can meet them there. Now get going."

I thought about grabbing a taxi, but the subway would probably be faster. I took the shuttle to Grand Central, then the Lexington Avenue local up to 59th Street. The uptown line was packed. The only place I could find to sit was wedged between a teenaged girl holding a large blaring radio and a middle-aged man reading a Jehovah's Witness pamphlet. I took the seat.

As we rumbled along, I tried to imagine Jerry Meredith as a murderer. It's kinda creepy to think about someone you once made love to taking another person's life. Was he the type? Not the Jerry Meredith I knew ten years ago. But people change. And anyway, love is blind.

When we pulled into the 51st Street station, the guy with the Jehovah's Witness reading material got off. His seat was taken by another teenager with a radio, this one playing something even louder. It made an interesting mix with the other noise. Sort of a stereo effect. I went back to thinking about Jerry Meredith.

He wasn't famous when I knew him. We were both reporters at the *Tribune* then, me on the city side and him in the business department. He wasn't a very good business reporter. But he was good-looking, personable, and women loved him—the perfect combination for TV. So Channel Seven hired him away, and within a year he was the anchorman there. Now he's a national household word.

Our affair was over a long time before that. I fell hard for him, but he was just passing time. We went our separate ways. I ran into him a year or two ago when I was covering some big society function. His wife was leading him around the room, showing him off like he was a trophy she'd won in a sailing race in the Hamptons over the weekend. We said hello, smiled at each other, and made awkward small talk for a few minutes. It was all very civilized.

The train squealed into the 59th Street station. I got off and pushed my way through the crowd on the platform toward the exit.

This is really no big deal, I thought to myself. Okay, I slept with the guy. We had this thing together. And then it was over. So what? Time heals all wounds. I was older and wiser now.

That's when I saw it. A huge ad for "The Morning Show" posted on the wall of the subway station: *You'll laugh, you'll cry, you'll get mad. It all happens every morning with Jerry Meredith.* There was a smiling photo of America's hottest daytime host looking down at me.

For just a second all the memories came rushing back. The sleepless nights. The frantic phone calls. The pain. The anger. Then it was all gone, just as quickly as it came.

"Yep, McKay," I told myself as I started up the steps and headed toward Park Avenue, "you're a lot older and wiser now."

Well, I was older anyway.

2
Blood on the Tracks

Park Avenue and 61st is only about a mile or two away from Times Square, but it might as well be in another universe.

Times Square is what New York City is really all about. It's dazzling, scary, fast-paced, and packed with excitement. Broadway theaters, street people, porn emporiums, tourist haunts. A few years ago the city launched an effort to clean the place up. They want to build new glass office buildings and get rid of a lot of the tawdry little businesses they think are an eyesore on the 42nd Street strip. Somehow that depresses me.

This part of Park Avenue, on the other hand, was like something out of one of those movies about New York from the fifties and sixties. Stately buildings. Quiet streets. Successful-looking people. You almost expected to run into Rock Hudson or Cary Grant or Doris Day. There was little sign of the New York City of the nineties—crime, drugs, poverty, AIDS. It would have seemed hard to believe things had changed at all.

Except that someone had murdered Eileen Clayton.

I didn't have any trouble finding the place where Jerry Meredith and Eileen Clayton lived. That's because I have a nose for news, a keen sense of direction, and an unflinching eye for detail. It's also because there was an army of press camped out in front. Reporters, photographers, press cars, mobile vans, video cameras, and even a helicopter hovering overhead. It looked like a staging area for the invasion of Normandy.

The Channel Six News crew consisted of Alan Sanders, the cameraman, and Artie Jacobson, who handled the sound. Sanders was young, black, and convinced he was just marking time until he got a break as a film director. He saw himself as the new Spike Lee. Jacobson, on the other hand, was in his late fifties and counting the days until retirement. I once asked him what his favorite part of the job was. "Lunch," he said.

They weren't hard to find. Sanders had the radio in the Channel Six NewsCenter mobile van turned up to full volume and playing rap music. He was talking to a young blond girl wearing a T-shirt that said CNN on the front.

"Yo, Jenny," Sanders said when he saw me. "What's happening?"

I shrugged. "You tell me."

"I gotta go to work," he said to the girl. "Catch you later. Maybe you and me can go check out some of those fine soul food restaurants we have in Harlem."

The girl smiled and walked away. She was wearing a tight pair of jeans and swiveled her hips as she moved. Sanders watched intently until she was out of sight. Then he turned toward me.

"Yo?" I asked.

"White girls like that jive talk," he told me. He was speaking perfect English now. "They like black men. Men who are bad. Who grew up on the mean streets of the city."

"Did you happen to mention to her that the mean street you grew up on was a suburban cul-de-sac in Larchmont and that your father makes $250,000 a year as a corporate lawyer for Exxon?"

"Seriously, do you think she bought it?"

"Absolutely. You sounded like a real homeboy. I did think

the soul food in Harlem might have been a bit much though."

I walked over to the van and turned down the volume on the radio. Jacobson was sitting inside working on a crossword puzzle. He did crossword puzzles all day long. The *New York Times*. The *Daily News*. The *Post*. When he was finished with them, he started on the scrambled words. Sometimes he even did the Connect the Dots on the children's page. He was always in his own little world.

"Wasn't that music driving you nuts?" I asked.

Jacobson looked up at me blankly. "What music?" he said. Then he went back to his crossword puzzle.

There were police cars parked out on the street and a couple of uniformed cops standing guard at the front door of Meredith's building. A crowd had gathered to see what all the excitement was about. There was even a guy with a cart and umbrella selling hot dogs. It was like a picnic.

"So what's the deal?" I asked Sanders.

"They're supposed to bring Meredith out in about twenty minutes. There's a lady ADA and a couple of detectives upstairs talking to him now."

I looked over at the cops by the door. "Anyone we know here?"

"A detective lieutenant named Jellinek. Remember him?"

I remembered Norm Jellinek, all right. We'd had a big fight at a crime scene about six months ago. He told us to shut off our camera. We said we would, but we didn't. The film ran on the six o'clock news that night, and he blew up at me.

"Maybe he's forgotten all about that by now," I suggested.

"It's possible," Sanders said.

I wandered over toward the front of the building and scouted around for Jellinek. He was standing off to the side, staring at the crowd that had gathered. I made a quick visit to the hot dog guy and bought a couple of dogs and some sodas. Then I walked over to Jellinek.

"Hi, Lieutenant," I said.

He whirled around and made a face when he saw me. "Oh, no," he groaned. "That's all I need. It's the worst goddamn day of my life, and now I get the final touch. The bigmouthed, brown-haired bitch from hell is here."

I had a feeling he might still be a little upset at me. A woman can sense that sort of thing.

"Here's a peace offering." I held out one of the hot dogs.

"A hot dog? That's supposed to make me forget about all the trouble you caused?"

"It's a great dog," I said. "Mustard. Sauerkraut. Mmmm . . . good."

Jellinek was a huge man, maybe six foot four and weighing around two hundred and fifty pounds. I knew from experience he was one of the world's greatest living receptacles for junk food. He looked at the hot dog in my hand, then grabbed it. I handed him a soda too. He took a big gulp from the bottle, then devoured half my peace offering in two bites.

"What's this going to cost me?" he asked, wiping mustard off his face.

"Just a little civility. Be nice to me. That bigmouthed, brown-haired bitch remark really hurt."

"All right, I'm sorry about that," Jellinek said. He took another bite. "Your hair isn't all that brown. It's more like dirty blond."

Well, at least he didn't seem mad anymore. McKay, you charmer, you. One hot dog and you've got him eating out of your hand. I guess the way to a man's heart really is through his stomach.

"Tell me what happened."

"Why not? It's all nice and neat and simple. Maid comes to work this morning, lets herself in and finds Eileen Clayton—all $800 million of her—dead. ME's still looking at it, but it looks like she had her skull crushed in by a model train engine worth maybe ten thousand dollars. Classy way to go, huh?"

"Who owns a model train engine worth ten thousand dollars?"

"Jerry Meredith. He's one of those train freaks. Got a whole hobby room up there with miles of track, little buildings and people alongside, and collectors' versions of all the great train lines in history."

"That's where she died?"

"Yeah, she was lying across the tracks right between the Orient Express and the Sante Fe Limited."

"You have landed on the Reading Railroad," I muttered. "Do not pass Go. Do not collect two hundred dollars. Do not do anything because you are dead."

Jellinek just grunted.

"And you figure Meredith did it?" I asked.

"He and his wife had been fighting, people tell us. We've got witnesses to that. Both here and at the TV station."

"Not bad for a start," I agreed.

"There's more. Meredith comes up a little short in the alibi department. He can't tell us where he was all night. He swears he's innocent. But all he knows is he showed up at home this morning and found out his wife was dead."

"Strike two," I said.

"Here's the best one. Eileen Clayton's lawyer says she called him yesterday. Wanted to change her will and start divorce proceedings against Meredith. She said she was throwing him out once and for all."

Jellinek finished off the hot dog and threw the wrapper onto the street. A breeze picked it up and carried it down the block. I wondered if I should point out to him that there was a fifty-dollar fine for littering. I decided not to.

"So there it is," he said. "Meredith had the motive, he had the means, and he had the opportunity. It's all nice and simple." He made a snorting sound. "So simple it stinks."

"You're not sure he did it?" I asked.

"It just seems too pat. We don't even have to do any investigating on this one. Someone handed it to us on a silver platter."

"I don't think he did it either," I said.

"Why?"

"I know Jerry Meredith. At least I used to. I don't see him as a killer."

He looked up toward the penthouse apartment and shook his head. "You know Katherine Grieco?"

"She's an assistant district attorney," I said. "Supposed to be a real hotshot. They call her Tiger Lady in the newspapers."

"Right. I guess you read her clips. Well, that makes two of you. You and her. Anyway, she's been assigned to this case. You should see her face. It's like letting a little kid loose in a candy store."

"She thinks it's good publicity for her?"

"Are you kidding? Talk show host murders his rich society wife. They'll make a TV movie about this one. This is going to make Ms. Grieco a very important national figure. All she has to do is put Meredith behind bars. And that shouldn't be too tough."

"What if he isn't guilty?" I asked.

"You want to know something? I asked Katherine Grieco the same question upstairs before."

"What was her response?"

Jellinek smiled. "I'm standing down here, ain't I?"

There was some activity going on now by the front door of the building. The press corps got ready to swing into action. "It's show time," Jellinek said.

They brought Meredith out a few minutes later. His wrists were handcuffed in front of him and he had a dazed look on his face. Like a man in a bad dream who just couldn't seem to wake up. He didn't look much like the calm, self-assured guy people watched on TV. Or like the man I remembered from ten years ago.

The police cars waiting to take him downtown were parked across the street and about halfway down the block. That meant Meredith had to walk through a gauntlet of press to get there. Katherine Grieco was right beside him. Like Jellinek said, the assistant DA was milking this for all the publicity she could get.

What she didn't count on, though, was what happened next.

Meredith stared straight ahead as he walked, with cameras going off and reporters shouting questions. He didn't respond to any of it. Then, as he walked past me and the Channel

Six crew, I called out his name. That's when he went to pieces.

He whirled around, and his eyes met mine. I guess I was like a life preserver in a sea of sharks. A friendly face. Someone who could gently wake him from his horrible nightmare. He broke away from the cops momentarily and moved toward me.

"Jenny, I didn't do it!" he shouted. "You've got to tell people that. I didn't kill her."

He was standing right in front of me now. He seemed frantic. Grieco screamed at the cops to keep him moving. Sanders and Jacobson were recording the whole scene on film.

"Why are they arresting you?" I asked.

"I don't know. I don't know anything. I just came home and they told me she was dead. I can't believe it. I'm not a murderer. You know that. You've got to make them believe me."

"Jerry, were you and your wife getting a divorce?"

He completely broke down now and started crying. He tried to reach out to me with his hands in the cuffs.

"I didn't kill her," he sobbed. "I swear I didn't kill her..."

Two cops grabbed him now and hauled him toward the waiting cars, with Katherine Grieco running right behind. They pushed his head down and shoved him into the backseat of a police cruiser. Then the cars squealed away from the curb and raced off with sirens blaring.

Sanders kept the film rolling until their flashing red lights were out of sight.

"Ho-boy," he said. "I think we've got ourselves a scoop."

3
Delta Burke Dieted for My Sins

I was living on the eleventh floor of a gleaming new highrise off Union Square.

They'd torn down my old place on the Lower East Side to make room for an office complex, as part of some urban renewal project. The owners tried to fight it in court, but the city got a lot of high-priced lawyers who convinced a judge it was needed for progress. I wandered by the new place the other day and checked out the directory in the lobby. Nearly all the offices were rented to high-priced lawyers. Just what New York City needs a lot of.

The urban renewal crowd had already been to Union Square. The place where I'm at used to be Klein's Department Store. It was a big old-fashioned landmark building where women who took the bus in from Brooklyn or the Bronx would buy clothes for their families at low prices. Now it was forty floors packed with Yuppies and stores selling goat cheese, designer everything and cappuccino.

Somehow I didn't think all this was exactly a huge step forward for civilization.

My apartment was a sublet I'd gotten from a guy at NBC who'd been assigned to Rome for two years. It had two bedrooms, a living room, kitchen, and a view facing north toward the Empire State Building. I'd turned one of the bedrooms into a study complete with desk, filing cabinet, and a computer. I bought the computer a year ago so I could write my Great American Novel. But so far all I'd done on it was play Where in the World Is Carmen Sandiego?

The place may not exactly be *House Beautiful*, but we call it home.

We is me and Hobo. Hobo's my dog. He's a black and tan dachshund that Tony, an actor I used to live with, found on the street. Tony split not long after that to go to Hollywood, and I got the dog. The last I heard, Tony was waiting tables at Spago, hoping someone would discover him as the new Tom Cruise. All things considered, I think I got the best of the deal.

Hobo and I talk together (well, I talk, and he listens), eat together, and sleep together. It's sort of like being married, only you don't have to worry about shaving cream in the sink every morning.

Hobo and I have this little ritual. Whenever I come home, I tell him a joke. Dog experts say this is good because the animal picks up your positive vibes and feels happy. What do I know about dog psychology? I just like to have a captive audience for my jokes.

I opened the door after finishing the Jerry Meredith story and Hobo ran to greet me. I said to him:

Okay, this guy goes into a doctor's office and complains he can't hear. The doctor tells him he needs to wear a hearing aid.

"Don't worry," the doctor assures him. "A hearing aid will solve all your problems. I use one myself."

"What kind is it?" the guy asks.

The doctor checks his watch. "Ten minutes after four," he says.

I laughed loudly and bent down to pet him. Hobo wagged his tail and licked my face.

After putting on his leash, I took him out for a walk. We went over to the park on 15th Street, made our way over to Broadway on the west side and then up to the Farmers' Market at 17th Street, where they sell fresh fruits and vegetables. I bought tomatoes, onions, and lettuce there and some eggs and mozzarella cheese at a deli on the corner.

When I got back, I clicked on the TV. I always have the TV on when I'm in the house. It's as natural as breathing for me. My TV schlock threshold is very high. I can watch virtually anything—"Gilligan's Island," "The Brady Bunch," "Three's Company." Except for "The Facts of Life." The minute I hear the theme song for "The Facts of Life" I leap for the remote control. I mean, you've got to draw the line somewhere.

What I wanted to see was myself. I'd set my VCR to record the six o'clock news. I rewound the tape now, pressed play and suddenly the WTBK News logo appeared on the screen:

ANNOUNCER: From the Channel Six Newsroom in New York, it's the News at Six on Six. With the Channel Six team of newsbreakers: Conroy Jackson and Liz St. John at the anchor desk; Chip Forte with the sports; and Stormy Phillips with the Action Six weather forecast. And now here's Conroy and Liz with what's happening.

The picture cut to their smiling faces.

Conroy Jackson is one of those Ted Baxter types of newscasters who've been around for twenty-five years and still have no clue what's going on. He's very distinguished-looking, sounds good, and our demographic surveys show the viewers trust him. He pretty much just reads the news. When he does ad-lib, it makes news directors want to jump out of high windows.

Liz St. John is our little piece of mindless fluff, a blond Barbie doll that every newscast in the country seems to think it needs for ratings these days. Liz is an ex-beauty contest winner and an ex-model who gives new meaning to the term "dumb blonde." Remember all those dumb blonde jokes that were making the rounds a while back. (Q: What do you call a blonde with half a brain? A: Gifted.) I think they started with Liz.

> **JACKSON:** Our top story tonight is the arrest of "Morning Show" host Jerry Meredith for the murder of his wife, real estate and business tycoon Eileen Clayton. Meredith's TV show—with a winning combination of talk and tabloid—ranks right up there in the latest ratings with "Oprah" and "Donahue." But none of his shows compare with the bizarre real-life saga that unfolded on Park Avenue.

God, I thought to myself, it's so obvious he's just reading that off a teleprompter.

> **ST. JOHN:** The bludgeoned body of Eileen Clayton was found this morning in her penthouse apartment by a maid arriving for work.

They went to a shot of the building.

> **ST. JOHN:** Our Jenny McKay was there when police arrested Jerry Meredith, and she has this exclusive interview.

I watched the scene of Meredith being led out of the building in handcuffs. The reporters shouting questions. The confusion. And then Meredith turning right into our camera to talk to me.

On TV it seemed even more dramatic than it had been. Sanders had really captured the look of panic and pleading in Meredith's face as he talked to me.

"Jenny, I didn't do it!" he screamed from the TV. "You've got to tell people that. I didn't kill her."

I put the recorder on freeze-frame and studied the picture

closely. His face. His expression. The way he tried to reach out to me. Then I rewound the tape and watched all over again. I'm not sure what I was looking for. A clue. A hint about what was really happening. Or maybe I just liked to see the two of us on the screen together.

I fast-forwarded the tape to where I was doing the wrap-up after they took Meredith to police headquarters.

McKAY: Channel Six News has learned that police are investigating reports that Mrs. Clayton had initiated divorce proceedings just before she died. A police source also told me that they had physical evidence linking Meredith to the crime. This is Jenny McKay, reporting live from the murder scene on Park Avenue.

The picture went back to Liz St. John and Conroy Jackson. They both gave more details on the story, then ran a thirty-second sound bite of a police spokesman saying Jerry Meredith had been booked, fingerprinted, and jailed on a murder charge.

When it was over, Conroy turned to Liz and said:

JACKSON: Speaking of murder, how about that weather out there today?

ST. JOHN: It's a killer, all right. It's really hot.

JACKSON: (imitating vintage Johnny Carson) How hot is it, Liz?

ST. JOHN: (laughing) That's what we're going to find out from our own Stormy Phillips. We'll be right back.

Then a successful-looking woman came on the screen, telling me how she was always on the go—being a mother, a wife, and a Fortune 500 executive. "I work hard, so I need a hardworking deodorant..."

I clicked off the VCR and made myself dinner.

I broke open three eggs, mixed them together with milk, vegetable salt, and pepper and poured the whole thing into an omelet pan. While that was cooking, I peeled off some lettuce and sliced a tomato and put them into a wooden salad bowl with low-cal Thousand Island dressing on top. By now the omelet was getting fluffy, so I dropped a few slices of mozzarella cheese and some chopped-up onion in the middle and folded it in half. Then I let it all cook for another minute or so until the cheese was melted. I thought about stuffing the thing with sour cream, too, but decided not to. I mean, I like Delta Burke, but I don't want to look like her.

I actually have this picture of Delta Burke taped to the door of my refrigerator. From her last days on "Designing Women." I mean, we're talking blimp here. Fat city. Thunder thighs. Stick her in a ring and she could be a sumo wrestler.

Now she goes on diets and exercise programs all the time, but none of it does any good. She's too far gone. Everywhere she goes, people talk about her weight. Comedians make jokes about it. The tabloids have a field day with her. So I leave the picture on the refrigerator door in case I get tempted to pig out. Seeing Delta in full figure makes me a lot more careful.

I took an Amstel Light out of the refrigerator, unscrewed the top, and carried it and the meal into the living room. I turned on the TV while I ate. "Murphy Brown" was on. Murphy was having an ethical dilemma about whether or not to reveal one of her sources. Me, I didn't have any ethical dilemmas. I barely had any sources. I took a sip of the Amstel and wondered how many fewer calories there really were in light beer.

The telephone rang. I turned down the sound on the TV and picked up the receiver.

"Hi, star," the voice on the other end said. "I caught you on the Six." It was Clare Lefferts. "So how'd you get that exclusive with Jerry Meredith?" she asked.

"I was just in the right place at the right time," I said modestly.

"Which is unusual for you," Clare pointed out. "You used to know Meredith, right? Before I met you."

"Yeah."

"Didn't you date him or something?"

"Sort of."

"Was it serious?"

I was starting to get exasperated. "Why is everyone making such a big deal out of this? I went out with the guy ten years ago. We slept together a couple of times. Then we went our separate ways and got on with our lives. We're not talking fucking Romeo and Juliet here."

There was silence on the other end.

"Jeez, Clare," I said finally, "did that sound like I was overreacting just a little bit?"

"A little."

"Sorry. I guess it did shake me up. I mean, I never thought of the guy as a murderer."

"Maybe he's innocent."

"You think everyone's innocent," I told her. "If you defended Charles Manson, you'd say he was just the victim of an unhappy family life."

Clare chuckled. "Not Manson. But maybe Squeaky Fromme. Listen, Jen, I have a good story for you to cover."

"I already have a good story. Jerry Meredith."

"Hear me out on this. There's a young woman in the Bronx..."

"Who's been terribly wronged by society."

"Exactly. She's in jail for stabbing her husband."

"That is against the law," I pointed out.

"The son of a bitch beat her up. He raped her after she refused to have sex with him when he was drunk. He held her hand over a gas burner as punishment for trying to run away. He made her life a nightmare. And then one day she stood up to him and defended herself. This woman symbolizes every battered wife in this country. If you interviewed her on TV, we could mobilize public support and make her an issue for..."

"Clare, I don't have time for this now. I'm working on a big story. Jerry Meredith's a very important person. So was his dead wife . . ."

"And some poor girl from the Bronx isn't?"

I sighed. "I'm going to hang up now and finish my dinner. If you want to try to right all the wrongs of society, more power to you. Me, I have enough trouble just keeping my own head above water."

"Can I say one more thing?" Clare asked.

"Go ahead."

She took a deep breath. "Her name is Elaine Rivera. She's being held at the Women's Prison on Rikers Island. You could visit her there any weekday from nine to five or on weekends until eight."

I didn't say anything.

"I figured sooner or later you'd want to know," she told me. "Just promise me you'll at least think about talking to her when you get a chance. Okay?"

"Okay, I'll think about it."

After I hung up with Clare, I had a serious decision to make. I'd already drunk one bottle of the Amstel Light with dinner. I had three bottles left in the refrigerator. If I rationed them carefully, I could make them last through the night. I'd drink one during the end of "Murphy Brown," another during "Northern Exposure," and save the last one for the eleven o'clock news. The only problem was that by the time "Northern Exposure" came on, I'd already drunk two more of the beers. I wondered if I should just go ahead and drink the last one right away. Or, I wondered, should I save it for the news? I also wondered if I was becoming an alcoholic.

I solved the problem by falling asleep in front of the TV.

It was a restless sleep. I dreamed I was assigned to cover a prison execution. There was a man strapped into an electric chair with a hood over his head. Someone yanked off the hood—it was Jerry Meredith. Meredith was looking at me with that same pleading look he had outside his apartment house.

"You've got to tell them I didn't do it," Jerry Meredith said. "That they're executing an innocent man."

Suddenly he broke free from the straps and reached out to me with his hand.

I screamed and pulled away. That's when I woke up.

Hobo was snoring peacefully at my feet. I got up from the couch, went into the kitchen, and found a pint of chocolate marshmallow ice cream in the freezer. My secret vice. I didn't even bother to put it into a dish. I just mainlined it with a spoon right out of the carton.

Forgive me, Delta, for I have sinned.

Then I gave Hobo his last walk and went to bed. I didn't dream any more that night.

4
Deadline U.S.A.

At 9:55 a.m. I was sitting in front of the midtown Manhattan Public Library on Fifth Avenue, reading the morning papers through a pair of oversized sunglasses and waiting for the front doors to open.

I was drinking a cup of coffee out of a foam container that I'd bought at a bagel shop on 41st Street. I'd managed to get out without buying any of the bagels. I was very proud of myself for that. I'd probably be even prouder if I hadn't stopped in the doughnut shop next door. Temptation, thy name is junk food.

I had on a brown patterned, ankle-length skirt, chocolate-colored blouse, and a rust-colored vest with rawhide fringe. I also was wearing beige sandals, a wide leather belt with a gold Western-style buckle, and big O-shaped earrings. I looked funky. Definitely funky. In fact, if I looked any funkier I could probably get a job as a veejay on MTV.

I'd come to the library to find out more about what Jerry Meredith and Eileen Clayton had been doing the past few years. I figured this was the best place to start.

At ten o'clock, a security guard with a ring of keys appeared, put one of them into the lock, and opened up the portals of knowledge. I dropped my coffee cup into a receptacle that said "Keep New York Clean" and walked inside.

There's a computer in the reference room on the second floor that lists all the newspaper and magazine articles written about someone. I found my way up to it, got comfortable, and punched in the name "Jerry Meredith." The screen went blank for a second, and then a long list of articles appeared. "Jesus," I muttered to myself, "this guy gets a lot of publicity."

Eileen Clayton had gotten even more: a lot of coverage in *Business Week* and the *Wall Street Journal* and financial publications I'd never heard of.

I diligently copied down all the data about the articles onto a yellow legal pad and took it up to the librarian's desk. A young girl with a bored expression sat there putting polish on her fingernails. I handed her the list of publications.

"Five at a time," she said, without breaking her concentration.

For a second, I thought she was talking about her fingers. But then I saw the sign: "Only five periodicals will be issued at one time."

"A lot of these are the same magazine, just different issues," I pointed out. "You could save me a lot of time if . . ."

"Five at a time," she repeated.

She still hadn't taken her eyes off her fingernails, which were now a bright pink.

I sighed, waited until she gave me the first five magazines on the list, and then walked over to a desk to read the articles. When I was finished, I brought them back and got five more. And so forth. I told myself it was good exercise. Probably work off some of the calories from that doughnut.

When put together, the articles told the impressive success story of Jerry Meredith. Some of it I knew, a lot of it I hadn't kept up with. He was forty-three years old and had been married three times. The first marriage was when he was twenty-two years old to a woman named Barbara Ann Forbes in Trenton, New Jersey, where he worked as a cub reporter on the *Trentonian* newspaper. They had two kids—a boy and a girl. Funny, he never mentioned anything to me about that when we were dating. I wondered how many other things he hadn't told me.

Wife number two was Janet Hutchings, a model who had appeared on the covers of *Vogue, Cosmopolitan*, and a number of other fashion magazines a while back. There were pictures of her with Jerry Meredith at Studio 54 and at a party thrown by Andy Warhol. A few years later she divorced Meredith, citing "adultery, mental cruelty, and emotional anguish." Something about coming home early from a photo shoot and finding him auditioning a pair of twenty-two-year-old actresses in their marital bed.

Then came the marriage to Eileen Clayton, which quickly turned into a national media event. They were written up in the gossip columns, *People, New York* magazine—and "Lifestyles of the Rich and Famous" even did a profile on them. Handsome TV anchorman marries richest woman in the country. It was beautiful. Better than Phil and Marlo, or Maury and Connie, or Donald and Marla.

The more recent clips talked about Meredith's meteoric rise as a talk show host. He'd stopped doing local news to start a talk show in New York. About a year ago, it had gone national, and he was now the hottest daytime host since Oprah.

"Some of the critics said that Jerry got his big break because of my money," Eileen Clayton said in one interview. "Well, you can't buy that kind of popularity. TV viewers are smart, they know what they like. And they like Jerry."

There was also some personal stuff about how much she and Jerry wanted a baby. She was forty-two and had never had one. Jerry sometimes talked to his TV audience about it, sharing some of the different methods, diets, and doctors' advice they were using to try and get her pregnant. But nothing ever happened.

Business Week and some of the other financial magazines told the story of Eileen Clayton's fortune. When she was nineteen, she'd inherited $10 million after her mother and father died in a plane crash. In twenty-three years, she'd parlayed that into a fortune estimated to be somewhere between $800 million and $1.2 billion. She owned a chain of department stores, a cosmetics conglomerate, a movie studio, TV stations, and massive amounts of ritzy real estate in New York City and around the world.

A lot of the articles used terms like *leveraged buyouts, stock options,* and *rollovers* that I didn't really understand. But I knew what a billion dollars meant. They also said she ruled her empire with an iron fist. There were stories of firings, humiliation of employees, and constant complaining if things weren't done to perfection. You had to grovel to work for Eileen Clayton, according to people who worked for her.

I wondered if her husband had had to grovel too. And how he felt about that.

By the time I was finished it was past noon and my stomach was starting to make strange sounds. The doughnut alone was enough to cause me gastronomical distress, but not filling enough to get me through lunch. I left the library, bought some newspapers, and walked up Fifth Avenue to a McDonald's. I ordered a Big Mac, some Chicken McNuggets, and a diet Coke and read the stories about Jerry Meredith's arrest while I ate.

Most of them mentioned me and the interview outside the apartment house. The *Post* even ran a picture of me with my microphone in Meredith's face. Wow, I was famous. I looked around the McDonald's and saw maybe a half dozen other people reading the *Post* too. I wondered if they recognized me.

Somehow I made it outside again without having to sign any autographs, found a pay phone, and dialed the number for the *Daily News*. I know a guy there named Jack Weinstein who writes a TV column. He owed me a favor or two from the days when we worked on the *Tribune* together.

A secretary said Weinstein was in a meeting. I gave her my name and said to tell him it was an emergency. A minute later, he came on the line.

"What kind of emergency?" he asked.

"A gastronomical one."

"What are you talking about?"

"I just ate a Big Mac and some Chicken McNuggets. And I had a doughnut too." I made a belching sound into the receiver. "Stop me before I eat again."

Weinstein laughed. "How ya doin', Jenny?"

"I need some help on a story. Can I stop by and talk to you?"

He said that would be fine. I walked over to the *Daily News* building on 42nd Street and then took the elevator up to their editorial offices.

Weinstein was sitting at his desk, waiting for me. "So how's the exciting world of TV journalism?" he asked after we exchanged hugs and I sat down.

"Exciting. How are you?"

"Well," he said, "the paper's almost gone out of business three times in the past few years. We've also had more gloomy warnings and dire predictions than I can count. Every day I come here, I expect there's going to be a padlock on the door and I'll have to go out and work for a living. But here I am."

"I remember when the *Tribune* folded," I told him. "You said you were finished with the business. You said you'd never let a newspaper break your heart again."

"It's a dying business, all right. Like being a blacksmith at the turn of the century and watching cars take over the roads. People don't need newspapers anymore. They don't read. They get their information in quick thirty-second sound bites on TV."

"Name the greatest newspaper movie of all time," I said.

He smiled. It was a game we used to play on slow days in the city room.

"*The Front Page*," he said. "The original as well as *His Girl Friday*, the remake with Cary Grant and Rosalind Russell. Forget about the one in the seventies with Walter Matthau and Jack Lemmon."

"*Deadline U.S.A.*," I told him.

"I forgot about that one."

"Humphrey Bogart is the managing editor of a newspaper that's going to fold the next day. God, I love that one."

"*All the President's Men*," Weinstein offered.

"Second place."

"I mean, it's got Robert Redford and Dustin Hoffman as reporters . . ."

"How about Jason Robards as Ben Bradlee? Wouldn't you love to have an editor like Jason Robards?"

We swapped more old newspaper tales for a while and then we got around to the Jerry Meredith story.

"You know much about him?" I asked.

"I'm a TV critic these days," he said, "not a reporter. I pretty much just watch shows and do reviews of them. Of course, I do hear things . . ."

"Like what?"

"Like Jerry had an eye for the ladies."

"Surprise, surprise."

"Huh?"

"Nothing. I used to know him. Any specifics?"

He shrugged. "People saw him out late at night. There are stories of him sneaking in and out of clubs with different women on his arm—none of them Eileen Clayton. There was also a rumor he was having an affair with someone on the set of his show."

"Who?"

"I don't know. Some production assistant, I heard. It's all just talk. But there was enough of it to make me think he wasn't being totally faithful to his marital vows."

"Do you think Eileen Clayton knew about any of this?"

"Apparently not. He was supposed to be very paranoid about that. I heard he signed some sort of prenuptial agreement where she could throw him out on the street with nothing."

"Well, at least he'd still have the TV show."

"I'm not sure about that. It was syndicated by an outfit called Vision World Features and made about fifty million a year. Now guess who owns Vision World Features?"

"Clayton Enterprises?"

"R-i-i-i-ght."

"So Eileen Clayton really had him by the balls, didn't she?"

"You might say that."

"Anything else?"

"There was some suggestion that Jerry Meredith was a little short of cash."

"How can a guy who's married to a billion dollars be short of cash?"

"When his wife's Eileen Clayton and she doles it out like an allowance. Anyway, I heard there supposedly were some tough guys hanging around the set talking to him. The word is he owed them money or something."

"For what?"

"Who knows? Drugs. Gambling. Maybe high-priced hookers." He waved his hand. "It's all just gossip. Hell, I don't know if any of it's true."

"Let's say it is. Where is his wife during all this? Just sitting home alone at night waiting by the window for Jerry?"

"Not exactly. Eileen Clayton was a busy lady too."

"You mean . . . ?"

"I had a drink one night with a guy who worked for her corporation. He got a little plastered and told me more than he should have. He said that when she went on business trips to Los Angeles his job was to fix her up with companionship for the night."

"With men?"

"Uh-huh. Big, beefy, hunky, muscular types. That's what she liked."

"What about in New York?"

"The same thing. She was seeing some guy named Bobby who worked at one of those clubs where guys dance naked for women . . ."

"You mean like Chippendale's?" I asked.

"Yeah."

"Did Jerry know about him?"

"Not according to this guy I was talking to."

"So Jerry Meredith is running around with other women, and Eileen Clayton's dirty dancing with some stud, and neither has any idea what the other one is up to."

"That's about the size of it."

"Oh, what a tangled web we weave," I said.

5
If It Walks Like a Duck . . .

A newsroom has always been one of the most exciting places in the world to me.

At the *New York Tribune*, when I first went to work there, the newsroom was like something out of *The Front Page*. It had wooden desks, battered old manual typewriters, bare floors covered with cigarette butts. The AP machine spewed out reams of wire copy, which could be punched onto sharp metal spikes that the editors kept on their desks. Once two of the editors got into an argument and had a spike fight in the center of the office, using them like swords. Another time a frustrated reporter picked up a typewriter and threw it out a window. It was great.

The Channel Six newsroom isn't anything like that. We've got carpeted floors, modular furniture, and computer terminals to write stories and store all the wire copy. If a reporter tried to throw a computer terminal out a window now, he'd either get a hernia or a shock.

We're located on South Street in lower Manhattan, along the East River and next to the Fulton Fish Market. The building used to be the home of a newspaper that died a long time ago. There's a legend that an old publisher built it down there because he had a scheme to beat the New York traffic jams by delivering the paper to Brooklyn and Queens by boat. Maybe the currents weren't right on the first trip or the captain got seasick or something, because it never worked out. But anyway the view was real nice—rolling waves, boats passing by, the Brooklyn and Manhattan bridges. And when I was on a big story, I still got that surge of adrenaline I used to get when I walked into a newspaper city room.

I sat down at my desk and announced in a loud voice: "Stop the presses!"

Barry Kaiser gave me a funny look. "No presses in a TV newsroom, Jenny."

"I know. I just like to say that. It makes me feel like Rosalind Russell in *His Girl Friday*."

"My, my, aren't we dressed for success?" a voice said.

I looked up. It was Stormy Phillips. Or our weather gal, as we call her on the air. Sexism is alive and well on TV.

"Clothes make the woman," I told her.

"I think Imelda Marcos said that first."

"What channel is she on?"

Stormy sat down on the edge of my desk and sighed. "Big meeting today. El Presidente Pesin will address the troops."

"Have you talked to him yet?" I asked.

"Briefly."

"What did you think?"

"It's going to be a great love affair."

"You mean between Pesin and us?"

"No, between Pesin and Pesin. He really likes to hear himself talk. All I got was stories about how he'd turned around stations in Boston and Washington, soared up the corporate ladder at CBS, and was the hottest thing to hit broadcasting since the invention of the Minicam."

"If he's so good, what's he doing at this armpit of a TV station?" I asked.

"He was a little vague on that point."

Stormy Phillips's real name was Susan Levin. She'd

graduated from NYU as a Phi Beta Kappa, then spent two years in law school before deciding she hated it. Now she did the weather. Her shtick was to dress up in sexy clothes to give the forecast. If it was hot out, she wore a skimpy bikini. When it rained, she paraded around in rubber. It scored very high in the ratings. Sex always does.

"Where's the queen of local news?" I asked her, looking around the newsroom for Liz St. John.

"She said something about getting ready for the meeting. She wants to make a good first impression on Pesin."

"I think I need to go to the bathroom," I announced.

That turned out to be a bad move. Liz St. John was there. She was getting ready for the meeting, all right. There was an array of cosmetics spread out on the counter in front of her. Powders, lipstick, blush. Lots of bottles with different color liquids in them. I watched as Liz carefully applied all this to her face in front of the mirror.

It was truly an amazing sight.

"Do you do that every day?" I asked.

"Three times a day," she said.

"How long does it take?"

"About thirty minutes. But it's time well spent. It keeps my complexion flawless for the camera. No pimples. No blackheads. No blemishes of any kind. You ought to try it. Then you wouldn't have to worry about stuff like that pimple starting on your nose."

"That's not a pimple," I told her. "It's a mole."

"It's a pimple."

"Look, Liz, I'm forty-one years old. I'm not a teenager who lives and dies every time I get a pimple. I've got more important things to worry about."

"Jenny," she told me solemnly, "there's nothing more important than your complexion."

The news meeting started promptly. Donald Pesin was obviously a stickler for punctuality. What he wasn't was a stickler for fashion or personal hygiene.

Pesin was what might be charitably called an easy dresser.

He wore a T-shirt that was too small and stretched against his belly. His pants were polyester and looked like he'd slept in them. There was a stain on the front of them that looked suspiciously like pizza, and the zipper didn't go all the way to the top.

He was grotesquely overweight, but not in the usual way. That's because he was both short and fat. The result was that when he walked, he sort of waddled like a duck.

I recalled the nickname people called him behind his back: Donald Duck. Pesin hated it. Sometimes people who didn't like him—and there always seemed to be plenty of those wherever he worked—tormented him by leaving little stuffed animal ducks on his desk. One guy even got fired for making a quacking sound in the newsroom as Pesin walked by. If you made even the slightest mention of ducks around Donald Pesin, he blew sky-high.

"All of you have probably heard of me," he was saying. "Some of your friends have probably said I'm a genius, others say I'm a son of a bitch." He paused for effect. "They're both right.

"Here's what I do. I fire people. I make people stars. And I turn failing news shows into ratings successes. I will do all these things here. If you want to be part of it, welcome aboard. Anyone who doesn't, leave now."

No one left.

"Believe me, I'm qualified for this job. I've run stations in the nation's biggest markets, and I've taught TV journalism at Columbia and NYU."

I leaned over to Stormy Phillips, who was sitting next to me.

"Well, you know what they say," I whispered. "Those who can, do. Those who can't, teach. And those who can't do either, go into TV."

She put her hand over her mouth to hide her smirking.

"Now this is going to be like a war," Pesin continued. "Think of the other stations as the bad guys, the Nazis. We're the good guys, the Americans. That makes me John Wayne.

And don't forget—John Wayne never lost a war."

I raised my hand.

"Miss McKay, do you have a question?"

"I once had another editor who used this same analogy, only he made the bad guys Klingons and us the Enterprise. Can we do it that way instead? That would make you Captain Kirk."

Pesin looked at me strangely. "Yes, I guess so."

"Who's Mr. Spock?" I asked.

"I think you're missing the point of what I'm . . ."

"Because I'd like to be Lieutenant Uhura. I always thought she was really cool." I put my hand up to my ear like she always did on the TV show. "They're not responding to our signal, Captain," I said.

Pesin ignored me and went on talking about how he'd single-handedly changed the face of TV broadcasting. Stars he'd created. Money he'd made for people with his brilliant, innovative thinking. At one point I looked up at the clock. He'd been talking for forty minutes. God, what a windbag.

"The most important thing you have to learn as a reporter," I heard him saying, "is what is news and what isn't news. Someone give me a definition of news."

He looked around the room. His gaze settled on me.

"McKay, you seem to have a lot of smart answers. What is news?"

"If a dog bites a man, it's not news," I said brightly. "But if a man bites a dog, it's news."

"That's a cliché," he snapped. "Give me a real answer."

I thought about it. "News is something out of the ordinary. Unusual. Interesting."

"Still not good enough. I want to hear how you know if an event is news. If I send you out on assignment, how can you tell if it's worth doing? Maybe it looks like news or sounds like news, but it really isn't. How can you be sure?"

"Well," I said slowly, "I usually figure it this way. If something looks like a duck, walks like a duck, and quacks like a duck, then"—I looked at him and smiled—"it usually is a duck."

No one said anything. No one laughed. No one even snickered. They just sat there in stunned silence. Pesin's face flushed a bright red.

Finally he looked around the room and said to everyone: "The meeting's over." Then to me: "McKay, I want to see you in my office."

"No problem," I said.

Maybe he wanted to talk about old "Star Trek" episodes with me. Or maybe he liked my outfit and wanted to pick up some fashion tips. Maybe he was going to fire me. Beam me up, Scotty.

Pesin's office was a lot like the man: a mess. He hadn't unpacked yet, so there were books piled on top of each other, stacks of papers and videotapes. But he'd already started putting stuff up on the walls. Pictures of him with celebrities, awards he'd won, letters of congratulation. This guy really loved himself.

"Sit down," he said.

I sat.

"Do you know the first thing I do when I take over a new job?" Pesin said. "I fire someone. I always fire someone. Do you want to know why?"

"Why?" I asked.

"Because it puts the fear of God in people. It establishes my authority. Like if I fired you right now for that little performance of yours out there, no one would ever talk back to me again."

He paused.

"Except I'm not going to fire you. Do you want to know why?"

"Why?"

"Because," he said, smiling, "I think I can use you. You're smart, McKay. A real smart lady. Not like some of the others. Take Conroy Jackson and Liz St. John, for instance. I mean, you put their IQs together, add ten, and you've still got a number lower than my golf score."

"So why not fire them?"

"Because they've got good marquee value. They're stars. That's what this business is all about. Star power. So I need them. For now."

He leaned back in his chair and looked out the window. A majestic sailboat drifted by on the East River outside, headed south for New York Bay and the open ocean beyond. I wished I could be on it instead of sitting here in Donald Pesin's office. Hand to the tiller, wind in my face, breathing the sea air. That was the life, all right. On the other hand, I'd probably just get seasick.

"Now in a few months," Pesin continued, "if things go the way I hope around here, I may not *need* Jackson and St. John as my stars anymore. Then I'm going to be looking for someone else to be a star. Someone like you."

"Me? Are we talking about the anchor job here?"

"Maybe. It all depends on what you do for me."

"What exactly is it that you're looking for?"

"A story, babe. Bring me a big story. Bring me the Jerry Meredith story."

"I'm doing that."

"You're reporting the Jerry Meredith story. I want you to break something on it. Something big."

"Like what?"

"Well, the cops say he killed his wife: the DA's office says that too. If we say he did it, that's not big news."

"You mean . . . ?"

"The whole world says he's guilty, right? So we prove that he's innocent." Pesin looked at me and winked. "Now, that's news," he said.

6
Requiem for a Billionaire

They held the funeral for Eileen Clayton at a church on East 67th Street. It was a hot, muggy August day in New York City, a week before Labor Day. The city was empty at this time of the year. Most New Yorkers were still out in the Hamptons or on Fire Island, trying to squeeze the last rays of sunlight out of summer. But a lot of them had come back to bury Eileen Clayton.

A few hundred mourners crowded into the church and sat on hard wooden pews as a minister eulogized her in terms that would make Mother Teresa blush. She wasn't just a billionaire. She wasn't just a corporate giant. She was a force for good in a world gone horribly wrong.

"Yes, Eileen was rich," the clergyman told the crowd, "but she was also rich in ways much more important than money. She was rich spiritually. She was rich in friends. And she was rich in human kindness. Eileen made a lot of money in her life, but she gave the world back so much more than she took."

He then proceeded to list all the charitable and benevolent organizations she supported. He did not say anything about the nude dancer she was dating. Or the young studs she got fixed up with whenever she traveled. Or the stories about the terrible way she treated her employees.

"There is a wonderful lesson for us in death," the minister continued. "Eileen's fame, her fortune, her power—they are all gone for her now. All that's left is her soul. And that will be true for all of us. Ashes to ashes. Dust to dust. For in death, we are all truly equal."

Somehow I always found that thought disturbing.

I looked around at the crowd. A lot of the city's movers and shakers were there. So were a lot of people from Eileen Clayton's business empire. And some media types who probably knew her through Meredith. I spotted Lt. Jellinek too. And Katherine Grieco, the assistant DA on the case, who probably saw it as a great photo opportunity.

The center of attention though was Jerry Meredith. He'd been released from prison on bail the night before in time to make it to the funeral. His lawyer told the court he was no threat to flee. He was a figure in the community. He was a solid citizen. And he was so recognizable from TV that he'd be quickly spotted anywhere he tried to flee. No one could argue with that.

I watched him during the service. He was dressed in a conservative dark suit, had a somber look on his face, and stared straight ahead as the minister talked about his dead wife. I tried to find some clues in his body language. Once, when the minister was talking about Eileen Clayton's love for the sea, Meredith put his hand to his eye as if he had something in it. Maybe he'd started to cry and didn't want anyone to see. Or maybe he did it deliberately to make people think he was in more grief than he really was. On the other hand, maybe he really did have something in his eye. Sometimes I think about stuff like that too much.

When the service was over, he was quickly surrounded by people expressing their condolences. I wasn't exactly sure about the proper etiquette of what to say in a situation like this. Was it, "I'm so sorry about your wife's death"? Or, "Happy to hear they let you out of jail on bail"? Or maybe, "Hope to hell you don't fry in the electric chair."

Cameras weren't allowed inside the church, so Sanders and Jacobson were waiting outside. I made my way by myself over to where Meredith was accepting condolences. When he saw me, he gave a big wave and started walking in my direction. He put his hand on my arm and dragged me with him as we started to make our way out of the church.

"Jenny, we need to talk," he said.

"Sure. I'm really sorry about—"

He cut me off in mid-sentence. "I want to do an interview."

"An interview? You mean on TV?"

"Sure. That's what you do for a living these days, isn't it?"

He leaned closer and whispered in my ear. "I need help, Jenny. Somebody's trying to set me up. And this woman ADA"—he looked over to where Grieco was standing—"she smells blood. My only chance is to get the message that I'm innocent out to the people who watch me every day on TV. I want them to believe in me. Then maybe I have a fighting chance to get out of this."

"You could use your own TV show," I pointed out.

"We're in reruns for the summer. We don't start new episodes until after Labor Day. By then, it might be too late."

"But why me? Why not Diane Sawyer or Sally Jessy Raphael? Everyone's following this story so . . ."

"I want you, Jenny. I know you. I trust you. I can count on you giving me a fair shake. That's all I'm asking."

"Okay," I said slowly. "When do you want to do the interview?"

He sighed. "I'm exhausted now. I've only been out of jail for a few hours. I'm going to go to sleep for about twenty-four hours. Then I've got to take care of some business on my show. . . . Let's say tomorrow afternoon. Is my place all right?"

"Whatever you want." I told him I'd be there with a camera crew.

We were at the door now. Cameras outside from all the TV stations and newspapers starting shooting Meredith. I was standing right next to him. I was going to be front-page news again. Sort of like Bonnie to his Clyde.

When we got to a waiting limo, he gave me a big hug before getting inside. The cameras caught that too.

"Thanks," he said.

"For what?"

"All your support."

"I'm just doing my job," I said. "This is strictly professional."

"If I thought that was true," he said, smiling, "I wouldn't be giving you the interview."

Then he got into the car and was driven off. I watched the limo disappear down 67th Street and make a right on Madison. When I turned around again, Katherine Grieco was standing there. Grieco was very tall—maybe five foot ten in flat heels—with short blond hair, and she wore no makeup. She looked at me coldly for a second and then introduced herself.

"I've heard a lot about you the last few days, Miss McKay," she said. "You're not exactly popular with the people I talk to in law enforcement."

"Neither are you," I told her.

She kept staring at me with that icy look.

"Let me give you a little advice," she said evenly. "Jerry Meredith's going down for this. He killed his wife. And he's going to be convicted of murder one. End of story."

"Gee, whatever happened to 'innocent until proven guilty'?"

"Don't mess with me, McKay."

"I'm just doing my job. Why don't you do the same? Do a little investigating, instead of just deciding Jerry Meredith's a bad guy. I already know a few things about this case. I know . . ."

Grieco shook her head in disgust. "You don't know anything, McKay."

Then she turned around and walked away.

Sanders and Jacobson had come up behind us and picked up on the tail end of the conversation. "Well, that was pleasant," I said.

"Yeah, you two really hit it off," Sanders said.

"Probably because of her sunny disposition," I told him.

Jacobson pointed to his watch and announced it was lunchtime. This was the highlight of the day for him. He didn't let a little thing like a spectacular murder case interfere with his mealtime. I mean, you could be talking about a Pulitzer prize-winning story with him, and he'd suddenly announce that it was Taco Tuesday at the Jack in the Box where he wanted to go eat. Sometimes it drove me crazy. Hey, it's no secret I love food too. But I love a big story even more.

"Let me ask you a hypothetical question, Artie," I said. "You've got your camera on John F. Kennedy and Jackie in Dealey Plaza on November twenty-second as the shots start to ring out. Just then a Mr. Frosty truck pulls up."

"Dilemma, dilemma," Jacobson said.

"Do you take one of the most famous pictures in American history or go buy an ice-cream sundae instead?"

Jacobson thought about it for a minute. "What flavor sundae?" he asked finally.

I decided to hang around for a while and schmooze with Jellinek. I told Sanders and Jacobson to go back to the office with the film of the funeral, then I wandered over to where Jellinek was standing.

"I'm a little surprised to see you here," I said to him. "But I guess that's an old cop ploy, isn't it? Go to the funeral of a murder victim to see if the real killer shows up to savor his work."

Jellinek took a stick of chewing gum out of his pocket, unwrapped it slowly, and popped it in his mouth. "You've been watching too many 'Columbo' reruns," he said.

"So, you made any progress on the investigation?" I asked.

"This may come as a surprise to you, McKay, but I don't think there's anything in the city charter that says I need to report to you."

"How about an exchange of information? I'll tell you what I know, you tell me what you know."

I figured I'd dazzle him with all the information I'd picked up. That would give me the upper hand.

Jellinek chewed hard on his gum. "Okay, you go first," he said finally.

"Did you know Meredith may have been seeing someone on the side?"

"Yeah."

"You did? Do you know who?"

"No, we're still trying to find out."

"How about this? Eileen Clayton was dating someone too. Some well-hung stud called Bobby who dances at a club for . . ."

"His name's Robert Santos. He works at a place called Cary's. We just talked to him."

"Oh." So much for the upper hand. "I guess you know everything I know then. How about the autopsy?"

"It says the Clayton woman died of a blow to the head. From one of the model train engines we found near the body."

"I already knew that." I sighed. "I guess we both know everything the other one knows."

"Did you know Eileen Clayton was pregnant?"

I stared at him in amazement. "Who?"

Jellinek shrugged. "Maybe her husband. Maybe Robert Santos. Maybe somebody else." He smiled at me. "Intriguing, huh?"

After I left the church, I didn't feel like going right back to the office. I decided to walk for a while. I headed downtown to the fifties and west over to Fifth Avenue, past Bergdorf Goodman and Tiffany's. I window-shopped at Tiffany's, dreaming about someone giving me one of the baubles there and feeling a little like Audrey Hepburn.

Next door to Tiffany's is Trump Tower, a fifty-one-story shining glass structure filled with posh clothing stores. I browsed there too, then had a tuna fish salad for lunch in the atrium. The atrium is a really cool place, with a sixty-foot-high waterfall and huge trees surrounding you as you dine. So much nicer than eating at my desk in the office and looking at Pesin or Liz St. John.

After I left Trump Tower, I went down to Rockefeller Center. That's where it really feels like New York. Lots of sightseers on the street, pointing their cameras at skyscrapers, and looking around for celebrities. Across the street people filed in and out of St. Patrick's Cathedral.

I was on my way to the subway station at 49th and Sixth when I saw a brown Lincoln driving slowly on the street behind me. Nothing unusual there. There's lots of brown Lincolns on the streets of New York City. And maybe he was going slow because he was looking for an address. Except that I'd thought I'd seen a car just like that trailing slowly behind me near Trump Tower too. Probably just a coincidence.

I made a right turn on 49th and walked over to the subway station. There was a newsstand outside, and I spent a minute or two buying some Life Savers and the late edition of the *Post*. When I was finished, I looked around one more time. Nothing now. The Lincoln was gone.

I shrugged and headed down the steps for the train ride back to the Channel Six studio.

7
Stars in My Eyes

I had a problem.

Donald Pesin wanted me to prove Jerry Meredith was innocent. But everything I'd come up with so far made him look guilty as sin. He was fooling around on the side. His wife was seeing a dancer. She'd gotten herself knocked up by someone. They had a big fight in which she'd humiliated him in front of people. And as long as she was alive, he couldn't get at any of her money. Whew! The way things were going you might as well just sign the guy up for a lifetime membership at Attica State Prison.

But it was news. Big news.

And so at 6:04 that night, after Conroy had delivered the other headlines at the top of the show (a massive pileup on the Long Island Expressway, a clash with cops at a gay rights rally, and a special feature on car repair rip-offs), Liz St. John turned to me and said:

ST. JOHN: Now for the top story of the day. Our Jenny McKay has spent the day investigating the death of billionaire Eileen Clayton and the arrest of her husband,

THE MOURNING SHOW 49

TV personality Jerry Meredith. She has this exclusive report for us. Jenny . . .

I was sitting next to her in the studio, wearing a blue blazer with a white patch on the front pocket which said: "Action Six News Team." My face was made up, my hair neatly combed. I felt perky. I felt peppy. I felt like Katie Couric on uppers.

McKAY: Thank you, Liz. Channel Six News has learned that Eileen Clayton was pregnant when she was murdered. And the father may not have been Jerry Meredith. Police sources say . . .

I went through it all. I just talked to the camera, I didn't use the teleprompter. I'm better when I do that. The teleprompter runs the text of what you're saying in big letters on a screen in front of you. The audience, of course, can't see it. When a teleprompter works well, the newscaster seems to be effortlessly talking without any hesitation. With me I always feel like I'm just reading . . . "See Dick run, see Jane chase Spot, see Jenny ruin her career . . ." So I only use it on stuff that's really complicated or boring. Jerry Meredith wasn't boring.

When I was finished with my report, the camera pulled back for a shot of Liz and me together at the news desk. This was the part where we're supposed to exchange clever repartee about the story. It shows that we're all one big happy family here at the Channel Six News Team. Buddies. Pals. Sisters in journalism.

ST. JOHN: Jenny, do police think the fact she was pregnant could have been a motive for murder?

McKAY: They're investigating that as a possibility.

ST. JOHN: Now does this mean that Jerry Meredith could be charged with two murders—his wife and the unborn baby?

I was stunned by that one.

McKAY: Uh . . . I don't think so. Eileen Clayton was only a few weeks along in her pregnancy. The fetus wasn't really formed yet. So the baby wouldn't qualify for life under the law.

ST. JOHN: Oh, you mean that abortion thing.

Right, that abortion thing. God, what an airhead.

ST. JOHN: Speaking of babies, we have some cute ones to show you next.

The screen cut to a shot of some baby seals sucking on their mother.

ST. JOHN: The Central Park Zoo proudly displayed its brand-new family of rare, exotic seals to the public for the first time today. As you can see, the little ones seem *udderly* oblivious to all the attention. We'll be back with this and the rest of the news. . . .

When the show was over, Donald Pesin came by my desk and congratulated me on the big scoop. I was a little embarrassed. I felt like everyone in the office was watching us. Gee, McKay, we thought you were a stand-up kind of woman. Didn't take any crap from assholes like Pesin. Maybe we should just call you Judas McKay.

"Terrific job," Pesin said. "I really love the pregnancy angle."

"It does add a certain poignant note to the story, doesn't it?"

"So what do you have next for me?"

I told him about Meredith saying he wanted to do an interview with me. Pesin's eyes widened in anticipation like a kid on Christmas morning. I thought for a second he was going to kiss me. That would have been hard to live down.

Instead he just stared at me for a second, then said: "Let's you and I go have a drink and talk about all this. I'm on my way to Elaine's. You go there much?"

Elaine's is where all the famous people in town hang out. TV stars. Media types. Actors like Woody Allen and Dustin Hoffman. If Elaine knew who you were, she treated you like royalty. If she didn't, you got seated somewhere between the kitchen and the ladies' room.

The last time I'd been to Elaine's was about a year ago. It did not go well. I was with the editor of a major woman's magazine, and Elaine herself came over and sat at our table. I was telling a long, very funny joke which required considerable body movement on my part. In the middle of the joke, I swung my arm around and accidently spilled an entire pitcher of beer into Elaine's lap. It took several minutes, three frantic busboys, and a lot of towels to dry out the front of her dress. I hoped she didn't remember.

"Not recently," I said.

"I've got a limo waiting downstairs. I'll meet you outside in fifteen minutes."

After Pesin left, Alan Sanders came by. "Well, well, aren't you two chummy?"

"He's very interested in the Meredith story," I said.

"I never figured you to be the ambitious type, Jenny. I mean, I know there's a lot of cutthroat, climb the ladder of success at any price, stab your coworkers in the back people in TV news. But not you. Or so I thought. I guess you never know what someone will do to become a star, huh?"

"Come here a second, Alan," I said. He leaned his head close to me. "Fuck off!" I yelled in his ear.

He laughed and walked away.

Stormy Phillips was sitting at the next desk. There was no expression on her face.

"You got a problem with me having a drink with Pesin?" I asked sharply.

"Nope. Have a drink with him. Listen to his ideas. Tell

him how great he is. There's just one thing I wouldn't do."

"What's that?"

"I wouldn't trust him."

As it turned out, I didn't have to worry about Elaine. She had no idea who I was. But she gushed all over Donald Pesin and so did everyone else. Lorne Michaels of "Saturday Night Live" was there. Billy Joel. Norman Mailer. Cindy Adams of the *New York Post*, the top gossip columnist in town, sat down at our table for fifteen minutes. She dished on everyone in the place, telling us who was sleeping with who and who wasn't sleeping with anyone. She was very funny. I really liked Cindy Adams.

I was drinking Amstel Light, Pesin had a vodka tonic. A waitress came by and asked if we wanted anything to eat. I gathered all my willpower and said no. Pesin ordered a cheeseburger with a double order of french fries.

"You're not hungry?" he asked when she left.

"I'm trying to stay on a diet."

"No kidding? You look pretty good."

"Thanks."

"Of course, you could lose a few pounds."

"So could you," I pointed out.

He laughed uproariously. His lips pulled back from his teeth when he did that, sort of like Mr. Ed used to when he talked to Wilber. I couldn't believe this guy. Nothing I said seemed to insult him. It's like he enjoyed showing how thick-skinned he could be.

"Tell me about Liz St. John," he said. "Is she as dumb as she seems?"

Boy, talk about a fastball right over the plate. I felt funny about swinging at it though. It was too easy. So I just smiled knowingly.

"Liz reminds me of a joke I heard about an empty-headed anchorwoman whose station was doing an AIDS awareness promotion," Pesin said. "Every show she had to deliver a message to the viewers about safe sex. Then one night she goes to this party where everyone's doing heroin. A guy shoots up and passes the dirty needle to a second guy, who mainlines, then passes the even dirtier needle to her. 'Aren't you scared of getting AIDS?' someone asks. 'Hell, no,' the anchorwoman replies. 'They're all wearing condoms.' "

He laughed loudly again.

The waitress brought his order, and he dug in eagerly. He put some of the fries on top of the burger and then devoured half of it in one bite. The guy was like a vacuum cleaner. I grabbed a few french fries off his plate, terrified I might lose a finger.

"I've been going over some demographic numbers on Liz," he said between bites. "She's got a certain popularity among men and certain lower-income groups who just want to see a pretty face on the screen. But to make a big move in the ratings, we need someone with more depth anchoring the news desk. Let's call Liz our Deborah Norville. What we need is a Jane Pauley. A Leslie Stahl. Easy on the eyes, but with intelligence too. The entire package. That's where you come in, McKay."

"You think I could do her job?"

"Down the road a bit. But first we've got to build you up. Get people to know you. This is a town that likes stars. So we make you a star."

"How are you going to do that?"

"By establishing your identity to the public with a big story."

"Like Jerry Meredith."

"Exactly. You've had two good exclusives. We're ahead of the field. Now we blow everyone away with the interview. Jerry Meredith talks exclusively to Channel Six's Jenny McKay. He weeps for his dead wife. He pleads that someone find the real killer. We promote the hell out of it. And then afterward we keep going until we . . ."

"Prove Meredith's innocent."

"Right. If you pull that off, you'll be in *People* magazine and on every TV talk show in the country. You'll be a star. And I'd like nothing better than to make a star like that my next anchorwoman."

"What if he's guilty?" I asked.

"Then prove that. It's almost as good if you find the proof that puts him away."

Pesin grinned at me. "Either way, we win."

It was almost eleven when I got home. I felt guilty. Guilty about eating the french fries. Guilty about schmoozing with Pesin like that. And guilty about leaving Hobo alone, since my dog-walker came in during the afternoon. I made it up to Hobo with a walk around the block and a heaping bowl of Mighty Dog English Grille dinner. Afterward, he licked my face happily. He never can stay mad.

Then I made myself a salad from the leftover lettuce and tomato in the refrigerator, carried it into the living room, and watched "The Honeymooners" while I ate. Ralph was telling Alice about one of his surefire, get-rich-quick schemes.

Hot ziggity, I thought to myself.

I'm going to be a big TV star.

And I'm going to get a chance to see Jerry Meredith again tomorrow.

What scared me was I wasn't sure which excited me more.

8
Women Who Date Their Lesbian Sisters!

The telephone woke me up the next morning. I fumbled for the receiver.

"Jenny, is that you?"

"Barely," I groaned.

It was Clare. "I wanted to catch you before you left for work," she said.

I looked over at the clock. It said 7:30. "Congratulations, you made it."

She ignored the sarcasm. "Can you come over for dinner Saturday night? Martin's got this friend that I want you to meet. He's . . ."

I rapped the phone twice on the end of the nightstand. "Sorry, I think we have a bad connection. I can't hear a word you're saying."

"Jenny, listen to me . . ."

"Clare, I've met your husband's friends before. Don't do this to me."

"But this one's different."

"Yeah, you said that about Howard Hummerman too."

"Hey, Howard's a very successful stockbroker on Wall

Street. He makes $200,000 a year, has a co-op in Battery Park, and drives a BMW."

"He's boring."

"This guy's not boring. He's . . ."

"I don't want to hear about it."

"His name is Pete Rousch, he's an American History professor at Columbia University, he's forty-four years old, and he's divorced."

"Terrific. I hope he has a wonderful life."

"Is that a yes or no?"

"Maybe," I said.

After I hung up, I took a shower, drank two cups of coffee, and began to feel like a member of the human race again. The next step was breakfast. I checked the refrigerator and found a package with three Oreo cookies left in it. That seemed a bit fattening, so I broke them open and just licked off the white flavoring.

A new low, huh?

What was next for me? Sucking whipped cream straight out of Reddi Whip cans? Maybe you'd find me down on the Bowery in a year or two begging people for spare change so I could go out and score some chocolate fudge brownies.

Then I got dressed. I wanted to look my best for the interview with Meredith. So I picked out a blue pin-striped Perry Ellis pantsuit that I'd bought at Bloomingdale's in a fit of fiscal irresponsibility last month. I put on a sky-blue silk blouse with it, navy blue heels, and an azure scarf with white polka dots sticking out of my left front pocket.

I checked myself out in the mirror. Chic. Stylish. Very happening. Like an Annie Hall for the nineties.

I asked Hobo what he thought of the whole look. "Woof," he said. Exactly the response I was hoping for. I took him for a walk around the park, put some dog biscuits in his dish, and then headed over to Third Avenue to catch a bus uptown.

Before going to see Meredith, I had decided to spend the morning talking to people at his TV show to see what I could learn there.

"The Morning Show" was shot in a building on 76th

THE MOURNING SHOW 57

Street and First Avenue. The set consisted of a desk where Jerry sat, a couch for his guests, a kitchen used in cooking segments, and about one hundred seats for the audience.

The producer of "The Morning Show" was a woman named Cheryl Wolcott. She was about thirty-five, with glasses hanging from a chain around her neck, and her hair pulled back into a severe bun in the back. She did not look happy. I don't think I improved her mood any.

"A reporter, huh?" she grunted. "I used to be a reporter once myself. Sometimes I wish I still was."

We were sitting in her office. The window was open, and I could hear horns honking on First Avenue.

"Thank God we're in reruns now," she said. "We've got some shows in the can too, so that buys us a little time."

"Jerry's out of jail on bail," I pointed out.

"I know," she sighed. "But how do you produce a morning talk show where the host has just murdered his wife?"

She suddenly realized what she was saying. "I mean he's been accused of murder," she said quickly.

"Well, look on the bright side," I told her. "Oprah was never arrested for killing anyone. Or Phil Donahue. Or Sally Jessy Raphael. This could be a bigger ratings bonanza than Murphy Brown's baby."

"You really think people would keep watching?"

"Hey, they watch 'Roseanne,' they'll watch anything."

Behind her was a bulletin board with a dozen eight-by-ten index cards posted on it. There were titles of future shows written on them in green magic marker. I read some of the titles: "My husband is a cross-dresser." "Women who are still virgins at forty." "Bedroom secrets of Hollywood stars." "How to Win Back Your Man from the Other Woman." "Women Who Date Their Lesbian Sisters."

"That last one is great." She laughed. "You get two taboos for the price of one."

"Are all these people for real?" I asked. "I mean, are any of them actors? Do you pay them?"

She shook her head. "We're inundated by people who want to reveal their innermost secrets on national TV. And there's millions of people out there who want to watch them."

I remembered reading somewhere that Cheryl Wolcott had been the one who came to Meredith with the concept for "The Morning Show." I asked her about that.

"It was my idea," she said. "Not that it was anything original. But I thought if you put together the right mix of tabloid confession, reality crime interviews, cooking tips, health advice, and celebrity spots . . . well, a lot of housewives would watch."

"It's that easy, huh?"

"Not quite. The most important thing is the host. You need someone really special to connect with the audience."

"Jerry Meredith," I said.

"Jerry's one of a kind. He's handsome, charming, funny. He's got that kind of likeable sex appeal that just oozes out of the TV screen and into people's living rooms. He's great."

"Do you think he's capable of murder?" I asked.

It was an easy question. All it required was a simple, "No, of course not." But Wolcott didn't do that. Instead she stared at me with a blank expression on her face.

"I've always made a point of keeping my relations with Jerry professional," she said finally. "I don't really know much about him personally. It seemed to work out better that way. Are we talking off-the-record here?"

I nodded.

"Jerry's a nice guy and all, but sometimes he uses a little too much . . ."

"Bullshit?" I suggested.

She smiled. "Something like that."

"I know what you mean."

I was starting to like Cheryl Wolcott. "Did you ever hear about him with another woman?"

"Just rumors."

"Someone told me he was getting it on with some production assistant on the show."

"I heard that one too. Like I said though, it was only a

rumor. Hell, the girl might have started it herself."

"How about Jerry's wife? Did you see much of her?"

"Eileen Clayton? No, not really. She was too busy making millions."

"When was the last time?"

She thought about it. "A few days ago."

"What happened?"

Cheryl Wolcott started to say something, then thought better of it.

"Something happened?" I asked.

She sighed. "I guess you're going to find out anyway. A lot of people saw it. They had an argument."

"About what?"

"She was going on about him spending money. How he was the only man in the world that could spend more money than she could make. And that it wasn't going to happen anymore."

"What happened then?"

"She stormed out. He didn't say anything to anybody, but he was really embarrassed about it. You could tell. Who wouldn't be?"

"Did he love her?"

Wolcott grunted. "Eileen Clayton was worth a billion dollars. I'd say he adored her."

"Do you have any idea why he'd be spending too much of his wife's money?"

"No."

I thought about what Jack Weinstein had said to me. "Did he do drugs or gamble heavily or anything like that?"

"I know he talked about sports bets a lot. The Giants, the Knicks—that sort of thing. But then a lot of people do that."

"Do you think it was anything major in his life?"

She shrugged. "Like I said, we kept our personal lives separate."

We talked awhile longer, then I stood up to say good-bye. She told me to call if I needed anything else and handed me a business card with "The Morning Show" logo and her telephone number on it. "Do you have a card?" she asked.

I searched in my purse and finally produced one. It said "Jenny McKay, reporter, *New York Tribune*." She gave me a strange look.

"I keep meaning to get new ones made up," I said.

I took the card back, wrote my number for Channel Six on the back, and handed it to her.

"Jeez, we've had a real run of bad luck around here," she sighed. "I mean, we've lost a director and an associate producer. And now this with Jerry. Things have got to get better."

"What happened to the director and associate producer?" I asked.

"Oh, the director, Andrew Cox, died last month."

I remembered the name from the same magazine article that had talked about Cheryl Wolcott. It described the two of them as the brains behind Jerry Meredith. Something about them being the driving forces of the show.

"What happened?"

"Andy was killed in a hit-and-run accident. It was the damnedest thing. He was crossing First Avenue as the light turned and—boom. Something like that really makes you think about how fragile all our lives are."

"And the associate producer?"

"Oh, nothing like that. We just had this one girl, Becky Bessard, who stopped showing up for work. Can you believe that? She's barely twenty years old, and she just walks away from a job on the top-rated daytime talk show in the country. Sometimes I don't understand kids today."

I nodded and started for the door. I was almost there when it hit me. I turned around again.

"At Channel Six an associate producer is pretty low on the totem pole. Really just a gofer. Or a production assistant."

"Same here. Why?"

"This Becky Bessard. By any chance, was she the one people were whispering about with Jerry Meredith?"

"Well, yes, I did hear some talk about her. Do you think . . . ?"

THE MOURNING SHOW 61

"I don't know. Did you go to the police when she stopped coming to work?"

"We called just to check, but they said there was no evidence of foul play. There was nothing they could do."

"I think I might look into her a bit more," I said.

"Maybe I will too," Wolcott said thoughtfully.

She saw the look of surprise on my face and laughed. "I told you I started out in this business as a reporter. An investigative reporter."

"Really?"

"Yep, I once got three councilmen indicted for graft in Altoona, Pennsylvania," she said proudly.

"So what happened?" I asked.

"I got a little sidetracked."

"I'd say you've been very successful."

"Yeah, well maybe it's time to get the old investigative reporting juices flowing again," she said. "Who knows? I might break the story before you do."

I spent some time afterward talking to other people on the show's production staff. Cameramen, lighting people, pages. No one heard Jerry Meredith confess to the murder of his wife. No one saw him washing blood off his hands after she was killed. No one caught him and Becky Bessard having sex on "The Morning Show" couch. A lot of people had seen or heard about Jerry Meredith's argument with his wife, but no one thought it was all that big a deal. "She was always giving him a hard time," one production assistant told me. "She was a real ball-breaker. To everyone." As for the Becky Bessard rumor, that's all it was—a rumor.

I walked out of the studio into the bright sunlight on East 76th Street. A little old lady was standing on the corner wearing a nun's outfit and Reeboks. She was holding a cup for money, next to a sign which said: "Save the world from Satan. Please help."

She looked at me hopefully and held out the cup as I passed. "I just want to save the world," she said earnestly.

I took out a dollar and dropped it in. I wasn't all that

sure she was really a nun. Maybe it was the Reeboks. But I figured one way or another, the money was going to go to somebody who needed it.

"You and me both, sister," I told her.

9
Lights, Camera . . . Questions

It had turned into a gorgeous summer day in New York City. The humidity had broken, and there was a refreshing breeze blowing in off the East River. I was stiff after sitting in Cheryl Wolcott's office, so I decided to walk to Jerry Meredith's apartment. I figured it would rejuvenate me.

It's a terrific section of New York City to walk through. The seventies were filled with singles out on the street and hip restaurants, which were just opening up for business. Couples in their twenties sat at checkered-cloth tables, looking like something out of a Woody Allen movie.

I guess you're supposed to envy the young their youth, but I don't. Being young isn't that great. You're twenty-one years old, confused about love, and unsure what you want to do with your life. Thank God, I'm long past that phase. Now I'm forty-one, confused about love, and unsure what I want to do with my life. There's a lesson to be learned there somewhere. I'm just not sure what it is.

By the time I got to Park and 61st, I was perspiring heavily and out of breath. I was definitely rejuvenated. In fact, if I was any more rejuvenated, I'd have to call 911. Maybe I should start thinking seriously about joining a gym.

Sanders and Jacobson were waiting for me in front of the building.

"I may be having a heart attack," I announced.

"Have it on your own time," Jacobson muttered. "I want to be wrapped up back at the studio by five, on the Long Island Expressway by six, and eating dinner at my house by six-thirty. Don't screw it up, McKay."

He and Sanders took their equipment out of the van, and we started for the front door. "There could be a bit of a delicate situation here," I said as we walked up the steps. "I don't know if you know it, but I used to . . ."

"Screw Jerry Meredith," Jacobson said.

"You heard?"

"The whole office has heard. Between that and your newfound friendship with Donald Pesin, you're Gossip Topic A in the Channel Six newsroom."

"What exactly are they saying about me and Jerry?"

"The word is the man broke your heart in a thousand pieces, as they say in the country song." He smiled. "Gee, this interview ought to be interesting."

"You know me," I said. "I'm the consummate professional."

Jerry Meredith answered the door himself. He was wearing an open-collared white shirt with red pinstripes, a pair of blue Calvin Klein jeans, and dark brown Dockside moccasins. His hair was wet and freshly combed. He looked refreshed and calm. The wild-eyed look of fear I'd seen the other day was gone.

"Jenny, it's so great to see you," he said, giving me a big hug. "At a time like this, you really appreciate your friends."

"I'm here as a journalist, not as a friend," I said, pulling away from him as quickly as I could. I thought it was important to say that. I could have added that friends don't not talk to each other for ten years, but I decided not to.

"Let's get something to drink," he said.

I followed him toward the kitchen, but not before taking a quick glance at Sanders and Jacobson, who began setting up the equipment in the living room. They both glared at me. Meredith was virtually ignoring them. Me, he treated like Joan Lunden. I knew I was going to hear about this later.

The place was spectacular. When I knew Jerry Meredith, he lived in a roach-infested studio apartment on West 73rd Street above a Chinese restaurant. Now he had about ten bedrooms, a chandeliered dining room, and a living room the size of a football field, not to mention other rooms filled with pool tables and pinball machines and his model trains. Jerry always loved toys.

"This place is breathtaking," I said when we finally got to the kitchen.

"Yeah, but it doesn't mean much anymore without Eileen. It just seems lonely. You know what I mean?"

"Of course. I'm sorry."

He opened the refrigerator. "You like beer, right? Is Budweiser okay?"

I wasn't sure if I should be drinking on the job. On the other hand, no one said I shouldn't. And the Budweiser in his hand looked very tempting. It was ice-cold from the refrigerator, with little beads of water starting to run down the sides. I took it from him, unscrewed the top, and chugged down a few swallows. Jenny McKay, this Bud's for you.

"Let me ask you the same question I did before," I said. "Why are you talking to me? You're big news—TV star arrested for murder. I mean, the networks and the tabloid shows are all clamoring for an interview with you. How come you didn't just call 'Hard Copy' or 'Inside Edition'?"

He opened a beer for himself and took a sip. "Like I said, I know you."

"Okay, but still . . ."

"Jenny, I know how you think, how you react to things. I know that if you decide I'm innocent and being railroaded, you won't rest until you find the real killer. That's why I have to convince you I'm telling the truth. If I can do that—then I can convince the rest of the people out there too. No matter what Katherine Grieco says."

"You figure she's really out to get you, huh?"

"I'm her golden goose," he said. "She looks at me and sees headlines, fame, and a bright political future."

I drank some more of my Budweiser. "Just between us old friends, Jerry," I asked, "did you murder your wife?"

"No," he told me. I looked at his face, trying to see if he looked innocent or guilty as he answered the question. But there was nothing there. He said it as casually as if he were discussing the weather.

"Where were you the night she died?" I asked.

He wasn't so casual anymore.

"I can't tell you that," he said.

"Why not?"

"Because I don't know."

He drank some more of the Budweiser and then sighed. "Look, I went to this bar and had a few drinks—a lot of them actually. I got pretty drunk. Anyway, I don't remember anything until the next morning, when I went home and found the cops at my place. End of story."

"What was the name of the bar?"

"I don't remember that either."

"That's not much of an alibi," I told him.

"Katherine Grieco said the same thing."

"What were you doing drinking all night in a bar?" I asked.

"Eileen and I had a fight, and I stormed out."

"What was the argument about?"

"Money. Sex. You name it. Eileen was used to getting her way. So am I. Sometimes that caused problems."

"Did she tell you about the baby?"

He shook his head sadly. "No, I never knew about that until after she was dead. I'm not sure she even knew about it. It was very early in the pregnancy, the doctors say."

I wrote all the information down in a notebook.

"Did you ever hear of a woman named Becky Bessard?" I asked.

Meredith nodded. "She was an associate producer on my show. Why?"

"The rumor is you were sleeping with her."

THE MOURNING SHOW 67

He smiled. "Don't believe everything you hear, Jenny."

"But you do know her."

"I know a lot of people."

Sanders stuck his head in the door. "We're all set up, Miss McKay," he said with exaggerated politeness.

"Are you ready?" I asked Meredith.

"Let's do it," he said.

The interview went great. For him. And for me. The minute the camera came on, he played to it like a true professional. He came across as a grief-stricken, decent and devastated man in love with his slain wife.

One high point came when I asked him the same question I'd asked him in the kitchen. Did he kill her? It wasn't just the simple "no" this time. He looked directly at the camera and said:

"Oh, my God, no! I loved Eileen so much. Eileen and I had so many dreams. Now it's all gone . . . our life together, our hopes of starting a family. And I'm actually being accused of murdering her."

His eyes glistened with tears. He wiped them dry and then continued in a choking voice.

"All of the people who watch my show know I never lie to them. I always tell it straight. And that's what I'm doing now. I want them all to know that I'm innocent. I pray that this nightmare will end and the truth can come out."

It was a pretty incredible performance. At another point I asked him about the report his wife had been pregnant at the time of her death.

"We tried so hard to have a baby," he said tenderly. "It meant so much to Eileen. To both of us. And now, when the miracle finally did happen . . ."

This time he broke down crying completely. "I'm sorry, I just can't talk about the baby now. It's too painful."

I'd never made anyone cry before in an interview. I felt like Barbara Walters.

When we were finished, Sanders and Jacobson picked up their equipment and got ready to leave. Me too. But Meredith asked me to stay there with him.

"Just for a little while," he said. "I can't handle being alone right now."

I looked at my watch. It was too late to do the interview for the six o'clock show tonight. The plan was to go back to the studio now, edit it, and then promo it for tomorrow night's newscast. I could do that later. So why not hang out here for a while with Jerry Meredith? He was the hottest news story in town. Maybe I could pump him for some more information.

After Sanders and Jacobson were gone, we sat on the couch in the living room and talked. About the case. About people we used to know. About our careers. I was still drinking beer and so was he. He seemed to be drinking a lot more than me, but who could blame him?

Then, without any warning, he suddenly reached over and put his hand on top of mine.

"Jenny, there's something I've wanted to tell you for a long time. I'm sorry about everything that happened between us. I was a real ass."

I pulled my hand away quickly. "Oh, I barely remember that," I said casually.

"I've known a lot of women in my life. Been in love with some of them, even married a few. But you were always special to me. I never met any woman quite like you. I want you to know that."

His hand was back on top of mine again. I looked at his eyes. They looked blurry. I wasn't sure if he was drunk or just getting emotional again.

Jesus Christ, I thought to myself, he's coming on to me. His wife's not even cold in the ground yet, and he's trying to make a pass at me.

"I've gotta run," I blurted out.

"Can't you stay awhile longer . . . ?"

"No, I need to edit the tape. I've got a deadline. We'll talk soon."

"Call me tomorrow," he said.

"I will."

"Promise?"

"I promise." I smiled.

I squeezed his hand as impersonally as I could, stood up from the couch, and then got the hell out of Jerry Meredith's apartment before I did something I would regret.

10
You Can Turn the World on with a Smile

"He did what?" Clare Lefferts said.

"Jerry Meredith came on to me."

"Right there in his living room? A few days after his wife's murder? One day after he's released from jail?"

"That about sums it up," I told her.

"Maybe it was just your imagination."

"It wasn't my imagination that was stroking my hand."

We were eating breakfast in the dining room at the Helmsley Hotel. Experts say that breakfast is the most important meal of the day. Eat a hearty breakfast, they tell you, then cut back for lunch and dinner. I had the breakfast part down pat. It was the rest of the day I still had a problem with.

The Helmsley Hotel is on 42nd Street next door to the *Daily News* building. Clare had an appointment at ten on 50th Street, so I suggested we meet there. Leona Helmsley might have gone off to jail, but she still set a damn fine table. I'd ordered eggs Benedict, home fried potatoes, and toast, while Clare went for the Belgian waffles. Of course, the bill for the two of us was going to be pretty steep. But as a veteran reporter told me when I was starting out in the business, "Kid, that's what expense accounts are for."

"Look, I'm not exactly a stickler for perfection when it comes to men I go out with," I said, pushing my muffin around the plate with a fork to pick up more of the hollandaise sauce. "I mean, I pretty much go along with comedian Merrill Markoe's theory on dating: 'Any date is a successful one where no one gets injured, catches a disease, or files any lawsuits.' But you have to draw the line somewhere. My line is I don't date murderers. It makes breaking up so hard to do."

Clare cut off a small piece of Belgian waffle and put it daintily in her mouth. She weighed 110 pounds and never gained an ounce. Eating with her always made me feel guilty.

"Do you really think he killed her?" she asked.

"No. Well, probably not. Christ, I don't know."

"It seems to me you've got a lot of personal baggage tied up in this case. Why don't you try to get off the story?"

"No way," I said.

I told her about my conversation with Pesin. How he seemed to like me. What he'd said about the anchor job. How he'd even asked my advice about other people at the station.

"You think this story's going to make you a star, don't you?" Clare shook her head. "Jeez, Jenny, I've never seen this side of you."

"Hey, what's wrong with wanting to be successful?" I said. "This is a big story, everyone's watching it. It could be my breakthrough. I could wind up as an anchor or get an offer from one of the networks or a show like 'Entertainment Tonight' or '20/20.' I've spent the last few years in this business doing crap assignments—everything from cooking segments to celebrity gossip. Now I've got a chance to really be a newswoman again."

"But you've got to keep seeing Jerry Meredith."

"I can handle that."

The waiter brought our check. I gave him my American Express card. I did this with some trepidation. American

Express had sent me an overdue notice just the other day that I hadn't had time to read. But I did note the word "delinquent" in the first sentence. The waiter did not break out into hysterical laughter when he came back with my card. He did not take out a pair of scissors and cut it in two. He did not call the police. Instead he just handed me a receipt to sign and thanked me for dining at the Helmsley Hotel. This was good.

"What about Elaine Rivera?" Clare asked.

"Who?"

"The woman in jail I told you about. Who was beaten up by her husband."

"I'm awfully busy, Clare."

"It would only take an hour or two."

"I promise I'll go talk to her. Soon. It's just that right now I've got a lot of things to do on Jerry Meredith."

"Like what?"

"For one, I want to have another conversation with the ADA handling the case. Katherine Grieco. Ever hear of her?"

Clare made a face.

"I met her at the funeral," I said. "She seems pretty tough."

"Katherine Grieco makes Hillary Clinton look like Rebecca of Sunnybrook Farm."

"Then there's Eileen Clayton's business. Everybody keeps telling me she stepped on a lot of toes. I need to find out more about that. Maybe money was behind her murder, not passion."

I took a deep breath. "Plus I want to keep in touch with Jerry. I mean, he is the key to this case and . . ."

Clare picked up her cup and downed the remains of the coffee in it.

"Oh, shut up," I told her.

"I didn't say anything," she said innocently.

"Yeah, but I know what you were thinking."

The station started the promos for my interview early that day. By midday, they were running them six times an hour—right in the middle of "The Brady Bunch," "Gilligan's Island," and the rest of Channel Six's award-winning daytime lineup.

It went for thirty seconds and started with the clip of Meredith being led out of his apartment on the day of his arrest. There was a freeze-frame on Meredith's face, then a voice-over said:

"Other stations just cover the news. Channel Six reporters make news. Our Jenny McKay gets the story behind the story in an exclusive interview with TV host Jerry Meredith."

Then came a tease from the interview with Meredith saying: "I did not kill my wife."

Finally they showed me at work in a busy newsroom typing on a computer. The voice-over said: "The Channel Six newsbreakers. Ahead of the news. Ahead of everyone else in town. Catch the excitement tonight at six, on Channel Six, right after 'Who's the Boss?' "

"Hey, that's pretty good," Sanders said in admiration as we watched it while I did some final editing on the Meredith tape. "That ought to get a few people to change the channel from 'Three's Company' on Channel Five, huh?"

"There's nothing wrong with 'Three's Company,' " I said.

"What are they running now—the early shows with Suzanne Somers as Chrissy?"

Suzanne Somers quit the show in a contract dispute, and they replaced her with some other nameless blonde. Then they got rid of Joyce De Witt too and left John Ritter as the star of the show.

"Without Suzanne Somers."

"I liked them better with her," he said.

"I can't believe we're having this conversation," I told him.

By the time I got to the set for the six o'clock newscast, I was feeling on top of the world. Barry Kaiser asked me to do a sound check by saying something into the microphone hooked to my Channel Six blazer. I started singing the theme song from "The Mary Tyler Moore Show."

"You think maybe this is a good time for me to throw my

hat up in the air and catch it like Mary used to do?" I asked Kaiser.

"Please, no hats," he said.

"Sorry, I forgot."

"Okay, here we go," he said to everyone in the studio. "Ten seconds to airtime. Let's make it a winner. Five . . . four . . . three . . . two . . . one . . ."

The pulsating sound of the Channel Six News theme came on, and we were under way. It was a piece of cake. I did a little bit of opening repartee with Conroy, and then they went to the tape of the interview. I watched myself on the monitor. I liked what I saw. Damn, I was pretty good. They let the interview run for a full eight minutes, which is an eternity in TV news. Then I did a little wrap-up on other aspects of the case, turned it back to Conroy, and we went to a commercial.

When the newscast was over, Donald Pesin strode into the newsroom.

"Now that is a goddamned scoop," he announced to everyone. "That is an exclusive. That is a blockbuster. That's the kind of story that just reaches out of the TV and grabs the viewer by the balls." He reached down and grabbed his own crotch for effect.

"Class always tells, doesn't it?" Stormy Phillips whispered next to me.

Pesin continued: "There's crews outside from CNN, Channel Two, Channel Four, and Seven and reporters from the *Post*, *Daily News*, and *USA Today*. They all want to talk to us about our Jerry Meredith story. Don't you just love it?"

Someone let the reporters in then, and Pesin held court for them all. He did interviews. He answered questions. He told anecdotes about TV news and quipped about how funny it was that all the press had to come to Channel Six for the story. A couple of times, he deflected a few compliments my way. But mostly it was his show. And he was a real expert at it. He played the press like a Stradivarius.

Later, after I'd repaired to the Bridge Café a few blocks away for a celebratory drink with some of the people in the newsroom, Stormy Phillips brought up something that had been on my mind too.

"It's funny, but I thought you were the reporter on the Jerry Meredith story. The one who was supposed to become a star. I didn't hear your name mentioned a lot back there when Pesin was doing those interviews. The only name I kept hearing was Donald Pesin."

"Okay, the guy sort of likes publicity," I admitted.

"Sort of likes publicity?"

"Pesin could have given me a tad more credit," I agreed.

"The guy's in love with himself. He doesn't care about anyone else. You remember what I told you?"

"Don't trust him."

"The advice stands," she said.

It was after eleven by the time I got home. I gave Hobo an entire can of Mighty Dog to apologize for being late with his supper, then took him for a walk around Union Square Park. The early editions of the *Post* were on sale at a newstand on the corner. The front-page headline said: JERRY'S TEARFUL PLEA: I DIDN'T DO IT! There was a picture of him taken off the screen talking to me. My name was in the third paragraph of the story. Donald Pesin wasn't quoted until the jump page.

Ah, it's great to be beautiful, talented, and famous.

The phone was ringing in my apartment when I got back. I picked it up and said: "Beautiful, talented, and famous speaking."

"McKay. It's Lieutenant Jellinek."

Lieutenant Jellinek? Why was Jellinek calling me at home? I didn't think he'd taken the trouble just to tell me how much he liked my work.

"Did you know a woman named Cheryl Wolcott?" he asked. "She worked for Jerry Meredith."

"Did?" I had a bad feeling.

"Yeah, she's dead. Went out a window on the fifteenth floor of her apartment building on West Eighty-third a few hours ago. She landed all over the street. It's not a pretty sight."

I took a deep breath. I'd met Cheryl Wolcott thirty-six hours ago. She seemed nice. I always wanted to be an investigative reporter, she told me. Maybe I'll look into this a little myself, she said. Now she was gone.

"People on the show said she was asking a lot of questions in the last day or so about the Meredith case and mentioned you a few times. We also found your card in her purse. You think you might want to come up here and tell me what you know?"

"I'm on my way," I said.

11
The Mourning Show

The way I figured it, there were probably a couple of dozen people working on "The Morning Show."

A director. Producer. Associate producers. Cameramen. Makeup people. Talent coordinators. Production assistants. Stagehands.

Maybe thirty, thirty-five people all together—forty tops.

At last count, the star was arrested for murder. His wife was dead. So was his producer. And from what Cheryl Wolcott told me before she died, the director was killed in a traffic accident a few weeks earlier and a production assistant mysteriously disappeared.

You didn't have to be a genius to figure out something very strange was going on with my old pal Jerry Meredith.

"That's a helluva body count," Jacobson said when I told him what happened. "They ought to call it 'The Mourning Show.' "

"Hey, remember that," I said. "Maybe we can use it for the tag line of the story."

"Are you kidding? I can barely remember my name."

I'd gotten both him and Sanders out of bed and told them to meet me right away at Wolcott's apartment building.

Jacobson had been sound asleep. Sanders was in bed too, but he wasn't asleep. I could hear a woman's voice and some high-pitched squealing in the background. Different strokes for different folks.

"I wasted a dinner and a movie on this girl," Sanders complained to me now as we stood on the corner of West 83rd Street and West End Avenue. "And then you call me before I get the payoff."

Jacobson muttered, "I'm starving. Aren't there any restaurants still open in this neighborhood?"

"It's great to work with professionals," I told them.

The cops had cordoned off the spot where Cheryl Wolcott landed when she went out a window on the fifteenth floor. A crowd of people stood around watching. The body was already gone, which was just fine by me. I wasn't sure what a body looked like after it fell fifteen stories, but I was content to go through life without ever knowing. It wasn't something we'd show on camera anyway. So Sanders and Jacobson just started shooting the scene, the outside of the apartment building and the cops and crowd milling around.

I went upstairs. Jellinek was in Cheryl Wolcott's apartment, along with the crime lab people. He was crawling around on his hands and knees near an open window, pointing out pieces of carpet and hair follicles for the crime boys to put into plastic bags. I came up behind him.

"Inspector Clouseau, I presume?" I said.

Jellinek looked around and sighed. Then he stood up. He did not seem pleased at what he had found on the floor. He did not seem pleased to see me. He did not seem pleased with life. Lt. Jellinek was not a happy man.

"Did you solve the case yet?" I asked him.

"Oh sure, we picked up a suspect a half hour ago, took him downtown to be booked, already had the trial, and gave him twenty to life. We were just waiting around now so we could tell you about it for the six o'clock report."

"You haven't solved the case?"

"Jeez, McKay, we only found the body an hour ago."

"Angela Lansbury solves all her cases in an hour on 'Murder, She Wrote,' " I pointed out.

"That's TV, this is real life. Sometimes I wonder if you know the difference."

"It does get a bit tricky, " I admitted.

I walked over to the window and looked down at the street below. The crowd was starting to thin out now. The show was over. I thought about Cheryl Wolcott looking out this same window a couple of hours earlier. I thought about her energy and her excitement when she talked about her days as a reporter. Now she was dead. And I couldn't shake the horrible feeling that it had something to do with the Jerry Meredith case and our conversation that day in her office.

"What do you think happened?" I asked Jellinek, turning back to him from the window.

"On the face of it, it looks like suicide. The Wolcott woman comes home depressed—maybe over the future of the show because of Meredith's arrest, maybe over her personal life or her finances or her health or something. Whatever it is, she sees no way out. So she takes a header out the window onto West End Avenue."

I made a snorting sound. "C'mon, Lieutenant, even you don't believe that."

"It could have happened that way," he insisted.

The apartment was two bedrooms, with one side facing downtown toward Columbus Circle and the lights of Broadway. The inside looked like some designer's vision of what a New York City apartment should like. All glass and chrome and metal. Modern and clean, but very stark and without any character.

I walked into the kitchen. The broiler part of the stove was open, and I could see two baked potatoes inside. There were also some lamb chops on a pan over one of the grills. And an untouched bowl of salad, with the dressing standing next to it.

"I guess she decided to cook herself a nice meal first, huh?" I yelled out to Jellinek. "Then she changed her mind and jumped instead?"

"Suicides do crazy things. I once found a guy who cleaned his apartment from top to bottom, paid all his bills, dressed up in a tuxedo, and then swallowed carbolic acid."

I came back into the living room.

"There's enough food there for two people. Maybe she was expecting a guest."

"Maybe she was just hungry."

"I think she was murdered," I told him.

"Yeah, me too," Jellinek said gloomily.

There was a yellow velvet couch, along with two pieces of metal that I think were what modern furniture passes off as chairs. Lt. Jellinek—all 250 pounds of him—plopped down on the couch with a thud. I wasn't sure it would hold the weight. I looked at the chair next to him and thought about sitting too, but decided against it. I was afraid if I ever got into that contraption I might never get out again.

"Let's talk about your business card being in Cheryl Wolcott's purse," he said.

"Sure."

"According to someone we just contacted from the show, the Wolcott woman was asking a lot of questions in the past day or so about Jerry Meredith and some other stuff. Why do you think she was doing that?"

I told him about our conversation and about the death of the director and the disappearance of the young production assistant.

"Did she figure there was some sort of connection between all this?"

"I think she felt it was a long shot, but she wanted to check it out."

"What do you think?"

"I think the odds just got a bit better."

Jellinek nodded. "That's an awfully lot of bad things to happen in a group of people that size in so short a time."

"Have you talked to Jerry Meredith yet?" I asked.

"Gee, there's a terrific idea. I wonder why I didn't think of it."

"You've already talked to him, and he has an alibi, right?"

"We sent a man over as soon as we found the body. He was at the Limelight, one of those fun spots where the beautiful people go to drink and dance the night away, from eight until eleven. Bartender remembers talking to him there. Wolcott went out the window about nine-thirty."

"So it wasn't him?"

"Maybe it was, maybe it wasn't. Maybe he slipped out the back, killed her, and then got back before anyone knew he was missing. Maybe he hired someone else to do it. Maybe he paid off the bartender to lie for him...."

"You're really fishing, aren't you?"

"I don't even have a motive for Cheryl Wolcott's death."

"Sure you do. She and I talked about Eileen Clayton's death, and she started nosing around it. She was asking questions on the set of the show. I think she stumbled onto something and someone..."

"That's just speculation, McKay."

"Okay, but it's intelligent speculation."

I thought about what he'd just told me.

"Don't you think it's a little strange that Jerry Meredith is out partying at the Limelight less than a week after his wife's death?" I asked.

"We all deal with our grief in strange ways."

"Maybe. But in public—during my interview and at the funeral—Jerry puts on a big show of grief for his late wife. The rest of the time he doesn't seem all that broken up by it."

"Hey, I thought you were the one who says he's innocent."

"Oh yeah. I forgot."

With a pained look on his face, Jellinek tried to get up from the couch. It was a big job—and I wasn't sure he was going to make it. For a second or two he teetered in midair—and I figured his body could go either way. Finally he made it onto his feet again. I wanted to cheer.

"Let me tell you something," he said quietly. "Katherine Grieco says Jerry Meredith murdered his wife. He did not have any help; he did it himself. Now his producer turns up dead too, and he's got an alibi for that. That complicates things a bit. Because if the two deaths are related, then maybe's he's not responsible for either one. Unless Cheryl Wolcott was a suicide that had nothing to do with Eileen Clayton or Jerry Meredith. That makes it all nice and simple again. Wolcott can be quietly buried, Meredith can go to jail for his wife's murder, and Ms. Grieco can go on to fame and fortune as a fearless, crime-busting district attorney. Do you see what I'm saying here?"

"It's going to be listed as a suicide."

"At least technically. If I come up with any solid proof that it's murder, I'll investigate that. But in the meantime I'm not getting in Katherine Grieco's line of fire. You should see her temper . . ."

"Yeah, we've met."

Jellinek said he'd go on camera for a live sound bite. Sanders and Jacobson came up from the street and set up their equipment. Both of them were still grumbling about working so late. I pointed out that the search for truth knows no curfew. They thanked me profusely for this insight and said they'd try to have a better attitude in the future—not!

Jellinek handled the interview like a pro. Yes, Cheryl Wolcott's death was officially being called a suicide. No, there was no evidence she'd been depressed about anything. Yes, all possibilities were still being investigated.

When we were finished, Jellinek yawned loudly. "I'm beat," he said. "I'm going home to bed."

That made it unanimous. Jellinek, Jacobson, and Sanders all wanted to go to sleep. This never happened to Lois Lane. I mean, she and Clark and Jimmy and Inspector Henderson never slipped off to cop a few z's in the middle of the show. Why couldn't life be like that? Everything wrapped up in a neat thirty- or sixty-minute package with a happy ending.

"Let's keep in touch," I told Jellinek.

"Why?" he asked.

"Well, maybe I'll come up with some new clues. Or you will. Then we'll exchange information. Join forces. Merge our crime-fighting capabilities. We're all on the same side in this, you know."

"You want me to wear a beeper or anything? That way if I'm in a meeting with the Commissioner I can drop everything and rush to a phone to find out what you want."

"I don't think you're taking my suggestion in the spirit it was intended."

"McKay, it's too late for this," he sighed.

He wandered away. So did Sanders and Jacobson, after packing up their equipment. It was too late to do anything with the tape, so we'd edit it in the morning. I took one more look around the apartment. At the window. The food on the stove. The bedrooms. I opened up a few closets. Nothing there. One of the bedrooms had been turned into an office, with a big walnut desk covered with papers. I wandered over to it.

I had absolutely no idea what I was looking for. Besides, I figured the cops had already done all this. Or else they would soon. But sometimes I can't help myself. I'm just naturally curious.

There was no suicide note. No confession that she had really killed Eileen Clayton. No key for a secret safe-deposit box. No map leading me to a buried treasure.

I was just about ready to give up when I found one thing that might be of some help. Two things actually.

The first was a staff list for "The Morning Show" with all the home addresses and phone numbers. Becky Bessard was on the list. She was listed at a place on East 27th Street. So was Andrew Cox, the director. He'd lived in Bergen County, New Jersey. I wrote the information down in my notebook.

The other thing I found was a restaurant guidebook for New York City. Nothing unusual about that, except that it was turned to the section for Brooklyn. Someone—probably Cheryl Wolcott—had put a circle around the listing for an Italian restaurant. There were plenty of Italian restaurants in Manhattan. Why did she need to go all the way to Brooklyn to eat? But it was probably no big deal. Maybe she had a friend in Brooklyn. Maybe she had business there. Maybe somebody told her they had the greatest food in the history of Western civilization. The name of the restaurant was the Colony Café. I wrote it down, along with the telephone number and an address.

I wasn't sure what to do next. I had a lot of leads to pursue. There was Becky Bessard. Andrew Cox. The Limelight.

Decisions, decisions.

I left Cheryl Wolcott's apartment, hailed a cab on West End Avenue, went home, and crawled into bed.

If you can't beat 'em, join 'em.

12
The Queen of Mean

The headquarters of the Clayton Corporation was in a skyscraper on Park Avenue, a few blocks north of the Pan Am Building. Well, it used to be the Pan Am Building. Now it's called the MetLife Building. I miss seeing the big, familiar Pan Am sign. Just like I miss Gimbel's, the Automat, and elevated subway tracks. I have a lot of trouble with change.

It was a little after noon, and people were spilling out onto Park for lunch. Some of them headed for nearby restaurants. Others bought sandwiches from street vendors and settled in with newspapers on benches to take in some of the afternoon sun.

I really wanted to join them. There was a little park in front of the Clayton Building, with a water fountain and a concrete wall alongside to sit on. I could buy me a foot-long hot dog buried in sauerkraut, a salty pretzel with mustard, and a copy of the *Daily News*, and spend an hour or two working on my tan. It sounded like heaven.

But I had an appointment at 12:15 with Glen LeBeau, who was the executive vice president for the Clayton Corporation.

I got it because I was charming, persistent, and resourceful. And also because Donald Pesin set it up.

I was in the editing room with Sanders and Jacobson working on the Cheryl Wolcott tape when Pesin came in.

"You had a busy night, huh?" he said.

"The city never sleeps," I told him.

"Let's see what you've got."

We'd started with the scene footage of the street where Cheryl Wolcott landed, then an exterior shot of her building. I did a voice-over which said:

McKAY: They're spelling "The Morning Show" M-O-U-R-N-I-N-G today. The top-rated daytime talk show suffered another tragedy when its executive producer, Cheryl Wolcott, died in a plunge from her fifteenth-floor apartment here on West End Avenue.

It comes just days after the arrest of "Morning Show" host Jerry Meredith, who's charged with killing his wife, financial czar Eileen Clayton.

And Channel Six News has learned there have been two other mysterious incidents around the ill-fated show in the past few weeks. The director died in a traffic accident. And a production assistant has disappeared without a trace. . . .

After that, the picture cut to the inside of Cheryl Wolcott's apartment and my interview with Jellinek, in which he tap-danced around the suicide question.

When it was over, I was back on camera saying:

McKAY: Murder or suicide? Although police are calling it an apparent suicide, sources in the department say they haven't ruled out the possibility of foul play in this or any of the other incidents.

What does all this mean in the Eileen Clayton murder case? Right now, no one here knows. Or if they do, they're not saying.

THE MOURNING SHOW

From West End Avenue, this is Jenny McKay reporting for Channel Six News.

The screen went dead. Pesin sat slumped in a chair staring at it. He was wearing a bright red madras sports jacket, blue and green plaid pants, and a mustard-yellow shirt. It was an awesome color combination. When he moved, it looked like a kaleidoscope. Watching him made me feel like I was on a bad acid trip from the sixties.

He was eating a bagel smothered in cream cheese and drinking coffee from an oversized mug with lettering on the side that said, "The Big Guy." Some of the cream cheese had dribbled down the side of his mouth. He used the sleeve of his shirt to wipe it off. Then he turned to me and said:

"It's great. Sensational. This story just keeps getting better, doesn't it?"

I said he was right.

"Okay, here's what we do," he said. "We put this on tonight, of course. But with lots of promos, lots of hype during the day. Stuff like 'Terror stalks America's favorite TV talk show. Details at six.'"

I said he was right again.

"Then you have to go after a dynamite follow-up," he continued.

"Well, first I'm going to check out the director and the production assistant. Then I can . . ."

"No, you're not," Pesin said.

"I'm not?"

He smiled broadly. "No, first you're going to do a profile of Eileen Clayton. A real profile this time, not that self-serving pap from the funeral. I met a guy named Glen LeBeau last night at Elaine's. He's the executive vice president for the Clayton Corporation, and he's got some dynamite stuff to say about her."

I thought back to my conversation with Jack Weinstein of the *Daily News*. When he told me about the nude dancer and what a tyrant Eileen Clayton was.

Pesin wrote down LeBeau's name and number on a piece of paper and handed it to me. "Call him right away."

"Sure thing," I said. "It sounds like a great idea."

Pesin took a big gulp of his coffee, belched loudly, and stood up. "You're doing great work, Jenny," he said. "Keep it up." Then he waddled his way out the door. Probably headed to a diner for breakfast.

"Quack, quack," I said when he was gone.

Sanders gave me a funny look. "I notice you didn't say that while he was here."

"What does that mean?"

"The legendary acid tongue of Jenny McKay isn't too active in front of Pesin these days."

"Are you saying I'm being a bit too deferential?"

"You're kissing his ass is what you're doing, McKay."

"Am not!"

"Oh, no?" He did an exaggerated imitation of me talking to Pesin. "Sure thing, Mr. Pesin," he gushed. "That sounds like a great idea."

"Well, it was a good idea," I insisted stubbornly.

I looked over at Jacobson, who was working on a crossword puzzle.

"Hey, Artie, you didn't think I was kissing Pesin's ass, did you?"

He put down his paper and looked at me. "Let me put it this way, McKay. If Donald Pesin would have stopped suddenly on his way out the door, you'd have a split lip right now."

I went back to my desk and called LeBeau. He said he'd be happy to talk to me today about Eileen Clayton. But he didn't want his name used.

"Let's do it off-the-record," he suggested.

"Sure."

"Even better, let's make it on deep background."

Ever since Watergate, people talk like that. Now, I have no idea what the difference is between "off-the-record" and "deep background." I'm not even sure there is one. But if a source wants to pretend he's Deep Throat, I'm happy to play Bob Woodward.

"No problem," I said.

LeBeau turned out to be a real pretty boy. Thirtysomething, blond hair, muscular body. He looked like he should be carrying a surfboard. Quite a hunk, if you liked that type. I didn't, but what did I know? I was still hung up on Jerry Meredith.

We sat in what used to be Eileen Clayton's office on the forty-fourth floor. He was sitting at her desk.

"Eileen was an amazing woman," he told me. "Brilliant, witty, powerful. She was a giant presence in everyone's life she came in contact with. We're all going to miss her so much."

"I heard she was a real bitch," I said.

LeBeau smiled. "Well, yes—that too."

"Tell me the ways."

He pondered that for a minute. I didn't figure pondering was something he did a lot of. Glen looked to me like a "party hardy" kind of guy. With the sun streaming in from the window behind him, I really pictured him on a beach somewhere with a girl in a bikini. Sun. Sand. A keg of beer. Beach Boys music playing on the radio. Surf's up, dude.

"Did you ever hear of a TV movie called 'The Queen of Mean'?" he asked finally.

"You mean the one about Leona Helmsley? Sure."

"If you take every horrible thing Suzanne Pleshette did as Leona Helmsley in that movie, multiply it by ten, and then throw in some more incidents so unspeakable that they defy belief—well, you start to get a picture of what it was like to be around Eileen Clayton."

"Aren't you exaggerating just a little bit?"

"I remember one day we had a meeting of the board of directors, and Eileen didn't like what they told her. So she made them sit there. First for an hour. Then two hours, then three and four. Pretty soon they had to go to the bathroom and were hungry and thirsty. But Eileen refused to let anyone leave the room. Finally Eileen told them to take a five-minute break—she took out a watch and told them she was timing it. You have all these guys in suits racing down the hall and fighting for urinals and stalls so they can get back without being late."

LeBeau shook his head. "Do you want to hear the best part? When they got their paychecks, Eileen had deducted five minutes' worth of pay from everyone—exactly the amount of time they were out of the boardroom."

"I'm starting to get the picture."

"I haven't even begun to paint the picture. Eileen got off on humiliating people. Belittling them. She was the royalty, and you were the serf. She said it all came down to money—and she had more than anybody.

"She fired people for the slightest thing—undercooking her meal, making a typing mistake in a report, or just for saying something she didn't agree with. Her face would turn purple with rage, and she'd start screaming about how stupid or incompetent or disloyal they were.

"She'd do this anywhere—in a crowded room of people, on the street, in front of someone's friends or family. Everyone else would just sort of cower in the background and be grateful it wasn't them on the other end of the tongue-lashing."

"How about her husband?" I asked. "How did she treat him?"

"That poor guy had it worse than anybody. Come over here, I want to show you something."

I walked over to where he was sitting behind Eileen Clayton's desk. He opened up a panel and showed me what seemed to be some sort of master control board.

"These buttons run everything in this room," he said. He pushed a couple of them to show me. "Lights. Air-conditioning. TV. And surprise, surprise—a hidden video camera and taping system."

"She secretly taped her conversations without anyone knowing it?"

"Uh-huh. Then sometimes she played them back for laughs. One of her favorite subjects was her dear hubby, Jerry Meredith. She'd browbeat the poor guy something terrible, totally emasculate him—then cackle with delight

THE MOURNING SHOW

as she showed the tape to people later. And he never knew anything about it."

I shook my head in amazement as I thought about what Jerry's life with Eileen Clayton must have been like. Maybe if he really did kill her, he could get off on justifiable cause.

"She sounds like a real sweetheart," I said as I sat down again. "How come you stayed around?"

"I escaped a lot of it because of the nature of my . . . uh, duties with her."

"What exactly were your duties, Glen?"

"I served as Eileen's personal assistant. I did everything from helping to analyze the world trade markets to managing the office. Why?"

"Well, I can't help but notice that you and a lot of the men who worked for Eileen Clayton are . . . attractive."

"Thank you."

"That was an observation, not a compliment."

"So what's your point?"

"I heard that Ms. Clayton had quite an eye for attractive males. Jerry Meredith for one. Maybe a lot of others on the side. Being a cynical person by nature, I suspect she didn't just keep you around because of your astute grasp of the international trade market and your typing skills. Were you sleeping with her, Glen?"

LeBeau stared at me across the desk. "I'm not going to dignify that with an answer."

"Okay, how about this then? Were you her toyboy? Her beefcake? Her love slave? Exactly what did you do to earn your executive vice president's salary?"

I wasn't sure if he was going to hit me or throw me out. As it turned out, he didn't do either. His face turned red first and then he chuckled. "You're really something," he said.

He looked down at his watch. It was past one. "How about finishing this conversation in a restaurant over lunch?" he said.

We went to the Bull and Bear, which is at Lexington and

49th Street. A maître d' there greeted LeBeau warmly and led us to a red-paneled booth in the center of the room, where we ordered drinks and studied the menu. There was everything on it from hamburger to filet mignon. I asked LeBeau who was paying. He said he was. That meant he was using Eileen Clayton's money, which I figured was really Jerry Meredith's money now. So I went for the filet mignon and some escargot for an appetizer. I figured Jerry could afford it.

"The answer to your question is yes," LeBeau said. "Of course I slept with Eileen. So did Michael, one of the guys you saw back there in my office, and Gary and Sandy and Victor and a lot of others. It was, as you guessed, part of the job."

"And what did you get in return? Besides sweet nothings whispered into your ear, that is."

LeBeau smiled. "Eileen wasn't big on sweet nothings. She was more apt to be talking business deals right up to the time she climaxed."

"That doesn't sound like much fun."

"It was for her. She loved money, and she loved to fuck. It was, as they say, what made the world go round for her."

"Like I said, what about you? What did you get out of it?"

"Some pleasant evenings. And, of course, a $250,000 salary, a Mercedes, unlimited expense account, and a beach house in Southampton."

I let out a low whistle. "Not bad."

I was going to say something else. I was going to say what that made him. But I decided not to. At least not until after he paid the check.

The waiter brought our drinks. LeBeau had ordered white wine. I was drinking Amstel Light. Out of a bottle. They bring you glasses at a place like the Bull and Bear, but I always drink Amstel Light out of a bottle. You can take the girl out of the saloon, but you can't take the saloon out of the girl.

"Do you think Jerry Meredith killed his wife?" I asked.

"Maybe. Probably. I suppose I'd have done the same thing if I'd been in his shoes."

"You mean because he knew about you and all the other men in her life?"

"I don't know if he knew or not. He might have found out. Or I suppose she could have told him just to make him crazy. That would be Eileen's style. She liked to do stuff like that."

"There was another man in her life too, wasn't there? Someone named Bobby Santos? He danced at a place called Cary's."

LeBeau nodded. "A bit of rough trade, that one."

"Was Eileen Clayton in love with him?"

"She was in love with herself. No one else."

"Is he the one who got her pregnant?"

"Who knows? There's plenty of suspects, aren't there?"

"Maybe it was you."

"No."

"How do you know?"

"I know."

"How can you be so sure?"

"Because I had a vasectomy."

I stared at him. "You're serious?"

"Absolutely."

"Why?"

"Eileen wanted me to have one." He smiled. "She hated to screw with a condom."

I shook my head. "Wow, you really earned that $250,000 a year, didn't you?"

"In ways you can't imagine."

He told me more stories while we ate. About the ways Eileen Clayton terrorized people. How she used men for her own sexual purposes. How she flaunted her money with everyone. Damn, it wasn't just her pregnancy that had a long list of suspects. A lot of people had plenty of reason to want the lady dead.

"Do you think her husband fooled around too?"

"Jerry? Not if he knew what was good for him."

"But if his wife was . . ."

"Eileen didn't believe in being fair. It was okay for her to have fun, but if she ever caught Jerry with another woman—well, he'd have been out on his ear with nothing."

"She could do that if there was a divorce?"

"Sure. Eileen was a sharp lady. I heard she made the poor bastard sign a killer prenuptial agreement. It tied him up so tightly he could barely buy a pack of gum without checking with her first."

A prenup agreement. Weinstein had mentioned some speculation about that too at the *Daily News*. It made sense. Someone like Eileen Clayton probably wouldn't get married without one. I made a note to myself to try to get ahold of a copy.

"I'll tell you something even worse," LeBeau said. "You know those secret tapes I told you about back in the office? The ones where she really humiliated him? Well, she loved to watch them in bed with me—while we were making love." He shook his head sadly. "I really felt sorry for him."

The waiter was back offering us coffee and dessert. LeBeau ordered some brandy. I agonized for a while between the cream puffs and the chocolate cheesecake, but finally settled on the key lime pie. I told myself it had less calories. I drank straight coffee with it.

"So what happens now?" I asked LeBeau. "Who gets Eileen Clayton's money?"

"I don't know. I'm sure there'll be a long legal battle."

"And you?"

"I guess I'm going to have to look for another job."

"Maybe you should put an ad in the paper," I suggested. "Something like this: 'Executive assistant available for ambitious, hard-driving female CEO. Types one hundred words per minute, makes great coffee, and does dynamite oral sex. References available upon request.' "

LeBeau laughed. "You're cute, McKay. Not drop-dead gorgeous, but cute. To be perfectly honest, I thought you were a little obnoxious at first. But you sort of grow on a person."

He smiled at me across the table. It was a high-voltage smile. The wine and the brandy were kicking in a bit now. I could picture him at long, intimate lunches with Eileen Clayton. He was good. He was very good.

"It's not that late," he was saying. "Why don't we . . . ?"

I held up my hand. "Don't even think about it."

"What?"

"Coming on to me."

"Why not?"

"You're not my type, and I'm not yours, Glen. I don't have enough money."

We drank our coffee in silence for a few seconds.

"I guess you and I aren't meant to be, huh?" he said finally. "We're just like two ships passing in the night. . . ."

"Why do people always say that?"

"Say what?"

"About it being like two ships passing in the night."

"Well . . ."

"I mean, why two *ships*? Why not say two cars passing on a dark highway? Or two people passing on a dark sidewalk? Have you ever actually seen two ships passing in the night? I haven't."

"It's just an expression. . . ."

"And why does it even have to be night? I mean, the idea is of two people or things headed in different directions that have a brief encounter. But the concept works in daylight too. And for that matter . . ."

LeBeau shook his head and signaled the waiter for the check. "You're right," he said.

"About what?"

"It would never work between us. You're too deep for me."

"A lot of men tell me that," I said.

13

Money Talks, Jenny Walks

It's a great feeling to have someone waiting for you when you come home.

Someone to talk to after a hard day at work. Someone to laugh with. Someone to share a cozy meal with. It makes the apartment seem so much warmer and friendlier and cheerful.

There was someone waiting for me when I got home that night.

That would have been good, except for one thing. I live alone.

The door was open, the lights on, and the TV blaring. I could hear the voice of Maureen O'Boyle on "A Current Affair" saying: "Rebecca told her husband she had a part-time job, but she didn't tell him it was as an exotic dancer. Wives who take it off to earn extra money. Next on 'A Current Affair!' "

Now there were three possibilities: 1) Maureen O'Boyle was actually in my apartment, 2) Hobo had figured out how to turn on the TV, or 3) Someone else was in my apartment watching my TV.

THE MOURNING SHOW

Hmmm.

The smart thing to do here was simply walk back down the hall the way I came, get on the elevator, and go to the lobby. Then tell the doorman to call the police. When the cops showed up, they could sort it out.

Yep, that was the smart thing to do, all right.

From long practice of hardly ever doing the smart thing, I pushed the door open and went inside.

There were two guys sitting on my couch in front of the TV. I'd never seen either of them before. One was playing with Hobo. He looked about my age, big, with bushy dark hair, wearing a loud Hawaiian shirt. The other guy was younger—maybe twenty-five—with a ponytail, dressed in jeans and a white T-shirt. He was eating some peanuts I'd bought the other day and drinking a bottle of my Amstel Light.

When they heard me come in, both of them looked up.

"Jenny McKay?" the bushy-haired one said.

"Don't hurt the dog," I said.

To be perfectly truthful, Hobo didn't seem to be in a great deal of danger. He was licking the guy's face and getting his stomach scratched. In between that, the one with the ponytail kept flipping him peanuts, which Hobo caught in his mouth. I was going to have to give Hobo a refresher course in guard dog duties.

"Nobody's hurting anybody," bushy-hair said to me. He stood up, and Hobo jumped off his lap and came bounding over to greet me. "I'm Doug, and this is Kevin," the guy said.

He stuck out his hand. I shook it.

"Hi, Doug. Hi, Kevin. I'm Jenny."

We stood there for a second.

"Let me guess," I said. "This is a meeting of the Future 4-H Club of America, and you want me to join?"

Doug laughed and looked over at Kevin. "They told us you thought you were quite the comedian."

"Doug . . . Kevin," I said slowly, "I don't want to be rude or impolite and please tell me if this offends you in any way, but... WHAT THE HELL ARE YOU DOING IN MY LIVING ROOM?"

"Gee, I'm sorry if we upset you," he said. "It's just that we didn't know how long you were going to be, and we didn't want to wait outside. So your super let us in."

"My super opened up my apartment?"

"Yeah. I think he somehow got the idea we were police officers."

"How would he do that?"

"Well, we sort of showed him phony badges."

It didn't take much to fool my super. They probably could have gotten in even without the badges. Well, that settled that. He wasn't getting any Christmas tip from me this year.

"Okay, you're here," I said. "Now what?"

"Vincent Guardere wants to see you."

"Who?"

"Vincent Guardere. He's a businessman from Brooklyn. Sheepshead Bay, to be precise. He has a matter he urgently needs to discuss with you."

I shook my head, walked into the kitchen, and checked the refrigerator. There was one bottle of Amstel left.

"A businessman from Sheepshead Bay," I said. "I love it."

I uncapped the top and took a long drink. "You can tell Vincent Guarddog or whatever his name is..."

"Guardere."

"Tell him to call me at my office and make an appointment. If I have time, I'll try to set something up. In the meantime, have a nice night. Have a nice life. Good-bye."

Doug cleared his throat nervously and looked at Kevin. "I'm afraid you'll have to come with us now," he told me.

"I'm busy now."

"Mr. Guardere simply won't take no for an answer."

I hadn't been afraid since I'd seen the two of them playing with Hobo. They didn't seem like they wanted to hurt me. But it could get ugly now. Unless I did what they said.

"Okay," I sighed, "but I have to walk my dog and feed him first."

"We already did that," Doug told me.

THE MOURNING SHOW

"You walked Hobo?"

"Well, we had to wait a long time for you to come home," Kevin explained.

There didn't seem to be anything left to say. We went down to their car—a brown Lincoln, just like the one I'd seen following me after Eileen Clayton's funeral—and drove to Brooklyn. Across 14th Street to the East River Drive, then over the Brooklyn Bridge. Doug drove, and Kevin sat in the backseat. I rode shotgun.

"Exactly what business is Mr. Guardere in?" I asked.

"He serves as a sort of intermediary for people interested in trying their hand at games of chance," Doug replied. "He facilitates their participation, you might say."

"He's a bookie," I said.

"That's sort of like saying Donald Trump manages an apartment house."

"Okay, he's a major bookie."

We were coming off the bridge now, making a left across Atlantic Avenue and then onto the Belt Parkway. So far, I knew where I was. You put me in deep Brooklyn, and I'm lost. Bensonhurst, Park Slope, and the neighborhoods across the river from Manhattan I know. I figured this was important in case I needed to throw open the door and make a run for it.

But I was only going to do that if I was in danger. I didn't see that happening. So far, the worst thing they'd done was tune the car radio to some station that wasn't K-ROCK. I had to listen to Frank Sinatra and Tony Bennett for the whole ride.

"Did you guys see *Goodfellas*?" I asked.

"Sure, great movie," Kevin said. He started doing an imitation of Joe Pesci: "Hey, Henry, here's a leg. Here's an arm. . . ."

"You guys aren't going to bring me back in the trunk or anything, are you?" I asked.

Doug smiled. "You know Mr. Mosconi, don't you?"

A bell went off for me. Mosconi, of course. Big Tony Mosconi.

"Yeah, I know him," I said casually.

A few years ago I did a big favor for Tony Mosconi, the number one mob boss in New York. His granddaughter was lost, and I put out an appeal over TV that got her back. I really didn't have a whole lot to do with it, but he's been grateful to me ever since. For a while, I even lived in an apartment he got for me. And he's helped me out on a few cases when I've reached dead ends.

Now it made a lot more sense why these guys were being so nice to me. I decided to revise my answer to the previous question.

"Actually Big Tony and I are really close. Thick as thieves, if you'll pardon the expression. I'm practically a member of his family. He loves me."

Doug nodded. "He told us you were all right. A bit of a pain in the ass, but basically okay. A guy could have a quiet little chat with you, and not see it turn up all over TV. That's what Tony said."

"Tony," I said, looking out at Gravesend Bay on our right as we drove through Bensonhurst, "is a great judge of character."

We finally stopped in front of an Italian restaurant in Sheepshead Bay. There didn't seem to be anybody eating in it, but I could hear noise and music coming from the back. A dapper man in a three-piece suit came out to meet us.

"I'm Vincent Guardere," he said when I got out of the car.

We shook hands.

"Thank you for coming." He glanced over at Doug and Kevin. "I hope it wasn't too much of an inconvenience for you."

"Well, these guys broke into my house, ate my food, drank my beer, and dragged me all the way out here against my will in the middle of the night."

"Is that a yes or no?" He smiled when he said it.

I smiled back. The only other mobster I knew was Tony Mosconi. Tony was fat and balding and smoked a big cigar. He looked sort of like Clemenza in *The Godfather*. But Guardere was different. He seemed more like a successful stockbroker or lawyer or corporation president. Except I knew he wasn't.

"Let's you and I go for a little walk, Miss McKay," he said.

"A walk?" I looked around. The streets were deserted, and it was getting dark. "Where to?"

"It doesn't really matter. We need to talk."

"I've had a tough day. I'm beat. How about we talk inside your restaurant? Sit down at a table, maybe have a drink or two . . . ?"

Guardere shook his head. "Walk," he said.

We walked. Him and me side by side, Doug and Kevin trailing about twenty paces behind us. It was a very bizarre scene, if you asked me. But no one did.

"You see," Guardere said when we were halfway down the block, "the authorities have recently taken a great interest in my business. I've found bugging devices in my restaurant, my home—even in our cars. There's no way to be sure we're not being monitored. Except this." He looked around. "They haven't figured out a way to bug the air yet."

I remembered John Gotti used to do the same thing. Held all his meetings in walks around the block. But it was too late. They convicted Gotti with a tape from his headquarters before he figured out what they were doing.

"What is your business, Mr. Guardere?" I asked.

"Gambling."

"Now what could that possibly have to do with me?"

"You and I have an interest in the same person."

"Who?" But I already had a hunch who it was.

"Jerry Meredith."

Bingo.

"Let me guess. Jerry owes you a lot of money for gambling debts. And you're getting worried."

We were walking faster now. I was having trouble keeping up. I was also getting winded.

"Jerry is a very charming fellow," he told me. "Glib, funny, personable. And a terrific talk show host too. Even I watch that show whenever I'm up in the morning."

"Yeah, he's the salt of the earth."

"Unfortunately he's a lousy gambler."

"How lousy?"

"$400,000 over the past six months. Wait a minute, the Mets lost last night. Make that $402,000."

I let out a low whistle. "Jesus. He bet all that on baseball?"

"Baseball. Football. Basketball. Soccer. Lacrosse."

"Lacrosse? He's a lacrosse fan?"

"There's an old story about gambling, Miss McKay. This guy bets on baseball and football games for twenty-one days in a row, and he loses every one of them. Twenty-one out of twenty-one. On the twenty-second day, he calls his bookie looking for some action. The bookie tells him there's no baseball or football games being played. Does he want to bet on hockey? 'Hockey?' the guy says indignantly. 'What the hell do I know about hockey?'" Guardere smiled. "You see my point?"

I was breathing heavier now. I definitely needed to start some sort of workout program.

"I still don't get it," I told Guardere. "Jerry's wife was worth a hundred jillion dollars. He's got a top-rated TV show. I know $400,000 is a lot of money to you. But it shouldn't be to him."

"That's what I thought too. So I kept extending his credit, figuring it was just a matter of time before he paid. And he kept losing. And losing."

"What happened when you asked him for the money?"

"He said he didn't have it."

"Why not?"

"Because his wife kept him on some sort of strict allowance. Can you believe that? And when I mentioned the TV show, he said she owned all the rights to that too. Poor bastard."

"So what did you tell him?"

"Money talks, bullshit walks."

"Clever response."

"Then he told me he thought he had a way to get the

money. But he needed some time. I said fine, but just don't take too long."

"Did he tell you what he was going to do?"

"No."

"Did you ask him?"

"I didn't care."

"Do you think his plan was to murder his wife?"

Guardere shrugged. It didn't matter to him. All that mattered was his money. We were coming up to the restaurant again after making a circle of a few blocks. I hoped he didn't want to take another lap.

"You're not going to want to hear this," I said, "but it may not make any difference. There were probably all sorts of prenuptial agreements and stuff that may mean he never gets to see any of her money."

"That's what lawyers are for. Anyway, out of jail he's got a chance in court to get his hands on my money. If he's in jail for her murder, I got no chance. That's the way I see it." He looked over at me. "Hey, are you okay?"

I nodded. I was leaning on the side of the car now, panting heavily. I looked up at the restaurant in front of us. The sign in the window said "Colony Café." The same name I'd seen in Cheryl Wolcott's apartment.

"You want anything?" Guardere asked. He sounded concerned.

I wanted to get in the car and go home. I wanted a stiff drink. I wanted to hug my dog. And I wanted to crawl into bed and sleep for about forty-eight hours.

"The question is what do you want from me, Mr. Guardere? Why am I here?"

"I've seen you on TV the past few days. You're on this campaign to make sure this murder rap doesn't stick on Jerry. I'm not exactly sure why, but that's what you're doing."

"I think he's innocent."

"Whatever. Anyway, we're on the same side on this. I don't want Jerry in jail and neither do you. Maybe we can join forces on this. Help each other."

"How can you help me?" I asked.

"With forty thousand dollars."

"Excuse me?"

"Forty thousand dollars is ten percent of what Jerry owes me. If he goes free and gets the money to me, I'll give you that as a finder's fee. Fair enough?"

"Fair, but not exactly ethical," I said.

"What do you mean?"

"Well, I've seen *All the President's Men* about twenty times. And I don't ever remember anything about Woodward and Bernstein taking payoffs on a story."

"So you won't take the money?"

"Mr. Guardere, I don't think Jerry Meredith killed his wife. And I'm going to do my best to prove that. If that helps you out of your financial dilemma, I'm very happy for you. But you don't have to pay me for it."

"I like the way you do business, McKay." He smiled.

Doug and Kevin drove me home afterward. Kevin told me he was taking law courses at Brooklyn College three nights a week. Doug had a wife and three kids at home on Staten Island, and another baby on the way. We really seemed to be bonding together.

They even let me change the radio. I wanted some Guns N' Roses music, but we compromised on the oldies station, WCBS-FM. By the time we pulled up in front of my building in Union Square, we were all singing along to "Get a Job."

Kevin got out of the car and opened the door for me.

"It was really nice meeting you," he said. "I enjoy watching you on TV."

Doug added, "I'm really sorry if we scared you in any way before. It's just business, you know?"

I said I understood. Then they got back in their car, waved, and pulled away. I watched until they were out of sight and then went upstairs.

The Colony Café, huh?

With my keen nose for news, I figured that might be a clue.

14
Clare Plays Matchmaker

The next day was Saturday, and I had a lot to think about.

I had a mobster who wanted to pay me $40,000 to prove Jerry Meredith didn't kill his wife. I had a dead producer—and a clue linking her to the mobster. I had a missing production assistant and a director who was the victim of a hit-and-run. I had a murder victim—Eileen Clayton—who seemed to have as many enemies as Muammar Qaddafi. And I had an ambitious assistant DA who wanted to reinstate the death penalty for Jerry Meredith, fry him in the electric chair, and make him pay the bill for the electricity.

I also had a date to go to Clare Lefferts's house tonight to meet Pete Rousch, the latest in her long line of blind dates for me.

I did not want to go to Clare's house for dinner. I did not want to meet Pete Rousch. I did not want to think about the Jerry Meredith case. I just wanted to stay home, veg out in front of the TV, and tell jokes to Hobo.

But I couldn't think of a way out. The last time I was supposed to go to Clare's to meet someone, I told her I had the flu. The time before that I used a toothache as an excuse. I was running out of ailments. Unless I came up with a new one, I was going to have to show up this time.

What I knew about Pete Rousch was that he was a history professor, he was in his forties, and he was just starting to date after a divorce. Clare told me he was bright, funny, and good-looking. On the other hand, she told him the same thing about me. Maybe we were both in for a surprise.

I spent the day cleaning my apartment. This is not something I do a great deal. I know there are some people who find it cathartic, they take out all their frustrations and anxiety by scrubbing the bathroom floor. Not me. I basically ignore housecleaning until the place gets so disgusting even I can't stand it anymore, then I clean it from top to bottom.

When I finished, I made myself a tuna fish sandwich, poured a glass of milk, and ate lunch in front of the TV. There was a movie on one of the cable channels called "—30—" starring Jack Webb as a managing editor. It's not the greatest newspaper movie ever made, but it does have its moments. Jack Webb still talks and moves like Sgt. Joe Friday on "Dragnet," the guy who played the fat detective Cannon is the city editor, and David Nelson is an eager copyboy. The only real flaw is the characters talk a lot about the ethics of the story they're working on. I've spent a great deal of time around newspapers. And I don't remember too many discussions about ethics.

The phone rang. I hoped it was Clare telling me she had to cancel for tonight. But it was Jerry Meredith.

"I was just thinking about you, Jenny," he said. "Do you maybe want to get together for dinner tonight?"

I swallowed hard. "Dinner?"

"Sure. We could get a bite to eat at this quiet little French place I know. Then maybe a movie. Or some dancing . . ."

"Jerry, your wife's only been dead for a week. Don't you think it's a little soon to start dating?"

"It's not a date."

"Yes, it is."

"It's just two friends . . ."

"Dinner is two friends. Maybe even a movie. But the dancing is really pushing it. . . ."

He laughed. "Okay, it's a date. So what do you say?"

"I'm busy tonight."

"Okay, we'll do it tomorrow night. . . ."

"Jerry, I'm not going out to dinner with you. It just wouldn't look right."

"How about brunch?"

"I've already eaten."

"Tomorrow then."

I thought about it. Brunch wouldn't really be a date. It would be more like a business lunch. And I did have a lot of questions for Jerry about the case. I thought about the newspaper movie I'd just seen. Jack Webb would probably disapprove of this. Going out with someone you're covering on a big story is borderline acceptable behavior at best. But I did turn down $40,000 last night. Hey, Jack—nobody's perfect.

"All right, I'll do brunch," I said. "But I'm picking up the check."

"Terrific. Let's meet at about one in the Oak Room of the Plaza."

The Oak Room of the Plaza is one of the most expensive places in town.

"On second thought, you pick up the check," I said.

After I hung up, I watched some more TV, read for a while, and took Hobo for a walk. Then I took a nap, a shower, and started to get dressed.

"The trick with an evening like this," I said to Hobo as I tried things on, "is to look casual, but not too casual. In other words, you should look like you just threw something on at the last minute. But you really have to spend a lot of time thinking about it. Understand?"

Hobo gave me his "where's my supper?" look.

I fed him and then put on a pair of black Calvin Klein jeans, a red silk blouse, a lizard skin belt I'd bought in the Village one weekend, and pair of pumps with three-inch heels that Clare called my "fuck me" shoes. That ought to impress Mr. Pete Rousch. Show him what he can't have.

Clare and her husband, Martin, lived in a two-bedroom co-op on Irving Place, with a view of Gramercy Park. Martin was a lawyer too. He was older than she was and once made a lot of money with some high-powered firm on Wall Street. Now he worked for the city, helping poor people hold on to their apartments against unscrupulous landlords or something. The two of them were so politically correct it made me feel guilty to be around them. They didn't buy vegetables that were trucked in across union lines. They took their money out of a bank that was doing business with South Africa. They didn't wear furs or leather. The only politically incorrect thing about Clare and Martin was their apartment, which was huge and gorgeously furnished and very self-indulgent. I once suggested to Clare that she had enough room to let three homeless families live there with them. She told me to fuck off. Clare may be dedicated, but she's not stupid.

Pete Rousch was there when I arrived. He was pretty much as advertised. Not drop-dead gorgeous, but he had an appealing, likeable look. Sort of a cross between Jerry Seinfeld and Garry Shandling. Clare introduced us.

"I thought all history professors had beards and smoked pipes," I told him.

"I shaved just for you."

Not bad. He answered my smart remark with his own smart remark. This guy had possibilities.

"Clare and Martin told me a lot about you," he said.

"Yeah, well they lifted the arrest warrant yesterday."

He smiled. "Clare said you were very outspoken."

"Did she really say outspoken?"

"Actually the term she used was smart-mouthed."

"What else did she tell you about me?"

"Not much."

"C'mon. . . ."

"All right." He laughed. "She said you weighed four hundred pounds, had killed eight other men you dated, and suffered from serious acne all over your body."

"What do you think now?"

"I think your skin has cleared up very nicely, you've been on a killer diet, and I'm not turning my back on you all night."

Clare came out of the kitchen carrying drinks for us. A scotch and soda for Rousch. An Amstel Light for me. She brought a glass with the Amstel Light. I ignored it and took a swig from the bottle.

"You're supposed to use the glass," she whispered frantically.

"Clare, don't tell me how to drink beer. I know how to drink beer."

She apologized for not being a better hostess, but said she and Martin needed to do some more work on the dinner. Then she disappeared back into the kitchen. I figured she had it all planned out this way so Rousch and I could get to know each other. We sat there silently for a few seconds after she left.

"This is really embarrassing, isn't it?" I said finally.

"Excruciating."

"I'm forty-one years old, and I still don't understand how this dating business works. I mean, are we supposed to talk about the weather? The economy? Or do we just take off our clothes and do it right on the floor before they come back?"

"I think you're supposed to wait until after the dessert is served."

Clare had brought out a tray filled with potato chips, pretzels, and peanuts and put it on a coffee table in front of us. I scooped up a handful of the peanuts and ate some.

"So what kind of history do you teach?" I asked.

"American. Nineteenth-century."

"I hope it's not about the Industrial Revolution. I hated the Industrial Revolution."

"Why?"

"I don't know. I just remember being bored in classes learning about it as a kid. Something about Eli Whitney inventing the cotton gin. It just seemed like a real downer period of American history. Worse than the Eisenhower administration. I liked the stuff about wars."

"The Civil War and its aftermath are my main area of specialization."

"No kidding? You mean the Reconstruction era?"

He looked at me with surprise. "Yes."

"I always thought if Abraham Lincoln hadn't been assassinated, the wounds of the war would have healed a lot faster," I said. "Andrew Johnson was a drunk and an incompetent. And they kept Jefferson Davis under house arrest. Lincoln had a plan to bring the country back together. But it took decades to do that after he died."

Martin came out of the kitchen. I guess Clare figured we'd had enough time together alone. So she sent him out as a sort of scout to assess the situation.

"What are we having for dinner?" I asked.

"Rack of lamb with mint sauce, cinnamon potatoes, buttered asparagus, and lemon crème pie for dessert."

"Yum-yum."

"Jenny, don't you ever eat in between times you come here?"

"No, I just live on love."

Martin sat down across from us.

"I hear you're working on a big story. The Jerry Meredith arrest. Clare says you think he's innocent."

"Well, of murder anyway."

"Can you prove it?"

"All I have to do is show there's reasonable doubt he's the killer. I think I can do that. There's a lot of other potential suspects I turned up."

I ran through some of the stuff I knew, but not all of it. I didn't mention my meeting with Vincent Guardere. I hadn't told anyone about that yet. Not even Pesin. Maybe that's because I wasn't sure how to handle it.

"I saw this guy Meredith on TV one day," Rousch said. "He was kind of obnoxious. A real showboat. And he seemed to be in love with himself. I didn't care for him."

"Jerry's not like that off camera," I said.

"You know him?"

"I used to. A long time ago."

"And you don't think he killed his wife?"

"No."

Clare announced it was time to eat. We sat down at the dining room table with real plates, cloth napkins, and even candles. I wasn't used to eating dinner like that. I usually ate off paper plates in front of the TV. I looked at my watch. It was nearly nine o'clock. Almost time for "Empty Nest." I wondered if I should ask Clare and Martin to turn on the TV. Probably a breach of etiquette.

"What have you done about Elaine Rivera?" Clare asked me as we ate.

"Who?"

She gave me a contemptuous look. "The woman in jail for stabbing her husband. You were going to look into her case. Remember?"

"I've been awfully busy, Clare."

"Oh right, I forgot you were a big star these days. And this stuff with Jerry Meredith is really important too. Much more important than some poor girl from the Bronx who finally stands up to years of abuse and . . ."

I held up my hand. "This is a very moving speech. You sure you don't want to put on some violin music for background?"

"You promised you'd go see her in jail, Jenny."

"No, I didn't. I said I'd think about it."

"Have you?"

"I haven't had time."

"When you were in newspapers, Jenny, you cared about people. Things mattered to you. You've changed ever since you got on TV. I really think you've compromised your principles somewhere along the way and . . ."

I sighed. "You're killing me here, Clare. I'll go see Elaine Rivera. I'll do an interview with her. I'll look into her case. I'll do anything you want, if you'll just ease up and let me eat in peace."

Clare smiled. "Good. How about tomorrow? She's in Rikers Island."

I cleared my throat nervously. "Uh . . . I'm busy tomorrow."

"Busy how?"

"I've got a brunch date."

"With who?"

"Jerry Meredith."

There was silence around the table. I looked over at Pete Rousch. He was playing with his asparagus. Way to go, McKay. You always know the right thing to say when you meet a new guy.

"What time?" Clare asked.

"One o'clock."

"So I'll meet you at Rikers in the morning."

"Sunday morning?"

"Sure. I'm Elaine's lawyer. I can get us visiting time then. Unless you're planning on going to church or something. . . ."

"I think I can fit you in between Communion and Sunday school," I said.

Clare changed the subject after that. I guess she figured she was blowing it. I mean, here she had me and this potential love interest together and she was screaming at me and bringing up an ex-boyfriend.

"Pete's writing a book." She smiled at him. "What's it about again?"

"The Battle of Gettysburg."

"That's an important moment in American history . . ." Clare started to say.

"It was the turning point of the war," I said. "The North had twenty-three thousand casualties in just three days of fighting, the South lost about twenty thousand men. But it was the last big major offensive Robert E. Lee's forces were ever able to mount. After that, he remained pretty much on the defensive until the war ended two years later. Isn't that right, Pete?"

Rousch nodded. Everyone was staring at me in amazement.

"And there was Pickett's charge," I continued.

"General Pickett was sent by Lee with fifteen thousand men to mount a massive assault on the Union's position," Rousch explained to Clare and Martin. "He almost succeeded, but was finally pushed back. That was the beginning of the end."

"If he'd made it," I said, "we might be eating grits and corn pone right now."

The evening broke up around eleven. Clare pointed out that Pete lived downtown, so he could walk me home to Union Square. Both of us just smiled and nodded. But when we got downstairs, he turned to me and said:

"We don't have to do this, you know."

"What do you mean?"

"Walk home together. I don't want to torture you anymore. You can tell Clare I did. . . ."

"It's only six blocks." I smiled. "What have we got to lose?"

There's all sorts of little cafés open on the sidewalks around Gramercy Park at night. Some people were still finishing up their dinners now. Others were strolling along like us, just enjoying a balmy Saturday night in Manhattan. I wanted to belt out a chorus of "I Love New York."

"So how do you happen to know so much about the Civil War?" Rousch asked as we walked.

I laughed. "I don't."

"But . . ."

"That was just an old reporter's trick back there."

"I don't understand."

"It's something I do when I want to win over a source or someone I'm interviewing. I find out what the person is interested in, then study up on it and pretend to be very knowledgeable. Clare happened to mention beforehand you were writing a book about the Battle of Gettysburg so . . ."

"You read a book about it."

"Actually I scrolled through the PBS Civil War miniseries this afternoon."

Rousch shook his head. "How long could you have kept going on about it?"

"I had about thirty seconds of conversation left. If you'd asked me one more question, things would have gotten embarrassing."

We were standing outside a café near Union Square now, not far from my apartment. There was an empty table.

"You interested in a nightcap?" Rousch asked.

I was and I wasn't. I guess my indecision showed through because he quickly retracted the invitation.

"Bad idea, huh? Sorry. I guess it's from listening to Clare all night trying to fix us up. You're not interested, are you?"

"Pete, you seem like a really nice guy," I said slowly.

"Thank you."

"You're good-looking, personable, successful—a woman would have to be crazy not to be interested in you."

"So why do I sense there's a big 'but' coming . . . ?"

"It's just that I'm sort of hung up on someone else right now. I don't know how that's going to work out. But I have to see it through to the end. And until that happens, I don't really have room in my life to start a new relationship. Do you understand?"

He nodded. "Is it the guy on TV—Jerry Meredith?"

"Yes."

"So give me a call sometime if you ever sort it out."

Rousch took out a piece of paper, wrote down his number, and gave it to me. Then he leaned down, kissed me on the cheek, and started walking toward 14th Street. I almost called after him, said I'd changed my mind about having that drink. But I didn't.

Damn.

Another good guy I let walk out of my life.

Well, he wasn't the first.

And he probably wouldn't be the last either.

15
Elaine Rivera

I went to see Elaine Rivera as promised.

Rikers Island Prison is a grim, imposing place to visit on a Sunday morning. Or anytime for that matter. It houses both men and women and really is on an island in the middle of the East River. To get there, you have to ride a bus across a bridge from Queens and undergo a security check. Then you meet the prisoner in a conference room. There are no bars or glass partitions to talk through like in the movies, but a guard is present the entire time.

Every once in a while, you hear about a prisoner trying to escape by swimming to freedom. Most of them don't make it. They either wind up turning back or their bodies wash up across the bay at LaGuardia Airport. There have been a few successful breakouts. But I never heard of a woman making it out of there.

Elaine Rivera was wearing a grey prison outfit that looked too big for her. She was twenty-five years old, with a dark, sensual face that had probably been pretty in better times. But now she looked tired. There were dark circles under her eyes, and her hand trembled slightly when I shook it.

"You've got to get me out of here, Miss McKay," she said. "I'm going crazy."

"I hope I can help."

"Clare says when you do my story on TV, people will see I don't belong here. I'm not a criminal. I'm a victim too."

"I know..."

"When will you run this? Tonight?" She looked around. "Hey, where's your camera crew?"

I glanced over at Clare. She was studying the floor.

"Clare may have spoken a bit prematurely," I said.

"What do you mean?"

"I just said I'd come talk to you, Elaine—no promises."

She was getting upset now. "But you have to. I mean, I need people to know about what's happened to me...."

"It's not up to me," I said. "I'm just a reporter. I have to talk to my boss after you give me the details of what happened. If he thinks it's a story, I'll come back with a crew to put it on the air. Do you understand?"

She nodded. She didn't like it, but she understood.

"So why don't you tell me about it, Elaine."

It was pretty much the way Clare had laid it out for me on the way over. Elaine Rivera's husband was named Ricky. He didn't really work, drank too much, and had a violent temper. At first he took out his anger on other people, but pretty soon he started using his fists on her when he came home. Elaine wanted to leave, but she was afraid and had no money. Then, a week or so ago, Ricky gave her the worst beating ever. She thought he was going to kill her, so she picked up a kitchen knife and stabbed him in the chest. When the cops showed up, they took him to the hospital and her to jail. Now Ricky was out, recovered, and living with another woman. Elaine was looking at a five-to-fifteen-year sentence for attempted manslaughter.

The American justice system—ain't it wonderful?

"It's horrible in here, Miss McKay. There's killers, drug pushers, prostitutes. Every morning when I wake up and remember where I am, I start to cry. I don't know how much more of this I can take."

The air was stifling in the room. There was an air conditioner, but it seemed to be out of order. A large fan whirring in the corner served as the only ventilation.

Elaine had the sleeves of her prison shirt rolled down, and it was buttoned all the way up to the top in front. That seemed strange to me. In this kind of heat, I would have rolled up the sleeves and opened the collar. I looked at other prisoners in the visiting room. Their sleeves were all rolled up.

"Do you use drugs, Elaine?"

She seemed surprised by the question. "No."

I reached over for one of her sleeves. She pulled away from me. "What are you doing?"

"I want to see your arms."

She looked over at Clare. Clare nodded her head that it was okay. Elaine rolled up her sleeves.

I was looking for drug marks—tracks from a heroin needle. There weren't any. What there was were bruises. Ugly black-and-blue splotches on the arm. When she opened the collar of her shirt, you could see more on her chest. They were starting to heal, but they still had a ways to go.

"Did Ricky do this?" I asked her.

"Like I said, he lost his temper sometimes. But he never hit me in the face. He was very careful about that. He wanted me to be pretty, so he could show me off to his friends."

Clare shook her head. "He's a bastard!" she spat out angrily.

"That he is," I agreed.

"Are you going to help me?" Elaine asked anxiously. "I don't belong in here."

"I'm going to try."

On the cab ride back to Manhattan, Clare said to me: "We've got to help her. There's women all over this city just like Elaine. Living in terror of their husbands or boyfriends, hiding their injuries. We've got to reform the laws of this country so they work for people like Elaine Rivera."

"Clare, stop being Miss Do-Gooder for just five seconds and listen to me. I'll try to do something on her. I'll talk to

Pesin about it. But not because I'm on some grand mission to change society. Only because it's a good story. That's all."

I told the cab to stop on Fifth Avenue and 59th Street, at the entrance to Central Park across from the Plaza.

"She really got to you, didn't she?" Clare said as I got out.

I thought about the bruises on Elaine Rivera's arms and body, about what it must be like to live like that from day to day, terrified that your husband would erupt at any second. Maybe break your arm. Or a rib. Or rupture a blood vessel. All because you didn't dust the coffee table or do the dishes fast enough.

I only went out once with a guy who hit me. He was drunk and apologized profusely the next day. But I broke it off with him right away. Because I knew it could happen again. In a week, a month, or a year. And even if it didn't, I would always be afraid of it.

I never understood why women stayed with men who hit them. But I sympathized with their situation. I mean, I know it's not easy to leave when you have no money and nowhere to go and are afraid of being alone. I didn't have that problem. But a lot of women did.

There's no happy ending for a battered woman in a marriage or any other relationship. Either the beatings keep getting worse and happening more frequently, or the woman fights back the way Elaine Rivera did.

And now she was sitting in a jail cell.

"Yeah," I told Clare, "she really got to me."

16
Sunday in New York

Eating brunch at the Plaza on a Sunday afternoon is about as good as it gets in New York City.

The place practically oozes class, elegance, and money. White-coated waiters moved effortlessly around our table, bringing us Bloody Marys, eggs, potatoes, and a plate piled high with croissants and bagels. I wished I could afford to eat brunch here more often. Hell, I'd do it every day if I could. But then I'd probably be fat, drunk, and broke.

"I'm going back to the show for the first time tomorrow," Jerry Meredith announced as we ate. "We'll start shooting some new episodes."

"Can you do that so soon without Cheryl Wolcott?"

He made a face. "I don't mean to sound insensitive here, Jenny, but Cheryl wasn't quite as important as she liked to think. TV is really very easy. All you need to do a talk show is the right host and some guests. I'm the host, and we've got plenty of guests lined up. It'll be fine."

I took a bite of my omelet. It was filled with sour cream and caviar, and I thought it was excellent. But then I say the same thing about the breakfast at McDonald's. Jerry didn't really have to spend all this money to bring me here. I'm a cheap date.

"What's your first show about?" I asked.

"It's called 'Women Who Love Too Much.' Like the title of the best-selling book. Only this is about housewives who are nymphomaniacs. They wait until their husband goes to work—then they have sex with the guy next door, the postman, and the supermarket checkout clerk."

"People really go on TV and talk about this stuff?"

"Sure. We've got three women who are going to bare their secret sex lives and a doctor to analyze it in medical terms."

"What about some of the other shows?"

"One is on the Eat-All-You-Want Diet. This guy wrote a book that shows you how to lose weight without giving up any of your favorite foods and without exercising."

"How do you do that?"

"You can't."

"Well, then why . . ."

"We sort of explain that at the end of the show. But that stuff really lures people in. It gets great ratings."

"Isn't it just a little bit dishonest?"

"What are you—from the Columbia School of Journalism? This is show business, Jenny."

I shook my head. "I don't understand TV. I work in it, but I really don't understand it."

"There's nothing to understand. That's what so great about it."

"I miss working at a newspaper," I said.

"Not me. Newspapers spend all this time writing long, boring stories that no one reads about world affairs and City Hall corruption and bond issues. TV is easy. That's why people like it."

"It's important sometimes that people make an effort . . ."

"Newspapers are dying, Jenny. Just go with the flow."

"I'd like to. I'm just never quite sure where to find it."

I waited until dessert and coffee to bring up some of the questions I had about the case.

"The way I see it, your biggest problem is your alibi," I said. "Basically, you don't have one. You say you went drinking all night and don't remember anything. That's a hard story to believe."

"Don't you think I'd come up with a better one if I was lying? Why would I make up something like that up?"

"I don't know," I admitted.

"The truth"—he smiled—"sometimes really is stranger than fiction."

We talked about the problems in the marriage.

"My wife was not a very nice person," he told me.

"Did you love her?"

He thought about that. "I guess so. At the beginning."

"And now?"

"We fulfilled each other's needs."

"That doesn't sound very romantic."

"Let's face it, marriage isn't a particularly romantic institution."

It was only when I mentioned the gambling debt to Vincent Guardere that he seemed to get rattled.

"How did you know about that?"

I didn't tell him about my meeting with Guardere. "I have my sources. I'm a reporter, remember?"

"Okay, it's true," he admitted. "I'm into this loan shark big-time. I've got a problem. Two problems actually. I love gambling. And I'm not very good at it. But it's going to be taken care of. I told Guardere that."

"Does Katherine Grieco know how much you owe him?"

He shook his head. "I don't think so. Why?"

"She might think it makes a helluva motive for murder."

"Grieco doesn't need any more motives to blame me for Eileen's death. She's already convinced I did it."

He looked across the table at me. "Are you going to go on the air with this?"

"No. Not now."

"When?"

"I'm not sure."

We spent the rest of the afternoon walking around New York. First through Central Park. Then browsing for books on Fifth Avenue. It was a beautiful way to spend a lazy, late summer afternoon.

When we finally got back to his apartment, he asked me to come up for a drink.

Now, up to this point things had gone very well. I wanted it to stay that way. I didn't want to do anything I might regret later. But I didn't want to leave either. So I had to make a decision.

You're a big girl, McKay. You've got plenty of willpower. You can handle yourself.

I went upstairs with him.

A maid was there this time. She brought us drinks, and then I excused myself to go to the bathroom. When I came back, I couldn't find Jerry. The maid pointed me toward the game room.

Jerry was inside playing with his train set. He seemed totally absorbed in watching the engines pull their cargos around the elaborate track. I remembered Jellinek telling me how some of the cars cost as much as ten thousand dollars apiece. I had a Lionel train set when I was a kid that I saved up my allowance to buy. This didn't look all that much different to me. Just a lot bigger.

"Isn't it a little weird for you being in here?" I asked. "I mean, it is the room where your wife was murdered."

"You think it's ghoulish?"

"A little."

"The whole house feels that way to me. Someone came in here and killed Eileen. It's not easy to forget that."

He had several different trains at once moving along the maze of tracks. The names of real lines—some current and some long dead—were painted on the sides of the cars. Penn Central. Silver Streak. Northern Limited. The landscape around them was just as detailed. There were miniature highways, buildings, cars, railroad stops, and people everywhere.

"This is quite an elaborate setup," I said.

"Do you like it?"

"It makes me feel a little like a kid again."

"I know." He shook his head. "Eileen hated my trains. Said they were a waste of time. She never came in this room except to yell at me to get off my ass."

"I heard she yelled at you a lot."

He shrugged. "It's no secret, I guess. We weren't exactly Ozzie and Harriet."

Two trains—a passenger and a freight—were chugging along toward the same crossing. For a second, I thought there was going to be a collision. But Jerry deftly flipped a switch and rerouted the freight train onto a side track. It was all very realistic.

"Do you think I killed her?" he asked suddenly.

"Hey," I said, "it's not me you have to answer to. It's the cops. And Katherine Grieco. And a jury."

"I know that. But I've got to start somewhere. It's like people trying to stop drinking learn at AA—you take it one day at a time. Not a week. Not a month. Not a year. Just a day. I need to do the same thing. Convince one person that I'm innocent and then work from there. You're the first." He smiled. "So what's your answer, Jenny? Am I a murderer or not?"

It was a question I'd thought about a lot in the past few days. I decided to be totally honest.

"No, Jerry, I don't think you killed your wife. I wouldn't be here today if I did."

He let out a breath slowly. "Whew, that's a relief."

I smiled. "Now all you have to do is convince the rest of the world."

When we came back out, the maid had left, so Jerry refilled our drinks himself. We sat on the couch in the living room sipping them in front of the TV. The Mets-Cubs game was on from Shea Stadium. The Mets were down by four runs, but had the bases loaded. Jerry groaned when the batter struck out. I wondered if he had bet money on the game.

Somewhere around the eighth inning—and about three Cubs' runs later—he made his move on me.

I felt his hand on my shoulder, then he pulled me toward him and put his lips close to mine. Not exactly a new move. I'd first seen it done in the backseat of a Dodge sometime in the summer of 1968. But this time I didn't go for it. I pushed him away from me.

"I really don't think this is a good idea, Jerry."

"Don't tell me you don't want to."

"I didn't say that."

I got up and walked down the hall back into the game room. I pressed a switch on the transformer, and one of the trains started up. As I watched it go round and round the track, Jerry came up behind me.

"These engines really cost ten thousand dollars apiece?" I said, trying to change the subject.

"Some do. Others a little less. And a few of them are very cheap, like the kind you'd get a kid for Christmas."

I looked at the different engines. "I really can't tell the difference," I said.

"An expert can. Most people just see a train set. That's why it's such a fun hobby."

He reached down and pressed another lever. The train's whistle made a tooting sound. Then he smiled and put his hand on top of mine.

"Let's do it right here," he whispered.

"Where?"

"On the train table."

"Jerry, I'm not going to have sex with you on the spot where your wife was murdered."

"Why not? Doesn't it sound exciting?"

The truth was I knew people who got off on stuff like that. One of the reporters covering the William Kennedy Smith rape trial in Palm Beach climbed the fence of the Kennedy mansion after the verdict and had sex on the exact patch of ground where Willie Boy was accused of tackling that woman. Another did the dirty deed on the site in Central Park where Robert Chambers killed Jennifer Levin.

But I wasn't that kind of person.

I didn't have sex with Jerry Meredith on the train table where his wife was murdered.

We did it in the bedroom. Not her bedroom either. One of the guest rooms. Maybe that doesn't seem important. But it did to me.

I realized then that this had been where we were headed since the first moment I'd seen him again. Maybe I never admitted it to myself. But I knew. It was like a piece of unfinished business between us. I needed an answer before I went on with the rest of my life. Did I still have the passion for Jerry Meredith I had ten years ago?

As it turned out, I did. At least that night.

Later, after we made love, we lay there in a bed next to a window overlooking a gorgeous view of the East Side.

"I still have a lot of trouble with your alibi," I said.

He laughed. "Boy, you never quit, do you?"

"What were you doing the night your wife was murdered, Jerry?"

He reached over to a nightstand for a cigarette and lit it up. "You're not going to like the answer," he said.

"Try me."

Jerry sat up in bed, smoked the cigarette, and looked out the window. It was starting to get dark now, and the setting sun cast a gorgeous reddish glow on the city. Finally he said:

"What I said was true. I went to this bar and got drunk. What I didn't say was that the bar was a singles place on First Avenue, near 77th Street." He sighed. "I met this girl there. Her name was Karen. We had a few drinks—a lot of them actually—and then went to her place around the corner. I spent the night there."

"So she's your alibi."

"Not really."

"Why not?"

"Two reasons. First, I was so drunk I don't remember her last name or where she lived."

"What do you remember?"

"She was a redhead, late twenties, had a bit of an accent— maybe from the South—and she was dressed in this kind of punk rock look with old blue jeans that had big holes cut out of them. She lived really close to the bar. It was a town house, I think. I had to open up the metal gate of a fence to get to the door and then we went up a couple flights of stairs. There was a balcony too. I remember standing out on it and feeling dizzy because I'd had too much to drink."

"Did you have sex with her too?" I asked sharply.

He shook his head. I must have looked skeptical, because he said, "Honest. I just needed a place to spend the night. That's all."

"So now all you have to do is track down this Karen and . . ."

"That's the second part of my problem. Even if I found Karen, I can't use her as an alibi."

I was confused. "Why not?"

"I might lose all Eileen's money if I did. You see, I signed this prenuptial agreement that . . ."

A bell in my head went off. "Has a clause about adultery."

"Yep. I forfeit all right to the money if anyone can prove that."

"But you said nothing happened."

"It didn't. But I'm not sure a court would believe that. The Clayton Corporation has a lot of high-priced lawyers. I can't take the chance."

"Jesus, Jerry, without that alibi you could be convicted for murder. That's a helluva lot worse chance to take."

"Maybe, but it's a chance that's worth about a billion dollars to me." He smiled. "Like I said, I love gambling."

It was dark out by the time I finally got dressed and left his place. I looked at my watch. Nearly 10 p.m. Poor Hobo was probably hungry and needed a walk. I stood there trying to hail a cab and thinking about everything that had happened.

Way to go, McKay. You had yourself a helluva day. You compromised your principles as a reporter. You embarrassed yourself as a woman. And now even your dog's mad at you.

So much for willpower.

17
Stupid TV Tricks

I sat at my desk in the newsroom on Monday morning and made up a David Letterman-like list of the Top Ten reasons why I was glad I left newspapers to become a TV reporter. I sometimes did this when I was upset about my life. Boy, was I upset about my life.

The list read like this:

10) Get to wear nifty Channel Six blazer.
9) No changing of typewriter ribbons required.
8) Feel like Mensa candidate being around Liz St. John.
7) Devastating Barbara Walters impression gets big laughs at parties.
6) Cool guys dig TV babes.
5) Donald Pesin better than Delta Burke as inspiration for staying on diet.
4) Tony Danza's show is our lead-in—and that just makes me feel tingly all over.
3) Emmys, Emmys, Emmys.
2) If Katie Couric can be a star, so can I.

And the No. 1 reason I'm glad I became a TV reporter ... (drumroll, please):

1) "I'm Jenny McKay, and you're not" is a great pickup line.

Pesin showed up around 9:30. I followed him into his office and sat down. He was carrying a takeout box from the diner downstairs, which he opened at his desk. There was a double order of pancakes inside along with a bag of potato chips. He put butter and syrup on the pancakes. Then he opened up the potato chip bag and poured them over the top. That was a new one, even to me.

"What's up?" he asked between bites.

"I've made some progress on the Jerry Meredith story."

"Tell me everything."

I did. I went through it all with him. The only thing I left out was the late-night meeting with Vincent Guardere.

"That's beautiful," he said when I was finished. There was syrup dripping down his chin. He wiped it off on his sleeve. Classy. "Anything else?"

"Just one thing." I swallowed hard. "I slept with Jerry Meredith last night."

That one stopped his eating. He stared at me with his mouth open. Believe me, it wasn't a pretty sight.

"You mean you had sex with him?"

"That's the way it usually works out."

"Where?"

"In his apartment."

I thought he'd be upset. I thought he might even fire me—or at least take me off the story. I thought he'd yell and scream a lot. But he didn't do any of those things. He just threw back his head and started laughing.

"Excuse me, did I miss something here?" I said. "I did a very bad thing. I violated one of the basic ethical rules of being a reporter."

He dismissed that with a wave of his hands. "You worry too much about that stuff, McKay. I don't care about goddamned ethics. All that matters is being first with the story. The way I see it, this puts you in a great spot to do that. That's because the spot you're in is in the same bed with the story." He slammed his fist down on the desk and laughed again. "Jesus, that's great!"

He told me to work up a piece for that night on Eileen Clayton and the way she rode roughshod over her business and her husband. Then to go after the ex-wives of Jerry Meredith, which he thought could be a dynamite followup. After that, we'd chase down a story on the missing production assistant and the dead director of "The Morning Show."

"There's one other thing I want to talk to you about," I said.

I told him about my meeting with Elaine Rivera. He didn't seem terribly interested.

"It's a small story," he said. "She's a nobody. We can do that anytime."

"But I think it makes an important point about abused women. . . ."

"Nobody cares about making points," he snapped. "The only points that matter are rating points."

"I know, but . . ."

"Save all your bleeding heart rhetoric about Elaine Rivera for the next NOW convention, huh?"

"Maybe if I just shot the interview in my spare time, we could take a look at it."

"No. I want you working full-time on Jerry Meredith. Understand?"

I nodded.

"You're doing great, McKay," he said. "I'm thinking more and more every day about you as my anchorwoman. Don't blow it."

I walked back out into the newsroom. Stormy Phillips was looking out the window at the sky. She had to decide whether to wear a bikini or a rubber dress for her forecast on tonight's show.

"Isn't meteorological science wonderful?" I said.

"Don't laugh. I know weather people who've talked on the air about a bright sunny day outside—in the middle of a snowstorm. All because they didn't bother to look out the window."

"You want to get a cup of coffee?" I asked.

We went downstairs to the diner. I told her about my date with Jerry Meredith. And my meeting with Pesin.

"Are you in love with Meredith?" she asked.

"I'm not sure. Maybe."

"Do you figure he's going to want to see you again?"

"I like to think so."

"So what's the problem?"

"I just feel kinda uncomfortable about it."

"Pesin doesn't mind."

"Pesin has the morals of Ivan Boesky. All he cares about is ratings. And making a name for himself."

"Welcome to the wild and wonderful world of TV." Stormy smiled.

I went back to my desk. Liz St. John walked past. She was wearing a khaki safari outfit, with something that looked like an ammo gun belt around her waist, and a wide-brimmed hat. She was telling people she bought it at Bloomingdale's over the weekend.

"You Tarzan, me Jane," I said.

She whirled around. "Go ahead, make your smart remarks. I'll have you know that *Cosmopolitan* calls this safari look the last word in fashion."

"Thank God. I couldn't take any more."

"You're hardly one to talk."

"What do you mean?"

"Look at yourself."

I was wearing a denim skirt, a T-shirt that said JIM MORRISON IS ALIVE AND LIVING WITH JANIS JOPLIN, and a pair of open-toed brown sandals. I'd also brought along a blue blouse to wear over the T-shirt when I went on the air.

"You look like some sort of refugee from the sixties."

"Hey, there was nothing wrong with the sixties."

"They were over a long time ago."

"And what a time they were. 'Incense and Peppermints.' 'Purple Haze.' 'Hey, hey, LBJ, how many kids you kill today?' "

She made a face. "Jeez, you're such a fossil. I just can't figure out why Pesin seems to like you better than me."

"I'll give you a little hint."

I started singing the LBJ ditty again, only this time I substituted Liz St. John's initials. "Hey, hey, LSJ, how many words you mispronounce today?"

Liz stalked off angrily. Sanders and Jacobson came over.

"Boy, you seem particularly prickly today," Sanders said. "Rough night?"

"The worst."

"Aren't you getting a little old for such a wild social life?"

"Everybody wants to put me in a nursing home. Maybe I should just drink some hot chocolate, play a little shuffleboard, and take a nap."

"Sounds good to me," Jacobson grunted.

"Do we have an assignment?" Sanders asked.

I said we were going to look for Jerry Meredith's two ex-wives. He said that sounded extremely interesting. Especially for me. I wasn't sure what he meant by that. But I let it pass.

They went to load the van while I did some research to get the addresses. I was just about to go downstairs to join them when the phone rang. It was Clare.

"How did you make out with the interview?" she asked. "Can we do it today?"

"I'm running into a little resistance."

"What do you mean?"

"My boss doesn't think Elaine Rivera's a story."

"That's ridiculous!"

"I know."

"So what are you going to do about it?"

"I'm working on him. Honest." I cleared my throat nervously. "Clare, there's something else I want to talk to you about. I need some advice."

"Legal advice?"

"Personal."

She sighed. "That's trickier. What's his name?"

"Jerry Meredith." There was a long pause. "I slept with him last night."

"Jesus!"

"I know, I know. It just happened."

"No, it didn't just happen. You wanted it to happen. You wanted it to happen from the first moment you got involved with this story. Well, now you've pulled it off. Proud of yourself, Jenny?"

"Not particularly."

"I don't know what's happened to you. You used to care about things that mattered. Now you're walking away from Elaine Rivera—who really needs your help—and you're falling into the arms of this creep Meredith. You keep going like this and you're going to wind up as empty inside as this guy Pesin you told me about."

"I didn't do anything wrong," I said stubbornly.

"Yes, you did!" She was screaming at me. "You slept with the guy you're doing a story about. A guy who's accused of murder. A guy whose wife was brutally killed just a few days ago. What kind of a journalist are you?"

"Pesin doesn't mind. And Stormy Phillips, another reporter here, thinks it's okay too. What makes you such an expert on journalistic integrity?"

"I'm just talking about integrity. Something you're a little short on these days."

She slammed the phone down angrily. I did the same thing.

Damn her!

Why did she always have to be so goddamned self-righteous? Why did she always have to be trying to save the world? Why did she always have to be such a do-gooder?

Worst of all, why did she always have to be right?

18
The Ex-Wives' Club

Jerry Meredith's first wife still lived in Trenton, New Jersey.

Her home was in a working-class neighborhood that had seen better days. There was a bowling alley on the corner, a check-cashing place next door, and several boarded-up stores. The buildings were old and bunched very close to one another. Her place was on the top floor of a two-family house. There was a battered old Dodge parked in front. Some spare tires and engine parts lay alongside the driveway.

"Not exactly Park Avenue, is it?" Sanders muttered as we got out of the Channel Six mobile van and walked to the door.

"No," I said.

"Just think," Jacobson said. "This could be you living here."

"What does that mean?"

"Well, it doesn't seem as if Jerry exactly leaves his ex-wives living in the lap of luxury."

"So?"

"So there but for the grace of God go you, huh, Jenny?"

He knocked on the door. A woman answered it. She was dark-haired, probably in her mid-forties, and had the kind of features that probably once made her pretty. But that was a long time ago. Now there was a tired, beaten-down look to her face. She was probably no more than a year or two older than me, but it seemed more like ten or twenty.

"Barbara Ann Meredith?" I asked.

"Barbara Ann Forbes. I use my maiden name."

"I'm Jenny McKay, and we're from Channel Six. I spoke to you on the phone about an interview. It's about your marriage to Jerry Meredith."

She smiled. "I didn't think you were here to ask me about my tea with Hillary Clinton."

We followed her into the living room. It was small and dark with old furniture that seemed to fit in with the rest of the neighborhood. There was a Bible on a mantel and a picture of Jesus Christ next to it. A TV set was on in the corner. It was tuned to "The Morning Show," and Jerry Meredith's face was on the screen.

"Jerry's really good on TV, isn't he?" I said, trying to make conversation.

"Jerry is an asshole."

Sanders snorted and had to put his hand over his mouth to keep from laughing.

I stared at her in amazement. "Don't sugarcoat it, Ms. Forbes. Speak frankly."

"All right. Jerry is a grade-A asshole. He's the king of assholes. If they had a Hall of Fame for assholes, Jerry would be the president."

I looked down at the TV screen again. "So why do you watch him?"

"Just so I never forget," she said grimly.

Sanders and Jacobson started setting up their equipment. I sat down on a battered couch across from Barbara Ann Forbes. I thought about Jerry's penthouse apartment and tried to picture him living in a place like this with her. He'd come a long way since then.

"Tell me about you and Jerry," I said.

They'd met some twenty years ago at the Trenton paper. Jerry worked there as a reporter. She was a receptionist, young and wide-eyed, and Jerry Meredith was the most handsome and exciting man she had ever seen. They had a passionate romance for six months until she became pregnant—so they got married and she had a baby girl named Elizabeth. A year later a second child—a son, Luke—was born.

After that, things started to go bad in the marriage. Jerry was restless in Trenton and wanted to make a big name for himself as a reporter to get a job in New York City. He started spending more and more time at the office—or so he told her anyway. Then one day he just never came home again.

"I never knew what happened to him until a year later when I happened to see his byline on a newspaper story out of New York. He could have changed his name, I suppose, to really disappear, but he didn't. He's got too big an ego for that."

She looked down at the TV set. Jerry was cooking a soufflé with a network sitcom star. They were laughing about the time they sat in adjoining boxes on "The Hollywood Squares."

"I went to see him at the paper. Told him he had a responsibility to support me and his two children. He just laughed. Said he'd hire a lawyer who'd drag it out in the courts for years. I couldn't afford to fight him."

"You could have gotten help. There are agencies . . ."

She smiled. "I know. Abandoned wives and their children have a few more options today. But this was a long time ago."

"So what happened then?"

"Nothing. I raised my kids as best I could. Elizabeth and Luke grew up. I grew older. Life goes on for us all."

"Did you tell them who their father was?"

"Of course. I wanted them to know what a son of a bitch he was." She looked at the TV screen. "They were reminded of it constantly. Imagine what it must be like to be growing up and seeing the father you never knew talking on TV every day. How do you think that made them feel?"

"Jerry never saw them again after he left?"

"No. He was too busy."

The cooking segment was over. There was a teaser for the next segment. It read: "Next—How to Tell If Your Best Friend Is Trying to Steal Your Husband. Stay Tuned to The Morning Show."

"Where are your children now?"

"My son Luke joined the Navy. He was confused and thought it might help him to find some answers. It didn't." She looked down at her lap. "He died six months ago of a drug overdose."

"I'm sorry." I didn't know what else to say. "And your daughter?"

"Elizabeth doesn't think much of me, I'm afraid. She left here shortly after Luke died. Said she was going to move to a new city and change her name and try to have a real life. I don't know where she is."

Jerry Meredith was back on the screen now. He was listening to a woman tell how her best friend seduced her husband. There was a compassionate, concerned look on his face. I thought about Barbara Ann Forbes sitting here in this little apartment watching him on TV day after day.

"Have you ever talked to him since that time in New York?" I asked.

"Once. Six months ago, after Luke died. I thought he should know."

"What happened?"

"He didn't really care. We were from another time. It was as if I was married to a totally different man."

"Did you ask him for money again?"

She nodded. "Not a lot. Just what he owed me. His debt to me and his family. Do you know what he told me?"

I shook my head.

"He said we'd have to wait in line."

On the ride back to New York after we'd shot the interview, Sanders said, "That is one bitter lady. I'm surprised she never took a gun and shot him."

"Maybe she did something better."

"What do you mean?"

"Well, if she killed Jerry, it would be over right away. What if she murdered his rich wife instead—and then made it look like Jerry did it? He spends the rest of his life in prison. Can you think of a sweeter revenge?"

"That sounds pretty sick. I'm not sure she's capable of it."

"You never know what a woman scorned will do."

The Manhattan skyline was in front of us. We paid the toll at the Holland Tunnel, crossed underneath the Hudson River, and got off at the exit for Canal Street.

"Where to now?" Jacobson asked.

"Now," I said, "it's on to wife number two."

Janet Hutchings was no longer a model. She'd moved to the other side of the camera and was working as a photo editor for a fashion magazine. We met at her office downtown. She was still beautiful, but the years were starting to show a little. It must be tough to be a model—your career is over by the time you hit thirty-five.

"Jerry's really got his ass in a sling this time," she said, laughing.

She was smoking a cigarette and sitting behind a desk covered with pictures of women in bathing suits and negligees.

"You might say that. I'm trying to help him."

"Why?"

"Pardon me?"

"Why are you trying to help Jerry?"

"Well, it's a good story if he's innocent. And I think he is. If I can prove it, it's a great exclusive for our station."

"Are you screwing him?" she asked.

I was startled. "That's a helluva thing to ask someone you don't know."

"Oh, but I know Jerry. And I know you too. In a sense."

"Have we met before?"

"Jerry used to talk about you when we were married. Whenever you had a big story in the paper, he'd brag about how he'd had you. Jerry likes to brag about his conquests. Didn't you know that?"

"I don't think my past history with Jerry is particularly relevant here."

"Oh, sure it is. And I'm not sure it's past history anyway. I figure Jerry's already done his number on you. The whole sensitive bit about how you were the one he really loved and how he's never gotten over you. Pretty soon you're feeling warm and wonderful all over. And the next thing you're in bed with him and believing he's innocent."

She ground out her cigarette in an ashtray that was already overflowing, then immediately took out another one and lit it.

"Smoking is a terrible habit, isn't it? Everyone says how bad it is for me. But I can't stop. Does that ever happen to you, Jenny? You just can't stop doing something you know is bad for you?"

I didn't like the way this interview was going. Janet Hutchings had caught me off guard. I wanted to act insulted and tell her she didn't know what she was talking about. But it was a little difficult under the circumstances. I tried to change the subject.

"Tell me about your marriage to Jerry," I said.

She laughed. "Well, we were officially married for three years. But it really only lasted about eighteen months. Jerry liked being married to a famous model in the beginning. But then the excitement faded, and he decided it would be neat to see how many other women he could score with. I ignored the first one, looked the other way for the next, and still tried to stick it out when there were too many to count. I had this naive idea of marriage—I really did. A house. Kids. A loving husband coming home every night."

"Like Rob and Laura Petrie on 'The Dick Van Dyke Show,' " I said.

"Yeah, that's it. Not anymore though. Now I know it's not like that...."

"Does Jerry pay you alimony?"

"You bet he does."

I told her the story of Barbara Ann Forbes.

"Well, I got myself a good lawyer," she said. "And if Jerry's a day late with his check or it gets lost in the mail or the postman gets in an accident or something, we're back in court. The judge is this woman who jails men who don't pay their alimony. I love it. It's one of the great pleasures of my life."

She leaned back in her chair and blew some smoke in the air.

"I think he did it, you know."

"You mean killed his wife?"

"Uh-huh."

"Why?"

"Because she found out about him, just like all the rest of us did."

Janet Hutchings looked over at me. She was enjoying my discomfort. She fanned some cigarette smoke from her face, leaned across the desk, and smiled.

"Whoops! There goes your big exclusive, huh, Jen?"

19
Wild Women Do

ANNOUNCER: It's the News at Six on Six. With the Channel Six team of newsbreakers: Conroy Jackson and Liz St. John on the anchor desk; Chip Forte with the sports; and Stormy Phillips with the exclusive Accu-Channel Six weather forecast. And now here's Conroy and Liz....

LIZ ST. JOHN: Three gunmen held up a jewelry store on Fifth Avenue in broad daylight today, getting away with a haul of nearly $3 million.

JACKSON: And city officials threatened a fifty-cent toll hike for motorists at the East River crossings unless federal officials help New York balance its budget.

ST. JOHN: But first, the top story of the day—which continues to be the Eileen Clayton murder case. Although her husband—talk show host Jerry Meredith—has been charged with the crime, our Jenny McKay has another special report which raises dramatic questions about the case.

Here's her hot new exclusive. And we do mean hot . . .

The scene cut to a picture of the outside of Cary's, with women standing in line to get in. Next was a shot of the inside—nearly naked men bumping and grinding on stage while the female audience screamed, whistled, and threw money at them. Amidst this pandemonium, I stood giving my report.

McKAY: These women are shouting "Take it off!" to the dancers on stage. And Channel Six News has learned that one of the dancers here did just that—and a lot more—for slain billionaire Eileen Clayton . . .

I probably ought to explain at this point what I was doing at Cary's.

When I told Pesin what I had from the ex-wives, he was not pleased. It made Jerry Meredith look like a really bad guy. Maybe even a murderer. That didn't help our story any.

"I want stuff that raises questions in people's minds about whether the cops arrested the right guy. So if this doesn't do it, let's try something else."

He was eating a cream puff as he talked. Or, to put it another way, he was talking as he ate a cream puff. Either way it was very messy.

"Like what?"

"Well, I'll tell you a little trick I learned about the broadcasting business a long time ago. It always works. When you don't know what to do next and you're at a dead end, but you want big ratings—try sex!"

"What kind of sex?"

"It doesn't matter. As long as it's naughty and titillating and yet mainstream enough to get on TV. In other words, lots of sizzle and innuendo, but nothing really hard-core."

I thought about what he was saying for a minute. Then it hit me. "Cary's."

"Exactly. Go do an interview with this guy Robert Santos that the Clayton woman was humping on the side. We'll dress it up with lots of shots of the dancers and the scene that goes on around it."

"I've never been to one of those places," I said.

He shrugged. "Neither have I. So what?"

"No kidding? I heard you used to be a dancer at Chippendale's. You've certainly got the body for it. Must be that cream puff diet you're on."

He smiled and took another bite. "You can't insult me, McKay. I've heard fat jokes all my life. I'm immune. Believe me, I know I'm not Arnold Schwarzenegger."

"Sorry. I can't help myself sometimes."

"Speaking of that, you could lose a little weight yourself."

I didn't like the sound of that. "Why? Do you think I'm fat?"

"No, not really. But you could trim off five pounds for the camera. Maybe even ten."

"Oh, God! I'm going to be obsessed about this all day."

"Don't overreact. But if we do move you into the anchor job, I want you looking your best. I want the whole package. Brains and beauty."

"Terrific," I muttered. "I finally get a break in this business and now I have to suffer for it by going on a diet."

"Hey," he said, stuffing the remains of the cream puff into his mouth, "sacrifice is what life is all about."

And so now there I was on the screen interviewing Robert Santos at Cary's:

McKAY: Bobby, how did you meet Eileen Clayton?

SANTOS: We get them all in here. Housewives and heiresses. She pulled up one night in her limo and checked out the talent. I was number one on her dance card. Both here and afterward.

McKAY: Where did you hold these romantic rendezvous?

SANTOS: What?

McKAY: Your dates. Where did you go on your dates?

SANTOS: You mean where did I have sex with her?

McKAY: Uh . . . okay.

SANTOS: Anywhere. The woman owned half of New York. It wasn't like we had to go to some SRO hotel.

McKAY: Do you think her husband knew about you?

SANTOS: I never worry about husbands. Life's too short.

McKAY: Bobby, Eileen Clayton was pregnant when she died. Do you think it was your baby?

SANTOS: Maybe. We'll never know though, will we?

McKAY: Here's a woman who was worth a billion dollars. She could have any man she wanted. Why do you think she came here? And why did she pick you?

SANTOS: Let me give you an example, Jenny.

He got up on the stage and began dancing. A bump-and-grind number to the song, "Wild Women Do." He was wearing a pair of tight pants, which he stripped off, leaving him clad only in a pair of bikini briefs.

What happened next had been carefully planned out with Pesin. I didn't like it. But a job is a job. I jumped up on stage with him, took out a handful of dollar bills, and stuffed them down in Bobby Santos's bikini briefs.

Then I danced around the stage with him to the cheers of the crowd.

McKAY: From the stage of Cary's, this is Jenny McKay reporting for Channel Six News.

The picture cut to the studio, where I sat at the anchor desk next to Liz and Conroy, watching the tape on the monitor.

JACKSON: Well, it's good to see you throwing yourself into your work like that, Jenny.

ST. JOHN: I'm jealous. The only man I get to be around is Conroy.

JACKSON: Well, you've never seen me in bikini briefs, Liz.

ST. JOHN: (feigning horror) Oh, Conroy, please!

She turned back to me.

ST. JOHN: Seriously, Jenny, you spent some of the station's hard-earned money on this assignment. Those dollar bills will probably have to come out of someone's salary. What exactly did you get in return?

McKAY: Well, there is this.

I pulled out a pair of bikini briefs like the pair Robert Santos was wearing on stage and held them aloft to cheers from Liz and Conroy and everyone on the set.

ST. JOHN: (still laughing) Coming up next—a bomb scare at Kennedy Airport. We'll be back after this message.

I truly believe this may have been one of the all-time low moments in the history of journalism.
There was a small crisis later in the show.
Chip Forte, the sportscaster, had a swollen lip. You see, Chip's shtick was making wacky sound effects during his sports report. The crack of a bat on a ball, a bone-crunching tackle or the swish of a basketball through the net—stuff like that.

THE MOURNING SHOW

Well, it turned out he was doing an interview with a wrestler called Max the Mountain Man when—in the middle of one of his sound effects—some spit landed on the guy's face. So the Mountain Man went berserk and punched Forte in the mouth. He could talk, but just barely. So he had to do the sports without any sound effects.

"That was a disaster," moaned Barry Kaiser after the show.

"I thought it was good," I said.

"All he did was read the scores. Nothing else."

"I know. It might be a whole new trend in TV journalism. It's called reporting the news."

Kaiser snorted. "What are you, some kind of revolutionary?"

The truth was I didn't want to discuss TV news with Barry Kaiser. I didn't want to talk to anybody. All I wanted to do was go home and sleep. And so, of course, the telephone was ringing when I walked into my apartment. I picked it up.

"Hi. Are we still talking?"

It was Clare.

"Sure. You're not still mad at me?"

"No. Look, I'm sorry. I stuck my nose into your business, where it doesn't belong."

"That's what friends are for," I told her.

We talked for a while. Clare said she had watched the Channel Six News that night. She was very diplomatic about my performance from Cary's. She said she thought it was "different." I said it sure was.

"By the way," I said, "I haven't forgotten about Elaine Rivera. I'm going to try to do something to help her as soon as I get my head above water."

"Good. I talked to her again today."

"How's she doing?"

"She's having a really rough time. My God. I can't imagine what it must be like in prison."

I thought about some of those movies about women's prisons they show on cable late at night. "You generally don't meet a nice class of people," I agreed.

After I hung up, I walked Hobo and told him a joke.

A guy goes to a psychiatrist for an exam. The psychiatrist tells him: "You're crazy."

"Hey, wait a minute," the guy protests. "I want a second opinion."

The psychiatrist thinks about it for a second, then says: "Okay, you're ugly too."

After we all stopped laughing, I fed him his supper. As for me, I wasn't sure what to do about eating. Pesin's remark about losing ten pounds was still bothering me. Maybe I should stick to a Weight-Watchers' TV dinner. On the other hand, maybe I should thumb my nose at Pesin by ordering a pizza and some chocolate marshmallow ice cream for dessert.

The phone rang again. I didn't pick it up. Let whoever it was leave a message on my answering machine. I could talk to them tomorrow.

The answering machine clicked on. There was a beep, and then: "Hi Jenny, this is Jerry . . ."

I grabbed for the phone.

"That was really mind-boggling watching that guy talk about my wife with you on TV tonight," he said.

He sounded a bit shaken.

"I'm feeling kind of lonely," he said. "Do you want to come up for a while?"

"It's awfully late," I said.

"How about I come down there then?"

"You mean to my place?"

"Sure. You want to?"

I thought about all the things I'd found out about Jerry Meredith in the past few days. About my conversations with Janet Hutchings and Barbara Ann Forbes. All the danger signs were there. This was a guy with a very bad track record when it came to the women in his life. And he might even be a murderer.

I wasn't sure what to do.

"Jenny? Can I come see you?"

"Sure," I heard myself say. Then I gave him the address.
I guess life really is a lot like TV journalism.
When in doubt, we turn to sex.

20
Missing Pieces

I was not a happy camper.

Basically, my professional and personal lives were in total turmoil. This was not a new phenomenon for me. I mean, you'd think I'd be used to it by now. But I'm not. I can never be happy unless everything is going absolutely perfectly. I'm always reaching for those stars.

On the cab ride down to work, I took stock of my situation on both fronts.

First the professional:

I was fast approaching a critical point with the Jerry Meredith story. Any big story works the same way. There's a big burst of interest in the beginning, then a series of follow-ups. After that, it takes a lot for a story to have what we call "legs." Most of the time it just sort of fades away because there's nothing left to say. Pretty soon another story becomes the top headline.

That was where I was afraid the Jerry Meredith story was headed. It had had a great run. But now I was running out of things to say on the air about it. Oh, in six months or so, Jerry would be tried for murder and the case would be big news again. But what was I going to do to fill those six months?

THE MOURNING SHOW 149

I came up with three possible solutions:

1) Move on to another story, like the Elaine Rivera arrest.

2) Call in sick for the next 180 consecutive days.

3) Come up with some startling new angle on Jerry Meredith.

Number one was logical and number two intriguing, but I finally settled on number three. I thought about it for a while and realized there were still some missing pieces of the puzzle. Like Andrew Cox and Becky Bessard, the dead director and the missing production assistant from "The Morning Show."

Were they somehow connected to Eileen Clayton's murder? Who knew? But it made for intriguing speculation.

The second part of my dilemma—the personal part—was a bit trickier.

I was not naive about Jerry Meredith. I'm no kid. I've been around the block a few times. I didn't necessarily believe that Jerry and I were going to walk off into the sunset—hand in hand—and live happily ever after.

On top of that, I was really uncomfortable about the ethical part of it. I was covering the biggest murder story in town. And I was sleeping with the prime suspect. No matter how hard I tried to rationalize my reasons for it, I didn't figure I was going to be winning any awards for journalistic integrity this year.

But I wanted to keep seeing him. I liked him. It was as simple as that. Despite all the logic against it, I really enjoyed being around him.

The head says no, but the heart says yes. Not to mention a few other places too.

An hour later, Sanders, Jacobson, and I were in the Channel Six mobile van heading north on the East River Drive to Andrew Cox's house in Paramus, New Jersey.

"Do you really think there's a connection between this guy and Eileen Clayton's death?" Sanders asked as we passed Gracie Mansion. On the other side, waves from the East River lapped gently alongside the highway. A sailboat drifted by with a fair-haired man and a young boy at the tiller. It was one of those moments that make you remember Manhattan is really an island, not just block after block of clogged streets and metal skyscrapers.

"Cox died in a traffic accident a few weeks before Eileen Clayton's murder. Becky Bessard disappeared a short time later. And then Cheryl Wolcott committed suicide—except I don't think it really was suicide. That's a lot of coincidences."

"You're saying somebody killed them all?"

"It's possible."

"Who?"

"Maybe Vincent Guardere."

"The mob guy?"

I nodded and told him about my encounter with Guardere and his people. I'd been thinking about it a lot lately. It made perfect sense. Guardere was mad at Jerry Meredith and suddenly people around him began having accidents. I wasn't quite sure why. Maybe it was a warning to Jerry to pay up or else. Maybe he wanted to scare him. I still hadn't worked the whole thing out in my mind yet.

"Obviously the logical outcome of this scenario is . . ."

"Vincent Guardere murdered Eileen Clayton," I said.

"Can you prove that?"

"I'm working on it."

We crossed over the George Washington Bridge and picked up Route 4 in Fort Lee, New Jersey, heading toward Paramus.

"Artie, you know much about New Jersey?" I asked.

Jacobson was sitting in the backseat with his eyes closed. He opened them now and looked around.

"Lots of good diners."

"Hey, that's right," I said. "Big portions, cheap prices. We can go wild for lunch. What's the best one?"

"The place where they used to shoot all those Bounty towel commercials. You remember—with Nancy Walker as Rosie the waitress? Well, that's a real diner. It's in this old railroad car. I ate there once, it's great."

"Where's it at?"

"They tore it down a few years ago."

I sighed. "Progress, I hate it."

Paramus is famous for being the home of the shopping mall. There really is no town. Just a collection of Toys "Я" Us, Caldors, and parking lots as far as the eye can see. But there were some nice residential areas too, once you got away from the crowds of shoppers. Andrew Cox's house was in one of them, a few miles from the Garden State Plaza.

Monica Cox was still having trouble adjusting to the fact that her husband wasn't ever coming home again.

"You know, my father died a few years ago," she explained as we drank coffee in the living room of her Cape Cod house. "He had cancer. It was a very difficult time for my mother and me, but we had plenty of time to say our good-byes. It wasn't like that with Andy. He was forty-five years old and he just went out one day and now"—her voice caught a little as she said it—"I'll never see him again."

I said something about how death was never easy, no matter how it happened. It didn't make a lot of sense. But then nothing ever does at times like this.

"Can you tell me exactly how it happened?" I asked.

Mrs. Cox shrugged. "There's not much to tell. It was a Sunday morning, and Andy got a call from someone at the show asking him to go to the office for something or other. I didn't want him to ruin the weekend. But he said there was no traffic now—he'd be in and out before I even missed him. According to the police, he parked his car on 76th and then was hit by a speeding car as he crossed the street to the studio. They never caught the driver."

"You know about the other stuff that's happened to people on the show?" I mentioned the deaths of Cheryl Wolcott and Eileen Clayton.

She nodded.

"Do you think there could be any connection between what happened to them and your husband?"

She looked confused. "Why?"

"I don't know," I admitted. "What kind of relationship did your husband have with Jerry Meredith?"

"A terrific one. Jerry really depended on him, you know. He used to tell Andy that he was really the reason for the success of 'The Morning Show.' That he couldn't do it without him."

Beautiful. Jerry bragged to me that the only indispensable part of the show was him—that nobody else mattered that much. Jerry really knew how to push people's buttons, all right.

I decided to try out a scenario I'd been playing over in my mind for the last few days.

"Did your husband like to gamble?"

"What do you mean?"

"Did he bet on sporting events? Football games? Horse races?"

She thought about it. "I think he was in some sort of office pool at work during football season. They each put up ten dollars a week and picked games on Sunday. And one weekend six months or so ago, we went to Atlantic City with another couple and Andy won a hundred and fifty dollars. He was so excited." She smiled sadly. "Why?"

"You never had any hint he was into big-time gambling, like with a bookmaker?"

"Andy? Of course not. He was very conservative about money. I don't think he ever even bought a lottery ticket."

"How about Jerry Meredith?"

"Oh, he loved to gamble. Everyone knew that. He was always talking about booking bets, according to Andy. But it didn't really matter if he won or lost, did it? I mean, he had all that money from his wife."

"Did your husband ever talk about a man named Vincent Guardere?" I asked.

She shook her head.

"How about Cheryl Wolcott and Eileen Clayton? What was your husband's relationship with them? Is there anything you can think of that might connect all their deaths?"

"No. Cheryl and he worked together, of course. But they weren't particularly close outside the office. And Eileen Clayton—I doubt Andy ever even spoke to her. We sort of moved in different social circles than her and Jerry."

"How about a woman named Becky Bessard? Did you ever hear of her?"

"Of course. She was a production assistant on the show."

"You knew her?"

"Not personally. I just talked to her the one time on the phone."

"When was that?"

"On the day Andy died."

I was confused.

"You mean you spoke to her after the accident?"

"No, before. Didn't I mention her name? She was the one who called from the office that day and asked Andy to come into work."

Becky Bessard had been there all along—bubbling under the surface of this case right from the very beginning.

I just hadn't paid much attention to her. It was like having a pebble in your shoe that doesn't bother you enough to take it out. Or getting a speck of something in your eye. Or feeling some slight discomfort in a tooth. You know it's there, but you don't always get around to dealing with it right away. And then—all of a sudden—it erupts into a real pain.

The pain I felt now was Becky Bessard.

She'd supposedly gone out with Jerry Meredith. She disappeared right around the time of his wife's murder. And now I'd found out she was the one who had called—maybe even lured—Andrew Cox to "The Morning Show" studio on the day he died.

So where in the hell was Becky Bessard?

The staff roster I found in Cheryl Wolcott's apartment listed her address on East 27th Street. The building turned out to be a high-rise on the north side of the street, between Third and Lexington.

The first thing I did when we got there was press the buzzer for her apartment. Hey, you never know. Sometimes the simple approach works. Becky Bessard could have come to the door wearing a bathrobe and hair curlers, wiping sleep from her eyes. Maybe she was sick. Or just vegging out in front of the TV and didn't feel like going to work. Or shacked up with some guy. But there was no answer.

Actually, I don't ever remember the simple approach working for me.

I checked the mailbox. It was stuffed with catalogues and bills. Another mailbox said SUPER over the top. I pushed that buzzer.

A minute later a squat, middle-aged man appeared. He was wearing green work pants, a white T-shirt, and holding a cigar. The T-shirt had a reddish stain down the front that looked like spaghetti sauce. The end of the cigar was wet with saliva. He looked around at us and our camera equipment with amazement. Then he put the cigar in his mouth, chomped down, and said between his teeth:

"Whaddya want?"

"Suave," I said.

"Huh?"

"Suave. The way you talk like that with the cigar still in your mouth. Did anyone ever tell you how much you look like Cary Grant?"

"What are you talking about?"

"Nothing. We're looking for one of your tenants. A young woman named Becky Bessard."

"So ring her bell."

"She's not home. She hasn't answered her bell or phone for several days, and we fear something may be amiss."

The super shrugged. I wasn't sure if he even knew what "amiss" meant. But it didn't matter to him anyway. I could hear the sounds of a cartoon show on TV from inside his apartment. It sounded like Daffy Duck. He probably wanted to get back to it in a hurry. You miss a few minutes of one of those suckers, and you lose the whole plot.

"I'm not a den mother," he said.

"How about you open up her apartment and let us look around?"

"I can't do that."

"Why?"

"A super has a bond with his tenants. A special kind of trust. He can't just go invading their privacy like that."

Terrific. I get the only super in New York City who has a code of ethics.

I reached into my purse and took out two twenty-dollar bills and a ten. I held them up for him to see.

"I'll pay you for your time."

He looked at the bills and thought about it for a second.

"I'd have to stay with you the whole time," he said.

"I wouldn't have it any other way."

He took the money.

So much for his special bond with the tenants.

The apartment was a studio. It was small, facing out onto a garden in the back, and had your basic young Manhattanite's furniture: a bed, a sofa, a floor lamp, and a few tables. But I really didn't pay a whole lot of attention to any of this. I was too stunned. The place looked like a hurricane had hit it. Drawers pulled out and turned over, clothes ripped up and thrown around—there was debris everywhere.

"Jesus," the super said in amazement. "What happened?"

"Either she's a rotten housekeeper," Sanders observed, "or someone else besides us is very interested in little Becky."

He quietly clicked on the video camera and began shooting the way the room looked.

I made my way through the mess, looking for something—anything—that might give me a clue as to what was going on. The closets were pretty empty. It looked like she'd taken some stuff with her. There wasn't much in the kitchen either, just a very old container of milk and some spoiled meat. Nobody had been living here for a while.

In the living room, I found an ID card from "The Morning Show" with her name on it. There was also a snapshot in the corner. It was the first picture of Becky Bessard I'd seen. She was beautiful, with dark, striking features, and a sexiness that came across even on the tiny mugshot-like picture. I stared at it.

"Becky, Becky, Becky," I muttered. "Where are you and what are you up to?"

Funny, but I had this strange feeling I knew her. That I'd met her somewhere along the way. But that was impossible. She wasn't on "The Morning Show" set that first day I interviewed Cheryl Wolcott. And no one had seen her since then.

I slipped the ID card and picture into my purse.

There was a scrapbook near one of the wastebaskets. It was filled with newspaper articles and pictures about Jerry Meredith and "The Morning Show" like a real fan would keep. Only someone had cut up all the pictures of Jerry's face and written obscenities with a magic marker on most of the pages.

"You figure Becky did that?" Jacobson asked.

"Maybe."

"It looks like your ol' friend Jerry broke her heart."

"Jerry does that sometimes."

Sanders walked over with the video camera on his shoulder. He'd been shooting me as I went through the place.

"So what now?" he asked.

"We go to the authorities."

"Jellinek?"

"Better than that."

"Who?"

"I think it's time to do something I've been dreading since this story began."

21
A Meeting with the Tiger Lady

Katherine Grieco had a great office.

It was on the top floor of a building on Centre Street, with a corner window overlooking much of downtown Manhattan. You could see City Hall, Trinity Church, and the World Trade Center in the distance. On the wall behind her was a plaque of achievement from the National Organization for Women. There was also a picture of her on the cover of *New York* magazine with a headline which said: "THE TIGER LADY DIGS HER FANGS INTO CITY'S DRUG WAR." Plus an assortment of other newspaper and magazine headlines and awards for her crime-fighting record. Katherine Grieco was only thirty-three years old, and she was already being mentioned as the next District Attorney. She was a woman on the move.

I was a woman on the move too. I just wasn't always sure where I was going.

But I had a new plan.

The plan was to join forces with Katherine Grieco. She was convinced Jerry Meredith murdered his wife. I didn't think he did it. So I'd show her all the evidence I had on the case and win her over to my side. Then we'd both try to find the real killer. Sisters in crime-fighting. Sort of like "Cagney and Lacey."

So there I was, sitting in a chair in front of her desk while she looked at me as if I were a bug.

"How'd you get in here anyway?" she asked.

"I told your receptionist I had an appointment."

"And she believed you?"

"I embellished it a bit."

"You seem to be very good at that."

"Thank you."

"It wasn't a compliment."

She stood up, walked over to a refrigerator against the wall, and took out a bottle of Perrier water. She unscrewed the top and took a drink. Then she sat down again behind her desk. She didn't offer me anything to drink.

"You know, I generally enjoy working with the press," she said, looking at some of the clippings on the wall. "I have a good relationship with most of the reporters in town. I think I help them do their job better. And sometimes they do the same for me."

"A vigilant press is society's best protector," I said.

She glared at me. "I don't like you, McKay."

"Okay."

"So why are we wasting each other's time? I don't have anything to say to you, and you obviously don't have anything I'd be interested in."

"*Au contraire*, Madame Tiger Lady," I said.

I ran through everything I knew. Becky Bessard. Vincent Guardere. The ex-wives. The enemies Eileen Clayton had. The rash of accidents, disappearances, and suicides of people on the show. Katherine Grieco listened politely. She did not interrupt me with any questions. She did not take notes. I guess she had a mind like a steel trap.

"You sure you don't want to try and tie this into the Kennedy assassination while you're at it?" Grieco said when I was finished.

That was not exactly the response I had hoped for.

"So what exactly is it you're trying to tell me, McKay?"

"That there's a helluva lot of people out there who could have killed Eileen Clayton."

She looked at me blankly.

"The facts are..." I started to say.

"Facts? You don't have any facts. All you've got is a lot of theory, supposition, and wild conclusions. You're all over the place on this, McKay—everywhere except where you should be. Focusing on Jerry Meredith as the guy who killed his wife. There's nothing that complicated about it. It's a very simple case."

She stood up and began pacing around the room as she talked.

"You want motive? I got plenty of motive. I got the prenuptial agreement. It states very specifically that if she finds out Jerry commits any kind of adultery, he gets nothing in a divorce settlement. Nada. Zip. A big goose egg. You figure Eileen Clayton might have found out he'd strayed from his marital vows?"

"So did she," I pointed out.

"Irrelevant. Her activities aren't covered in the agreement. It's one of the little perks of going into a marriage with a billion dollars in your bank account."

I swallowed hard. "I know about the prenuptial agreement. But I thought..."

Grieco shook her head disgustedly. "You thought? That's your trouble, you don't think, you... you... ninny."

Ninny?

"As for Vincent Guardere, why would he want Eileen Clayton dead? She's his best way of getting the money he's owed. If he was going to murder anyone, why not kill Meredith? Right?"

I said that certainly made sense.

"And you think we didn't check out a lot of the other people? Even the ex-wives. Both of them have airtight alibis for the night of the murder. Not that they really needed them. There's no motive. Just like Guardere, the only person they'd want to kill is Meredith."

"What about the other deaths—Andrew Cox and Cheryl

Wolcott? And the disappearance of Becky Bessard?"

"Here's a radical thought—maybe they're exactly what they seem to be. Just isolated incidents that have nothing to do with Eileen Clayton. People do get hit by cars. And they commit suicide. And they go off somewhere without telling anyone. There doesn't have to be a conspiracy involved. Hell, maybe Lee Harvey Oswald really killed JFK."

"That's bullshit."

"No, you're the one who's full of bullshit. You come on like you're on this noble crusade to free an innocent man. And all the time you're sleeping with the guy."

I couldn't believe what I had just heard. I felt my face turning red. "What are you talking about . . . ?" I stammered.

"C'mon, McKay. You think I don't know what's going on between you and America's favorite TV host?"

"How . . . ?"

"Meredith's a murder suspect out on bail. We like to keep tabs on what he's doing. A lot of interesting stuff turns up. In this case, it was you."

"It's not like it seems," I told her. "I used to know Jerry a long time ago."

"Really? So this must be great for you. You get a big story and a big romance, all rolled into one. Neat."

"Are you . . . ?"

"Going to tell people about this? Well, that depends."

"On what?"

"On how willing you are to be a good citizen."

I didn't like where this was headed.

"I'm running a murder case here," she said. "Like I said before, it's really not a complicated one. Meredith was fooling around on his wife, she threatened to cut him off without any money, and so he killed her. Now I'm going to convict him and send him to jail for the rest of his life. If the Governor happens to restore the death penalty before that, I'll put the son of a bitch in the electric chair. That's it. End of story. We're not talking about a 'Murder, She Wrote' episode here. There's no hidden suspects lurking around who really did it. And you're not Angela Lansbury. You're just a goddamned pain in the ass—who seems to be causing trouble every time I turn around."

"It's called investigative journalism," I told her.

"Don't throw that journalistic ethics crap at me, McKay. It's a little hard to take too seriously when I know you've been playing hide the salami the whole time with my murder suspect."

She leaned across the desk now and looked at me with an icy glare. I suddenly realized how devastating she must be in a courtroom when she moved in for the kill on a witness. It was like something out of "Perry Mason." And I was the poor schmuck squirming and stammering in the witness box.

"I'll tell you what's going to happen now," she said. "You're going to stop causing trouble, McKay. You're going to get off the Jerry Meredith story. You're going to tell your bosses you've exhausted all the possible leads, which is certainly the truth. Then you're going to move on to some other topics. God knows, there's plenty of things to talk about in this city: AIDS, the homeless, drugs. This story's over for you. Let us get on with our job."

"And if I don't?"

"Then I'll make sure every gossip columnist in town knows about you and Meredith. I can do it with a few phone calls, you know. How do you think that'll make you look? A little unprofessional, huh? Sort of hard to spout off about journalistic ethics when everyone's snickering that you're just looking to get laid."

She had a tight little smile on her face as she said it. God, she really loves this, I thought.

I smiled back at her and groped for the perfect response.

"Fuck you, bitch," I told her.

Succinct, yet effective. Jenny McKay, master of the clever riposte.

Grieco just sighed. "You think you're really a tough lady, don't you?"

I didn't say anything.

"Well, I wrote the book on tough, McKay."

She reached over and pressed the intercom button for her receptionist. "Bernice, have Security come to my office. I have an unauthorized visitor here."

A few minutes later two security guards came into the office.

"Escort Miss McKay here out of the building," Grieco told them. "I don't think she'll give you any trouble. Will you, Jenny?"

I looked at the two guards. Neither of them exactly sent shivers of fear through me. One guy was in his fifties with a huge bald spot on his head and a potbelly. The other was so thin and frail he reminded me of Barney Fife on the old "Andy Griffith Show." The two of them looked like the night security detail at Kmart.

I figured I could probably take both out if I had to. But I decided to go quietly instead.

"Well, that settles it," I said to Grieco as I stood up. "You're not getting my vote for District Attorney."

The two guards led me out through the receptionist area, where Bernice stared at me like I was Amy Fisher stalking Mary Jo Buttafuoco with a gun.

"They'll never take me to the big house alive," I told her in my best Jimmy Cagney imitation.

Bernice never cracked a smile.

22
Talk of the Town

I didn't feel like getting out of bed the next morning.

My clock radio alarm clicked on a little before eight. I reached over, swatted the off button like it was a fly, and rolled over again. Outside I could hear the sounds of New York City waking up. Garbage trucks, people out jogging on their way to work, Howard Stern coming out of somebody's radio. The start of another big day in the Big Apple. Time to rise and shine. Up and at 'em, New York.

But I didn't want to be up and at 'em. I didn't want to go to work. I didn't even want to listen to Howard Stern. All I wanted to do was pull the covers up over my head and go back to sleep. I could sleep all day until it was dark. Then it would be time to go to bed again. Perfect.

Sleep, as W. C. Fields once said, the most beautiful experience in life. Except drink.

But it wasn't that easy. I'd forgotten about one thing. As I started to drift back to sleep again, I had this vague sensation of someone kissing me. It wasn't Jerry Meredith. It wasn't Mel Gibson or some other fantasy lover. This guy had a helluva beard. I opened my eyes.

"Hobo," I said.

Sure enough, it was my dog frantically licking my face. He wanted to be walked. He wanted to be petted and played with. Most of all, he wanted to be fed.

Breakfast waits for no woman.

I groaned and pulled myself into an upright position. So far, so good. I sat there for a while feeling proud of myself. Then I put on a robe and slippers and made my way into the kitchen to turn on the coffee. While it was heating, I fed Hobo and padded my way over to the front door to pick up the newspapers I have delivered in the morning.

I paged through them as I sipped the coffee and ate a bowl of Cheerios. The cereal box said Cheerios were low in fat, low in sugar, and high in oat content—a healthy way to start the day. This made me feel good. In fact, I felt so good that I poured myself a second bowl. I figured that would make me twice as healthy.

The *Post* had me on Page Six. The headline was "STRANGE BEDFELLOWS." It said:

> Jerry Meredith doesn't waste a lot of time on mourning. The daytime TV host, free on bail after being arrested for the murder of his wife, is already dating up a storm—and it looks like he's getting more than just romance out of the deal.
>
> Sources say the lucky lady is none other than Channel Six TV reporter Jenny McKay—who (surprise, surprise) has recently done a series of reports raising questions about the District Attorney's case against Meredith and suggesting that poor Jerry's being framed.
>
> But the TV audience isn't being told the full story.
>
> A law enforcement insider told Page Six that in recent days the couple has been spotted dining out, taking long walks in the park, and cozying up at each other's apartments.
>
> "She's head over heels for the guy. They had an affair a long time ago, and now she's rekindled the whole thing again. What Jerry Meredith's motivation is, one can only guess. But it doesn't hurt to have a very close

friend in the media pleading your case before a million viewers."

Prosecutors in Assistant District Attorney Katherine Grieco's office are said to be licking their chops over the revelation. They say it totally destroys the credibility of Channel Six's TV campaign on the Meredith case and makes his conviction even more likely.

"How can anyone believe a single word of what this McKay woman says when she doesn't even tell people she's sleeping with the guy?" said one person close to the case. "The public has a right to know where she's coming from on this story. And that's Jerry Meredith's bedroom."

There were similar pieces in the *Daily News* and *New York Newsday*. Katherine Grieco had been a very busy lady after I left her office. I pushed aside the bowl of Cheerios and looked down at Hobo.

"God, I think I'm really going to hate today," I told him.

By the time I got to the office, I was already a hot topic of conversation.

"All the other TV stations have been calling," Barry Kaiser told me. "They want to come over and do some sound bites with you. What do you want to do?"

"Is Pesin in?"

"Not yet. He called and said he was stopping for a quick breakfast on his way in."

"Oh great. That means he probably won't be here until dark."

"So you want to talk to these TV people or not?"

"Stall them until I can ask Pesin. That's why he gets paid the big bucks. To make the big decisions."

Kaiser gave me a funny look. "You sure you really want to talk to Pesin?"

"What do you mean?"

"Well, he may not be happy with you."

"People rarely are," I said.

Liz St. John came over to my desk. She had a big smile on her face like the cat who'd swallowed the canary. It sometimes seemed to me like her happiness was in inverse proportion to my unhappiness. And vice versa.

"So who's the bimbo now?" she said.

I sighed. This was not getting any better.

A while back, Liz had broken a big exclusive about a politician who was going to announce he was running for a higher office. When I asked her how she'd found out about it, she admitted that she was sleeping with the guy's press secretary. I was pretty relentless with her for a long time after that. I lectured her about journalistic ethics. I called her "The Big Easy." And I kept talking about how she should be elected to the bimbo-casters hall of fame.

Now I had a feeling—call it a wild hunch—that all this was going to come back to haunt me.

"This isn't as bad as it looks," I said.

"Really? Because it looks pretty bad."

"There are some extenuating circumstances."

"Like what?"

I glared at her. She still had that stupid smile on her face.

"You mispronounced eleven words last night," I said.

"What?"

"On the newscast. I kept count. Or at least I did until I ran out of fingers. I didn't want to take off my shoes, so I lost track at eleven. Actually the final total may have been quite a bit higher."

"No one's perfect," she said defensively. "I'm on the air for a whole hour. I have to say a lot of very complicated foreign names and cities sometimes. Everyone makes a mistake or two."

"One of the words you mispronounced was Manhattan," I pointed out.

Liz shook her head. "Are you going to tell me what the extenuating circumstances were with you and Jerry Meredith?"

"No."

"Why not?"

"Because it would take too long to explain to you what extenuating means."

She stalked off. My telephone rang. At first when I picked it up, I didn't hear anything on the other end. Then there were a series of low moans. And a woman's voice that kept saying, "Oh yes, that feels so good!" It was one of those sex phone lines. Somebody had called it, then patched it into my extension.

"Funny," I said in a loud voice as I slammed the receiver down. "That's a real riot."

Pesin came in a few minutes later. He was carrying a bag of food from McDonald's under his arm. As he passed by me, he tapped me on the shoulder and said, "My office. Now."

When I got to his office, he'd already unpacked the McDonald's bag. There were three Big Breakfasts inside. Eggs, sausage, potatoes and English muffin. The cholesterol special. Pesin poured the contents of all three onto one big plate. There was also a jumbo coffee. He poured four sugars and heavy cream into that. Nature's perfect meal.

"Things seem to have gotten a little bit out of hand," I said.

"What do you mean?" He started downing the sausages with one bite each, popping them into his mouth like peanuts.

"All the stuff in the papers this morning."

"Yeah, I saw that. How'd it happen?"

I told him about my encounter with Katherine Grieco at her office.

"Do you want me to resign?" I asked quietly.

Pesin looked confused. "Resign? Why? You got a better job offer somewhere? Hey, we'll match anything. . . ."

"No, I just thought it might be best for the station. To avoid any embarrassment or bad publicity."

Pesin had already finished the meal. He pushed the plate away, took a big gulp of coffee, and belched softly. Then he began to laugh.

"You still don't get it, do you, Jenny?"

"I beg your pardon?"

"This isn't bad publicity. There is no bad publicity. Publicity, by its very definition, is good."

"You mean you're not mad at me?"

"Mad? I'm ecstatic. I'm thinking of assigning all our reporters to sleep with the people they're covering."

I smiled.

"We wanted to make you a part of this story, we wanted viewers to think of you and Channel Six News whenever they heard about the Jerry Meredith–Eileen Clayton case. Well, we've succeeded beyond our wildest dreams. All this stuff in the papers, the other TV stations wanting to talk to you . . . Who do you think people are going to be watching at six o'clock tonight to find out what happens next? You. And Channel Six News."

"But it's not really ethical. It's not good journalism . . ."

"You're not in journalism anymore, Jenny. You're in television."

He finished off the coffee and then pushed the cup and the remains of the meal into a wastebasket alongside his desk.

"The big thing we have to decide now is how to take advantage of all this, what you should say when you go on the air tonight."

"I'm going on the air tonight?"

"You better believe it."

The final decision was to go on the offensive. Fight fire with fire. Attack, not retreat. Go for the jugular. So this is what I told the viewers on the newscast:

McKAY: A campaign of character assassination has been launched against this reporter in the past twenty-four hours by a woman in the District Attorney's office named Katherine Grieco.

There's been a flood of newspaper articles and TV reports—cleverly attributed to "law enforcement sources"—which say that I'm carrying on a secret romance with TV talk show host Jerry Meredith. The sources claim that's why this station and I have broken a series of stories raising doubts about Meredith's guilt in the murder of his wife, billionaire Eileen Clayton.

Here are the facts of the matter:

I do have a personal relationship with Jerry Meredith. I have known Meredith for more than ten years. I have seen him socially in recent days. Yes, I have gone out to eat with him, walked in the park with him, and been to his penthouse apartment. None of this is wrong or against the law—despite what Katherine Grieco may want you to believe.

More importantly, I have never allowed any personal feelings I may have toward Jerry Meredith to interfere with my reporting of this case.

The bottom line is this: Through exhaustive investigative work, I have raised a number of disturbing questions about Ms. Grieco's quick arrest of Meredith for his wife's murder. These still have not been answered. And there is a strong possibility that the real murderer of Eileen Clayton is still out there.

I think you viewers—whose taxes pay Ms. Grieco's hefty salary—should demand that she spend more time finding out the truth about this case and less worrying about who I'm dating.

One final thing. I will not stop working on this story. I will not be bullied by the DA's office. I will not abdicate my responsibility as a journalist.

To paraphrase Thomas Jefferson, aggressive reporting is the cornerstone of a free democracy. . . .

I thought the Thomas Jefferson reference might be going a bit too far. But Pesin liked it.

Personally I figured the ol' Jeff-meister didn't exactly have this sort of thing in mind when he talked about freedom of the press a few hundred years ago. I mean, what would our Founding Father say if he suddenly showed up in the 1990s and saw me quoting him on the six o'clock news to defend my sex life?

On the other hand, he'd be confused about a lot of things. TV. VCRs. Cable. Why Jay Leno is hosting "The Tonight Show." How Tom Arnold became a star. It'd take him so long to figure out all that stuff that he'd probably never even get around to me.

The best part of doing it, though, was the look on Liz St. John's face. She figured I'd really dropped myself in the shit this time. But instead I was a bigger star than ever. And worst of all, she had to introduce my report and smile sweetly at me on camera.

When we went to a commercial break, I jotted a note down on a piece of paper and shoved it in front of her. It said: "Life's a bitch, ain't it?"

When I got back to my desk after the newscast, there was a deluge of messages from people wanting to talk to me. Newspaper reporters. Other TV stations. And one from Jerry Meredith. I dialed his number.

"Wow!" he said when he came on the line. "That was unbelievable."

"Yeah, a new first in broadcast journalism. It sort of puts me right up there with Walter Cronkite, doesn't it?"

"Do you want to get together tonight?"

"And do what?"

He laughed. "Oh, I'm sure we can think of something."

"I've got to go home first," I said. "I need to walk my dog. And feed him."

"No problem, it's still early. I'm going over to the Limelight about ten. Meet me there."

"Gee, I'm not sure the Limelight's such a good idea. There are always photographers there. People will talk...."

"They're already talking. So what do we have to lose?"

I thought about that.

"You're right," I said. "When you're right, you're right."

I told him I'd see him there at ten.

I'd just hung up when the phone rang again. It was Clare.

"I could do without your usual scathing review on this one," I told her.

She didn't say anything. Then I heard her crying.

"Clare, what's wrong?"

"She's dead."

"Who?"

"Elaine Rivera."

I clenched the phone tightly and closed my eyes. "What happened?"

"There was a fight in the cafeteria. One of the women had a knife. Elaine wasn't even part of the argument, but she got caught in the middle. She was dead by the time they got her to the prison infirmary."

Clare started to cry again.

"I told her I'd get her out of that hellhole, Jenny. I never did. I let her down."

I wasn't sure what to say. Maybe because I felt the same way.

On the face of it, it was the kind of murder that hardly caused a ripple in a place like New York City. People die violently here every day. They get strangled, shot, stabbed, shoved in front of subway trains, and set afire. Or maybe some kid drops a cinder block off a roof on top of them. I even remember one guy getting it with a bow and arrow.

Most of them, like Elaine Rivera, never even make the news. I mean, she wasn't famous. She wasn't rich. She wasn't particularly interesting or unusual in any way. She was just another crime statistic.

Except that I'd met this one.

I met her and I liked her and I felt sorry for her. Most of all, I promised I'd help her.

Another in a long list of broken promises for ol' Jenny McKay.

I talked with Clare for another ten minutes or so, trying to calm her down. Then I went home, poured myself a drink, and tried to figure out something I could do about Elaine Rivera's death. I couldn't think of a damn thing.

So I headed for the Limelight.

23
Late Night at the Limelight

The Limelight is on 20th Street, at the corner of Sixth Avenue. It's an old church that was converted into a nightclub several years back. Now it's one of the New York "in spots"—the kind of place where everyone from Shannen Doherty to Zsa Zsa Gabor goes to get their picture taken looking beautiful.

There's an annoying phenomenon that takes place at trendy joints like this. The happening people get to go right in, while everyone else has to wait outside. There are always long lines of suckers out front, desperately hoping that some bouncer will choose them from the crowd. It all depends on who you are and how you look. Based on that, most of the people outside the Limelight now had about as much chance of walking through the front door as I had of being *Sports Illustrated*'s swimsuit issue cover girl. But they still stand there patiently through heat and cold and rain. Me, I can't figure it. I won't even stand in line to go to a movie.

Fortunately I didn't have to stand in any line at the Limelight. I was one of the beautiful people. I was on television. And I was there to meet Jerry Meredith, America's favorite daytime talk show host. I pushed my way through the sea of anxious faces, identified myself to a person at the door who was either a man dressed in woman's clothing or vice versa, and went inside.

There was loud music and flashing lights and lots of people dancing. I found Jerry holding court at the bar. Photographers and celebrity reporters were gathered around him. When I showed up, they started taking pictures of both of us and talking to me. I was big news. If Pesin loved today's papers, he was going to be in ecstasy tomorrow.

"How you doin'?" he whispered in my ear.

"Terrible."

"What's wrong?"

I told him about Elaine Rivera.

"Did you know her very well?"

"We only met once."

"So what's the big deal?"

"She . . . she touched me, Jerry. I could have helped her. I should have helped her. But I didn't."

"Have a beer," he said. "It'll make you feel better."

A while later—after the press had finally drifted away to meet their deadlines—we were still standing at the bar. The bartender, whose name was Ivan, put the latest in a long series of drinks in front of us. I was starting to get very drunk.

"I hate television," I announced. "It's all so phony."

Jerry laughed and sipped on his drink.

"You know what really bugs me?" I said. "The way TV people thank each other after they do a story. You know. 'Thanks for that report, Jim. Good job.' Can you imagine doing that in a newspaper? Putting a paragraph at the end of a story thanking the reporter for writing it? C'mon, that's what they're being paid for.

"And how about the quips? The whole happy news team concept. A couple of ninnies giggling up there on the screen about the weather or the traffic or the color of the anchorman's tie. It's like being at a really bad cocktail party with a bunch of bores. Only these people are getting paid big bucks to do it.

"Then there's the ones in love with themselves like Liz St. John. They preen to the camera. They smile constantly. They exaggerate every gesture and inflection, artificially punching out the words like William Hurt's character in *Broadcast News*. Camera-fuckers is what I call them. I hate 'em all."

Jerry chuckled at the state I was working myself up into.

"The camera is your friend, Jenny. You should learn to feel more comfortable with it."

"Don't you ever miss the printed word? The idea of writing a wonderful sentence or paragraph or story, putting it down on paper? Then knowing it will be there for years—not gone in an instant like television. God, I miss working at a newspaper."

"Newspapers are overrated," he said. "Nobody reads them anymore. Hell, no one reads anything these days. People get all their news and entertainment on the screen."

"Now there's a comforting thought for the nineties."

Ivan came over to refill our drinks. I'd started with Amstel Light, then switched to scotch. Jerry was drinking Jack Daniel's. Somewhere about an hour earlier I'd lost track of how many rounds we'd had. It looked like it was going to be a long night.

"Tell me about Becky Bessard," I asked him suddenly.

No reaction. Jerry just sipped his drink thoughtfully. "I told you before—I barely knew her."

"I don't believe you."

He shrugged.

"That's the story you're gonna stick with, huh?"

"It's not a story. It's the truth."

"I've been to Becky Bessard's apartment. It was very interesting."

I told him about the scrapbook she kept about him. All the clippings and the pictures.

"Okay, so she was a big fan." He seemed a little uncomfortable now though. "And probably a little crazy too. Just like most of the women I meet."

"What's that supposed to mean?"

"I'm not talking about you, Jenny."

"I met your two ex-wives."

"Janet and Barbara Ann." He smiled. "Janet's a real ball-breaker, isn't she? She goes back to court if my alimony check isn't there when she checks her mailbox on the first of the month. Maybe the mailman's just late—it doesn't matter to her. And she doesn't even really need the money. She just loves to stick it to me. That's what she lives for. Janet. Barbara Ann. Even poor little Becky—who you say developed this unrequited crush on me. I sure do seem to attract the nut cases."

"How come you didn't tell me about your marriage to Barbara Ann Forbes when we were going out together ten years ago?"

"It didn't really seem to matter. I mean, I'd almost forgotten about it myself. That was a whole different lifetime for me. I mean, you've been down to Trenton to see her. Can you imagine me living like that?" He shuddered. "God, what a nightmare."

"You had two kids," I pointed out.

"That was a long time ago too."

"You never asked about them? Wondered how they were growing up?"

"No."

"One of them died a year ago, you know."

"Yeah, so I heard."

He saw the stunned expression on my face. "Look, I know that sounds bad, but it's just the way it is. It's not like any of these people are really my family anymore. If I ran into them on the street today, I wouldn't even recognize them. So why lie and pretend that they mean something to me that they don't?"

I thought about Barbara Ann Forbes raising their two children all alone in that depressing little house in Trenton. About Janet Hutchings and her hatred for the man who'd ruined her life. And then I said out loud something I'd been thinking about for a while.

"This is just a theory," I said. "But what if one of your ex-wives really wanted to get revenge against you? What would they do?"

"Shoot me."

"That's the simple way. But then you'd be dead. And you really wouldn't suffer for very long. If they really wanted to torture you—if they wanted to make your life a living hell—how else could they do it?"

Jerry thought about that for a second. "By taking away everything I have."

"Exactly. Your money. Your career. Even your freedom."

"You think one of them might have killed Eileen? And tried to frame me for it?"

"It's possible. Diabolical and farfetched, maybe. But possible."

"Jesus, you could be right!"

I tried to imagine Janet Hutchings or Barbara Ann Forbes murdering Eileen Clayton. And Andrew Cox and Cheryl Wolcott and maybe Becky Bessard too. Somehow it didn't quite click.

There was something wrong with the picture.

Something I was missing.

Alcohol does funny things to your brain. When you're drinking it, you feel very smart. Most of the time, in the cold light of the next morning, you realize all those brilliant ideas you came up with are really pretty dumb.

But this time was different. I'd somehow jogged something out of my subconscious. Maybe if I wasn't drinking I'd have thought of it earlier. Or maybe the booze helped.

But suddenly I knew.

I knew where I'd seen Becky Bessard before. Or at least someone that looked a lot like her.

"I've got to make a phone call," I said.

Jerry looked at his watch. "It's one-thirty in the morning."

"This won't wait."

I found a pay phone and dialed information for Trenton, New Jersey. When I finally got her, she was asleep, of course. But I said this was a matter of life and death. Then I laid it all out for her. For a second or two, she didn't say anything. I wondered if she was going to just hang up and go back to sleep. But she didn't. Barbara Ann Forbes told me everything.

It was thirty minutes later when I got back to the bar. Jerry was deep in conversation with Ivan. They were discussing Porsches. Ivan said he got his new one up to 120 mph over the weekend. Jerry said he'd once hit 125, and then he turned to look at me.

"God, I thought you'd gotten lost," he said. "Who were you calling?"

"Your ex-wife."

"Janet?"

"No. Barbara Ann."

"Her? You think she's the one who killed Eileen?"

I shook my head.

"Tell me the truth about Becky Bessard."

"Like I said, I barely knew the girl. She just worked on the show and . . ."

"Cut the crap, Jerry."

He looked startled.

"It's just you and me talking here," I said. "There's no camera, I don't have a tape recorder—I'm not even taking notes. You can deny it later if you want. I've got no proof. But I have to know the truth. You slept with her, didn't you?"

Jerry looked down at his drink and sighed. He'd had a few more while I was on the phone. He seemed pretty drunk.

"Hey, she was young. She was beautiful. She was very hot for me. I'm only human."

"How many times?"

"A few."

"What happened then?"

"She started getting really serious. Talked about how she was going to tell Eileen the truth about us. I couldn't believe it. She was just this little sexpot I was having a few kicks with. And now she was going to blow everything for me. So I had to end it. I gave her some money—a lot of money—and told her to go away."

"How'd she take that?"

"Badly. You saw the scrapbook. The way she cut my head up and wrote all those disgusting things."

He finished off the rest of his drink. His eyes were glazed now.

"What a pity," he said. "She was so beautiful. I guess it's like Woody Allen says, 'Great beauty drives women crazy.' "

I glared at him.

At that moment I knew how Janet Hutchings and Barbara Ann Forbes felt about him. And maybe Becky Bessard too.

"What's wrong?" he asked.

"You stupid son of a bitch—you don't know, do you?"

"Know what?"

"Becky Bessard is your own daughter."

24
Trenton Again

I had a headache that wouldn't quit. My mouth was all parched and dry. And I was dead tired after only a couple hours of sleep. I was not in good shape.

But I had a scoop.

I popped a couple of aspirin into my mouth, unscrewed a bottle of seltzer to wash them down with, and looked out the window of the Channel Six mobile van as we headed south on the New Jersey Turnpike toward Trenton. The beginning of the trip was through the industrial flats near Newark. Then you got to the rolling plains and rural countryside of the middle of the state. And finally it turned to factories and smokestacks again as you got close to Trenton.

Sanders looked over at me from the driver's seat. "Long night, Jenny?"

I made a whimpering sound.

"The trick is to take the aspirin before you start drinking," he told me. "That way you don't even get the hangover. It always works for me. How about you, Artie?"

Jacobson stirred in the backseat. "I like to eat a good meal before I start. That lines your stomach and you can drink all night and still wake up the next morning feeling fresh as a daisy. The more you eat, the better. A rare steak. Some greasy potatoes. Rolls drenched in butter..."

I was getting nauseous. "Look guys, I know you mean well, and I really appreciate your advice, and please don't take this the wrong way, but—SHUT UP!"

We drove in silence for a little while.

"Let me get this straight," Sanders said. "Becky Bessard is really Elizabeth Forbes—the daughter of this woman Meredith was married to twenty some years ago. And Becky—or Elizabeth or whatever—had sex with Meredith. Only he didn't know it was really his own daughter that he was banging like a gong?"

I nodded.

Sanders let out a low whistle. "That's heavy."

"The heaviest."

"And you think the girl is the key to everything that's happened?"

"I do."

"So where is she now?"

"That's the $64,000 question."

The house in Trenton didn't look any better than it had the first time we were there. The little patch of grass in front seemed browner. The Dodge was still there, and so was the spare tire and engine parts around it. Next door a guy in a sleeveless white undershirt was sitting on the steps drinking a beer. It wasn't exactly the kind of neighborhood where you expected to run into Robin Leach.

Barbara Ann Forbes let us in, and we sat down again in the tiny living room.

"I have to know about your daughter," I said.

She nodded.

The last vestiges of beauty were still there on Barbara Ann Forbes. Looking at her now, I realized why I'd finally recognized the same features that I'd seen in the daughter's picture. And also why it took me so long to realize it.

"I'd like to do this on camera," I said. "Is that all right?"

Another nod.

It didn't matter to Barbara Ann Forbes. Nothing seemed to matter to her now.

Sanders and Jacobson set up the equipment as she sat there quietly, her hands folded together in her lap. When Sanders was ready, he gave me a sign, and we started rolling. I asked Barbara Ann Forbes when she'd last talked to her daughter.

"Elizabeth called me. After you were here the last time."

"Where was she?"

"I don't know."

She looked around the room. At the walls with paint peeling off them. The grimy window looking out on the yard with the Dodge sitting on the lawn. The picture of Jesus on the mantel and the Bible next to it.

"This is a good house," she said. "I tried to make it that way. I tried to raise my children the best I could. I taught them about religion. And the difference between right and wrong. But I was all alone. I had no husband. Very little money. It was so hard."

She looked at me. "Do you have any children, Miss McKay?"

"No."

"You give them everything you have. You work for them, you worry about them, and you love them. But no one can ever be sure how things will turn out. Or what will happen to your children."

"What did happen?" I asked.

"Elizabeth was very confused growing up," she said. "She had a lot of . . . well, problems. Mostly relating to her father."

"I thought she never really knew him, that he left when she was an infant."

"The doctors call it a father fixation. When she found out who he was, she became obsessed with him. It only got worse the more famous he got. She'd tell everyone who saw him on TV, 'That's my dad.' Most people didn't believe her. How could a big star like Jerry Meredith have a daughter living like this?"

"It's understandable," I said. "A lot of kids in single-parent families have real problems relating to what happened to the one who's not around. It sometimes takes years to get over. Until they grow up and move on."

She shook her head. "It just got worse as she grew up."

"What do you mean?"

"At first, she was fascinated by Jerry. But then her attitude changed. She began to get angry at him. For what he did to me. For the way he abandoned her and her brother Luke." She gestured toward the picture of Jesus. "I taught Elizabeth about religion, I used to read from the Bible to my children every night before they went to bed—but there was no forgiveness in her heart toward her father. I'd walk in and find her screaming at him on the TV screen. Or she'd take pictures of him out of newspapers and magazines, then cut up the head and write terrible things all over them."

I thought about the scene in Becky Bessard's apartment. It was all starting to come together now.

"Things got worse when she was a teenager," her mother was saying. "I took her to a doctor—a psychiatrist. It cost a lot of money. I'm still paying the bills for it."

"Did it help?"

"The doctor thought it did, but I was never sure. I mean, all they did was talk. It wasn't like he could just give her a shot or a pill or something to fix what was wrong. And the more she talked about all this stuff with her father, the more she thought about him. It became her whole life. I was angry at the doctor, angry at Elizabeth for being like she was, and angry at Jerry for causing the whole mess." She took a deep breath. "And then Luke died."

"Your son?"

She nodded. "He had problems too. He got in with a bad crowd and started doing drugs. Marijuana. Cocaine. And finally heroin. They found him in a bed in some seedy hotel with a needle in his arm. The authorities said it could have been an accidental overdose. Or maybe suicide."

There were tears in her eyes.

"How did this affect Elizabeth?" I asked.

"Horribly. She read the Bible all day long—but I don't think she was getting the word of God from it. I think she was listening to the Devil now. There were ugly things going on inside her. She said someone had to pay for Luke's death. She didn't blame her brother for the overdose, she didn't blame his friends, she didn't blame me. Do you know who she blamed?"

"Jerry Meredith?"

"Yes. She sat there in front of the TV staring at him. I asked her what she was thinking about, but she wouldn't talk about it. She wouldn't go back to the doctor. And then one day she just left. She announced she was going to change her name, move to another town, and start a new life."

"And so she went to New York. And got a job on 'The Morning Show' as Becky Bessard."

"I didn't know that then."

"When did you find out?"

"When she called me."

"What did she say?"

Barbara Ann Forbes started to cry now. We sat there with the camera rolling as she tried to compose herself. Finally she took out a Kleenex, wiped her eyes dry, and said in a flat, matter-of-fact voice, "She told me she wanted to get back at him. She wanted to ruin him and his career."

She dabbed at her eyes some more with the Kleenex. "You have to understand, Miss McKay, that my daughter is a very beautiful young woman. I guess it was in her genes. It's the one thing Jerry gave her—good looks. And people used to tell me I was attractive too. A long time ago. Men like Elizabeth. And she likes the fact that they do. It gives her a feeling of power over people she never had as a child. She learned she could get men to do things because she was so beautiful. And so . . ."

I suddenly knew what she was going to say.

"She seduced Jerry."

"Her own father?"

"Yes. She said it was all part of her plan. She'd get pictures of them together. Pictures of them . . ."

"In bed?"

She nodded. "Elizabeth was going to use them to destroy him. To destroy his career. To destroy his marriage. Only something happened that changed everything."

"What?"

She started crying again. This time it didn't stop for a long time. I looked over at Sanders. Neither of us could believe we were getting all this on camera.

"She said . . ." Barbara Ann Forbes said as she finally composed herself, "she said that she'd fallen in love with him."

Then the tears began again.

My God! What a tangled mess. This family made Woody Allen and Mia Farrow look like Ozzie and Harriet.

"But she said he'd broken her heart too. Just like he'd broken mine all those years ago. Now she didn't think she could go on. She talked about giving up. About going to see Luke again."

"You mean killing herself?"

"Yes. She didn't say it in so many words, but I knew what she meant."

"What did you tell her?"

"I begged her to come home. To tell me where she was. But she said it was too late. She'd done some terrible things. I said we could work things out. No matter what she'd done, I could forgive her."

"Even sleeping with her own father?"

"Yes. I don't care about anything but my daughter, Miss McKay. She's all I have left."

"What did she say?"

"She said she'd done something worse than sleeping with her father. Something she couldn't undo. Something no one could forgive her for—not even God."

There was a silence in the room. I looked over at Sanders and Jacobson. They were both staring at Barbara Ann Forbes in rapt attention, just like they were watching it on television—waiting for her next words.

"What did she do?" I asked.

"Elizabeth told me," Barbara Ann Forbes said as the camera captured all of it, "that she'd killed some people."

25
Becky Bessard

"This is dynamite," Pesin said.

He reached over and rewound the tape to the beginning again, then pressed the play button. He seemed transfixed by the image of Barbara Ann Forbes telling the story of her daughter on the screen.

The two of us were sitting in the Channel Six editing room. Pesin had a jelly doughnut sitting on a table next to him. He hadn't eaten a bite while we watched the tape.

High praise, indeed.

"I called Lieutenant Jellinek and fed him everything I had," I told Pesin. "He's going to put out an APB to pick up Becky Bessard. But he says he'll hold off a public announcement on it so we can break the story on the air at six."

"What are the charges going to be against her?"

"Suspicion of murder."

Pesin cackled with delight. "I love it."

"Jellinek figures this will knock the stuffing out of Katherine Grieco's murder case against Jerry Meredith. It was all circumstantial anyway. And now you've got this girl's own mother quoting her as saying she confessed to murder."

THE MOURNING SHOW

"Can you imagine what Grieco's reaction is going to be when she finds out about this?"

"It's what I live for." I smiled.

Pesin pressed the pause button on the video machine. Barbara Ann Forbes's face froze in mid-sentence on the screen. I stared at it, wondering where Becky Bessard was right now. If she was even still alive.

"Let me tell you a story," Pesin said. He leaned over and took a bite of the jelly doughnut. Pesin loved to tell stories. He had a lot of them, but they all had one thing in common. They were always about himself.

"I solved a case like this a few years back when I was at Channel Two," he said. "The cops, the DA—no one had a clue. This guy pulled off a big heist in the Bronx. Only the cops couldn't prove it. He claimed he was eating lunch at the time—he said he'd had an egg cream at a place just off the Grand Concourse, then gone next door for a slice of pizza. Now I grew up in the same neighborhood. I knew that block like the back of my hand. You can't buy an egg cream there—you've got to walk a block south. And to get a slice of pizza you go two blocks in the other direction. When the cops confronted the suspect with this, he broke down and confessed everything. Pretty clever, huh?"

I smiled and said it was clever.

Actually I didn't think it was that clever at all. It didn't make much sense to me. It didn't really prove anything. And—to be brutally honest—it sounded suspiciously similar to something I'd seen on an episode of "Matlock" a while back.

But what the hell—the guy liked me. He was going to help my career. There weren't that many people I could say that about. So why not just go with the flow?

"I knew I could pull this case off too," he was saying. "I had a feeling about it from the very beginning. I've got a great instinct about stuff like that."

I?

"Excuse me," I said, "but I had a little to do with this story too. I figured out about Becky Bessard. I took on

Katherine Grieco. I slept with Jerry Meredith. All in the line of duty. Let's keep that in mind when we're handing out congratulations for this one."

"Sure, sure," he said quickly. "I meant *we*. You did a good job too. But you're not finished yet."

"I know that."

"You've still got to . . ."

"Find Becky Bessard."

"The perfect ending to the perfect story."

As it turned out, I didn't have to find Becky Bessard after all. She found me. Sort of.

Lt. Jellinek called to tell me about it just before we went on the air one night.

"I'm heading for the George Washington Bridge," he yelled over a car phone. "You better get up here right away."

"What's at the George Washington Bridge?"

"Becky Bessard. She's threatening to jump."

"Jesus!"

"A police car should be in front of your building right now. It'll give you an escort up to the bridge."

"Okay. But why all this special attention?"

"She's asking for you," he told me.

"Becky Bessard?"

"Yeah. She saw your broadcast about her. She says she has something she wants to say."

"I'm on my way."

The WTBK studio is on the southern tip of Manhattan, the opposite end from the George Washington Bridge. But it's also right next to the East River Drive. Within minutes we were on the drive, heading north through the evening rush hour traffic with the police car—siren wailing and lights flashing—leading our way. We got to the bridge just as the six o'clock news was about to start.

"We'll do a live remote with you from the scene," Barry Kaiser said over the radio. "You get yourselves ready. Set up the shots of the bridge, the girl threatening to jump—then we'll cut into the news and go to you live. Okay?"

"Roger," Sanders said into the phone.

I was already out of the van and running toward the spot on the bridge where they were trying to talk Becky Bessard down from her perch.

She'd climbed about twenty feet up one of the spans and was standing there above the Hudson River. There were a lot of cops and emergency service people looking up at her. All the traffic on the bridge had been stopped while they tried to deal with the crisis. This was no small thing at six o'clock at night. You could hear horns blaring all over the place.

It didn't seem the way someone should die. With a massive traffic jam and a lot of angry people. But I guess once you're dead, it doesn't really matter.

Kaiser's voice crackled in my ear.

"Are you ready to go yet?"

I was standing next to Jellinek now. I looked around for Sanders and Jacobson. They were right behind me. Sanders had the camera pointed at Becky Bessard on the span above. He gave me a thumbs up sign.

"Let's do it," I told Kaiser.

Back in the studio, Conroy Jackson was saying:

JACKSON: . . . we have a late breaking story. Becky Bessard—now the chief suspect in the deaths of three people, including the wife of TV star Jerry Meredith—has been cornered by police on the George Washington Bridge. She's threatening to jump and has demanded to talk to Channel Six's own Jenny McKay, the reporter who broke the story of her involvement in the killings. For a live report, we go right now to Jenny at the George Washington Bridge. . . .

The camera cut to a shot of me on the bridge. You could see the water and the cliffs of the Palisades behind me.

McKAY: Conroy, a tense life-and-death drama is being played out here this evening. Becky Bessard, who has emerged as the key player in the tangled Jerry Meredith murder case, is in a standoff with police. She's threatening to jump into the water below. Authorities said the only demand she's made is to tell her story to me on TV. That's what we're going to try to do now.

The screen showed a shot of Becky clinging to the cables on the bridge and looking down at the water below. Her hair was blowing in the wind, and there was a blank expression on her face. I wondered if she was on drugs. She looked like she hadn't slept in a week.

I moved into a position as close as I could. Jellinek had a megaphone in his hand. He pointed it at Becky and said:

JELLINEK: This is Lt. Jellinek of the New York City Police. We have Jenny McKay here from Channel Six and she wants to talk to you. Is that all right?

Becky looked down at me and nodded.

BESSARD: Am I on television right now?

McKAY: Yes, you are. This is all being broadcast live on the six o'clock news. Everyone can hear what you're saying.

BESSARD: You're the one who went to see my mother.

McKAY: That's right.

BESSARD: My poor pathetic mother. The first to be cursed by Jerry Meredith.

McKAY: Jerry is your father . . .

BESSARD: My father and my lover. My enemy and my friend. My happiness and my pain. He is everything, and he is nothing. . . .

She seemed to be rambling now.

McKAY: You had a love affair with him, didn't you?

BESSARD: It's not what I wanted. I wanted revenge. I wanted him to pay for what he did to my mother. To Luke. And to me. I wanted it to be painful, and I wanted it to be slow.

McKAY: You were going to destroy his life and his career. Isn't that right, Becky?

She nodded.

BESSARD: I wanted to take away everything that mattered to him. Just like he did to us.

McKAY: Did you kill people, Becky?

BESSARD: Yes, I killed them.

McKAY: Andrew Cox? Cheryl Wolcott? Eileen Clayton?

BESSARD: I killed them all.

She started crying. The she started talking again. At first I couldn't make out what she was saying. But then I realized what it was. She was praying. She was reciting from the Bible. I remembered the picture of Jesus on the mantel of the little house in Trenton.

BESSARD: Yea, though I walk through the valley of the shadow of death, I shall fear no evil. For Thou art with me. Thy rod and Thy staff, they comfort me. . . .

We all stood there, not sure what to do next. Me, Sanders and Jacobson, the cops. Everyone was afraid to interrupt her or make a move because she might jump. I tried desperately to think of what I could say to her when she finished praying. How I could save her life.
But it was too late for that.

She finished with the words: "... surely goodness and mercy shall follow me all the days of my life."

Then she stood there for a second, silhouetted against the evening sky.

Suddenly she pushed herself out from where she was standing and toward the water. She did it casually and without any warning. Like it was the most natural thing in the world. Like a young bird leaving the nest for the first time.

It was one of those moments that would be shown over and over again on news shows around the country for weeks to come. They'd freeze-frame it. Do it in slow motion. Play sad music by Leonard Cohen or somebody as a backdrop as Becky Bessard, whose real name was Elizabeth Forbes, plummeted toward the Hudson River.

A classic moment in live television. Just like Jack Ruby shooting Lee Harvey Oswald. Or Budd Dwyer shooting himself at a press conference in Pennsylvania. Or Reginald Denny being beaten by a mob during the Los Angeles riots.

Except that this time I was there.

Some people think that when a person jumps from a high place their whole life passes in front of them on the way down. Others say there's no truth to that—it's just an agonizing and painful way to die. There's also a theory that a person loses consciousness in the first few seconds of the descent and never feels anything after that.

I always wondered what it was like for Becky Bessard. Was she thinking about Jerry Meredith? Her mother? The people she killed? Or was she finally at peace with herself?

But I'll never know the answer.

She was dead by the time they pulled her out of the water.

26
Let's Be Careful Out There

The cops had pretty much sorted it out by the next day.

"We retraced our steps on all the murders, and Becky Bessard popped up everywhere," Lt. Jellinek told me.

"That sort of shoots a rather large hole in Katherine Grieco's case against Jerry Meredith, doesn't it?"

"I think Grieco may be jumping from the George Washington Bridge herself later today."

"Is she going to drop the charges against Jerry?"

"What other choice does she have? Becky Bessard confessed to the murders on television before she killed herself. How do you beat that?"

We were sitting in the squad room. Around us I heard snatches of conversation about "perps" and "a ten-eleven in progress" and booking procedures. Every once in a while someone brought a suspect through the room. It was sort of like being in Capt. Furillo's office on "Hill Street Blues."

I'd brought along a bag of doughnuts and some coffee from a deli on Second Avenue to cement my new friendship with Jellinek. He'd already polished off one glazed, one jelly, and a jumbo coffee with four sugars and heavy cream. Now he was ready to make his move on a sugar cruller.

"Tell me what you found out about Becky," I said, taking a sip of my coffee. I'd eaten a couple of doughnuts myself. Three actually. But I put Sweet'n Low in my coffee.

Self-discipline is the code I live by.

"You already know she was the one who made the phone call to Andrew Cox that got him to the studio the day he died. She was also the person who identified the body at the scene. None of that seemed very significant before. But it sort of jumps out at you when you go back through the files now.

"Next, we come to Cheryl Wolcott. Cheryl talks to you and becomes suspicious about what's going on. So she decides to do some investigating on her own—and that leads her right to Becky Bessard. That landlord you talked to says Wolcott turned up there asking questions on the day she died. We figure Becky found out, followed her back to her place, and decided to shut her up for good.

"And then there's Eileen Clayton—billionaire, super bitch, and wife of your close friend, Jerry Meredith. One of the help at the building just identified a picture of Becky Bessard. He says she was there to see Eileen Clayton the day before the murder."

"The day before?"

"Yeah."

"Why would Eileen Clayton even talk to someone like Becky Bessard?"

"Who knows? But it establishes a link between Clayton and the Bessard woman. Let's say they met and argued over Meredith. Then Becky comes back the next night to get rid of her for good."

I shook my head sadly. "That's an awful lot of killing over one man."

"Becky started out wanting to destroy Meredith's life. So she killed what she figured were the two most important people responsible for the success of his show. And she went after the woman who gave him his money. It was her way of revenge for the way he'd abandoned her and her brother and her mother."

THE MOURNING SHOW

"Only somewhere along the line she fell in love with him."

"And then he broke her heart all over again. It doesn't make a lot of sense, does it?"

"Love rarely does."

Jellinek looked down at the now-empty bag of doughnuts. He picked up a few crumbs with his finger and licked them off. Waste not, want not.

"You want to hear a funny kicker?" he said. "The train engine Becky Bessard used to kill the Clayton woman wasn't worth ten thousand dollars after all. It turned out to be just a cheap plastic toy. Meredith kept a couple of them around for gags. So this lady who's worth a billion bucks winds up getting it with something you could buy at Toys "Я" Us."

"There's something tragically poetic about that."

"By the way, Meredith still doesn't admit to having had an affair with Becky. He says that was all in her imagination."

"I'm not surprised."

"Didn't you say he admitted it to you?"

"It was very late, I was very persuasive, and he was very drunk. Now he's sober, and he's got one thing on his mind—Eileen Clayton's billion-dollar estate."

"And the prenuptial agreement says he can't have it if he committed adultery while she was still alive."

"Exactly."

"Who can prove anything anyway?" Jellinek said. "Becky's dead. And even if she wasn't, it's just her word against his. No pictures of anything have turned up. All he has to do is keep denying it and the money is his. Adultery's a tough thing to prove."

"You figure he'll wind up with the billion dollars?" I asked.

"Probably."

"I wonder."

He smiled. "Who knows—you play your cards right and you might be able to share it with him. Jenny Meredith? It's got a nice ring to it."

"Doubtful," I said. "Very doubtful."

"Do you think he'll deny Becky Bessard to you—claim you misunderstood him that night at the Limelight?"

"I don't know." I stood up. "Maybe I'll go ask him."

I shook Jellinek's hand and thanked him for his help on the story. I told him we made a great team. If he needed any more help in catching criminals, he should just give me a call, the way the cops do with Jessica Fletcher on "Murder, She Wrote." He didn't say anything. I guess he was just overcome by the emotion of the moment.

On my way out, I thought again about how much the police squad room reminded me of a scene out of "Hill Street Blues." People running around, barking orders, yelling into phones. Sort of like a newsroom.

Maybe this could be a whole new career for me. Forget about journalism, I'd concentrate on law enforcement from now on. I mean, everyone on "Hill Street Blues" always seemed to be having a great time—Furillo, Esterhaus, LaRue, the whole gang.

The only problem was I was forty-one. That's a little old for being a police rookie. A lot of cops are retired by the time they're forty-one.

I was standing at the door now. I looked around at all the hubbub in the room and said in a loud voice—just the way Sgt. Esterhaus used to during roll call in "Hill Street Blues"— "Hey, you guys, let's be careful out there."

Absolutely nobody paid any attention to me.

Just like in the newsroom.

They were getting ready to shoot "The Morning Show" when I got to the studio on East 76th Street.

Someone was warming up the audience. There were signs telling people when to laugh and when to clap and even when to cry. Welcome to the wonderful world of TV in the nineties. This stuff made "The Gong Show" look positively cerebral.

Jerry Meredith was backstage in his dressing room. A young, attractive woman was putting makeup on his face as he sat in front of a mirror. I wondered if he was screwing her too.

"Jenny, you did it!" he boomed with delight when he saw me. He jumped out of the chair and gave me a big hug. "You really pulled it off. You proved I didn't kill Eileen. Now I'm going to be a free man again."

I hugged him back. The makeup woman was watching us closely.

"I'm doing the whole show today on the case," he announced.

"You mean on your wife's murder? And your daughter's death?"

"Yeah, it'll be terrific." He seemed really pumped up. He sat back down in the chair, and the woman resumed putting pancake powder on his face. "Our ratings ought to go through the stratosphere on this one. I want you to be on the program too."

"Me?"

"Sure. You were a big part of it all." He smiled broadly. "C'mon, Jenny, let me make you a star."

"I don't think so."

"Why not?"

"There's enough stars in this city."

He gave me a puzzled look. "What does that mean?"

"Jerry, don't you think it's just a little bit . . . exploitive . . . to do this?"

"For Christ's sake, Jenny, lighten up for once in your life. It's just TV. People want to see this sort of thing. So I'm giving it to them. The real story behind the headlines. It'll be great."

"The real story, huh? Does that include your relationship with Becky?"

He looked over at me with surprise. Then he signaled the makeup woman to stop what she was doing. He told her he needed to be alone with me for a few minutes. She gave me a dirty look and left. Jerry shut the door behind her.

"You're lying about what happened between you and Becky," I said.

"I don't know what you're talking about."

"Sure you do. The other night in the Limelight you told me you slept with her."

"I was drunk. I didn't know what I was saying."

"Jerry, it's just the two of us here. There's no TV cameras. Tell me the truth."

Jerry came over and sat down next to me. He put his hand on top of mine.

"Jenny, we're talking about a billion dollars here."

"Who cares?"

"A billion dollars! You have to care about a billion dollars."

"Why, Jerry? Why do I need a billion dollars? Why does anybody need a billion dollars? I mean, how much money does a person really need to be happy? How many houses can you own? How many Jaguars or Porsches? How many yachts? That's not what I want out of life. All I need to be happy is a comfortable roof over my head, a refrigerator filled with things to eat and drink, someone I care about to share it with, my dog, and I guess a good TV. That's it. I've got very simple tastes."

"I can make you happy."

I laughed. "You mean you and me together for the rest of our lives?"

"It could happen. . . ."

"Sure. Just like it did with Janet Hutchings and Barbara Ann Forbes. Right?"

"What do you want from me, Jenny?"

"The truth about Becky."

He stood up and checked himself out in the mirror. "I've got a show to do," he said.

"Doesn't it bother you at all?" I asked.

"What?"

"The girl died because of you."

"Hey, I had nothing to do with that. She was screwed up. She murdered three people. I had nothing to do with any of it. She was a kook."

"She was your daughter."

Jerry looked at me blankly. There was no remorse there. No sadness. No emotion of any kind. He walked over and kissed me on the lips. I waited for the thrill I felt when he'd done that before. But this time there was nothing.

"We'll talk after the show," he said.

Then he was gone.

I wandered out a while later and found a place off stage to watch the taping. When I got there, Jerry was talking to the audience about his wife and his daughter and his two closest friends, Andrew Cox and Cheryl Wolcott. He said the loss of them had been almost unbearable. He hoped he could find the strength to bear up under the grief and somehow carry on with his life. His voice trembled a bit as he said these things, and at several points he wiped tears from his eyes. There was a monitor on the wall where I could see shots of the audience reactions. They were crying too.

It was all very emotional. Very poignant. A classic TV moment.

"Have you heard the news?" someone behind me was saying. "Jerry just got a big offer from Hollywood to do a TV movie about the whole thing. They want him to play himself."

"Hooray for Hollywood," I muttered.

27
Everyone's Famous for Fifteen Minutes

Pete's Tavern is on Irving Place, which is a tiny street that runs for six blocks, just south of Gramercy Park.

Pete's is probably my favorite bar in New York City. The front room is dark and wood-paneled and reeking of history, with a big round table by the window where O. Henry is supposed to have written some of his most famous short stories. I was never sure if this claim would hold up to any serious historical investigation, but I was willing to go along with the legend. There are booths where you can eat and drink beer. And the crowd's a nice mix of neighborhood regulars and singles looking for companionship.

I wasn't looking for companionship. I wasn't looking for history. I was looking for a place to drink beer.

Clare and I sat at a table underneath a big color TV set and talked about Jerry Meredith and Elaine Rivera.

"You seem disillusioned," Clare said.

"That's a polite word for the way I feel."

"What did you think? That Jerry was going to give the money back? Or hand it all over to charity? And then pick you up at your door in a golden chariot to whisk you away to some magical land where you'd live happily ever after?"

"I can dream, can't I?"

"That's your problem, Jenny. You live in a dream world. A fantasy place where you believe in fairy godmothers and princes and the Easter Bunny and happy endings."

"Hey," I told her, "I haven't believed in the Easter Bunny since I was twenty-one."

"So what are you going to do about you and Jerry?"

"I don't know." I told her about what happened at the studio that afternoon. "For a long time I didn't want to see any of his faults. I guess I was blinded by all the charm and fame and glitter of his life. But now the blinders are off. I can see that the emperor—or in this case the TV star—has no clothes."

"Meredith didn't kill anyone," Clare pointed out.

"I know that now."

"So?"

"He let people down. He's morally bankrupt."

Clare made a face. "Let me get this straight. You were in love with the guy when you thought he could be a murderer. Now you think he's a bad guy, even though you know he had nothing to do with the killings. That really doesn't make any sense."

"Welcome to my life."

There was a news show on the television above us. A picture of Jerry Meredith appeared on the screen. Then it switched to an interview with Donald Pesin. I couldn't make out everything Pesin was saying, but it was something about how he had single-handedly spearheaded the Channel Six investigation that broke the story wide open.

"I feel like I've screwed everything up over the past few weeks," I told Clare.

"What are you talking about? You broke the story—you pulled it off. You're a helluva reporter, Jenny."

I shook my head. "My priorities have been all wrong. I've been concentrating all my energies on people like Pesin and Meredith. I've been blinded by big money and fame and pizzazz, all the things I like to say I don't care about. The result was I didn't have time for the things I should have cared about. Like you and Elaine Rivera."

"Nobody's blaming you for Elaine Rivera's death."

"Sure they are. I am."

"It just happened. Neither you nor I could have done anything to change that. I realize that now."

"How do you know? Maybe if I'd done the interview with her, she would have gotten out of jail. Maybe it would have sparked a public outcry. Maybe I'd have touched a chord in the public consciousness and saved thousands of other women—just like Elaine Rivera—who are the victims of abuse by their husbands."

"That doesn't seem very likely."

"Why not? I'm a helluva reporter. You told me so yourself."

I sighed. "You know what really ticks me off about Jerry Meredith? He doesn't show the slightest bit of remorse about the death of his daughter. Or the fact that he slept with her without realizing who she was. Christ, that's what pushed her over the edge."

"As a father figure, he doesn't exactly make you think of Ward Cleaver," Clare agreed.

"And he's probably going to walk away with a billion dollars."

"Well, look on the bright side—at least he won't get the entire billion."

"Why not?"

"It'll be ten thousand dollars short. Isn't that what you said the antique train engine cost that Becky Bessard used to smash Eileen Clayton over the head?"

"Not true. It turns out that Jerry's luck held there too. She used one of the cheap ones to kill her. I guess the rich just get richer, huh?"

Someone had changed the channel on the TV set. "Nightline" was on now. Pesin was on that too. Pesin was everywhere. He was telling Ted Koppel that he was in negotiations with Hollywood to act as a consultant on the TV movie they were making about the case.

Pesin and Meredith. Beautiful. They'd make a great team.

"Didn't you have a little something to do with this case?" Clare asked as she watched the show.

"Sure. He just mentioned my name. When he thanked the countless people too numerous to mention who had helped him on the story. That's me."

"The man sure knows how to grab the glory."

"It's like Andy Warhol once said: 'Everyone can be famous for fifteen minutes.' Only Pesin doesn't know when his time's up."

He was talking now on the screen about the role of television journalism in society and telling an anecdote from his past to illustrate the point. I thought Ted Koppel looked bored. But maybe it was just my imagination.

"It's sort of odd, isn't it?" I said.

"What? Pesin being on two channels at once? Not really. It's a big story. Everyone seems to want a piece of it."

"No. I meant the fact that the train engine Becky used to kill Eileen Clayton wasn't one of the expensive ones."

Clare shrugged. "I don't know."

"There were a couple of hundred expensive train engines and cars in that room where she died—and only one or two cheap ones. So what are the odds that one of the cheap ones would wind up being the murder weapon?"

"A couple of hundred to one, I guess," she said.

"That's right. Unless you knew something about trains."

"You think Becky Bessard knew a lot about model trains?"

"No. But Jerry Meredith did."

"Jerry Meredith didn't kill his wife. His daughter did."

"There's another thing. Jerry Meredith once told me that his wife hated that train room—never went inside unless she had to. So why was she there with Becky Bessard that night? No, it makes much more sense if it was her husband there—and Eileen Clayton went in to confront him over something."

"Becky's already confessed that she did it, remember?"

"She said, 'I killed them all.' She didn't say, 'I killed Eileen Clayton.'"

"C'mon . . ."

"There's something else too. Jerry told me he always attracted crazy women. And the night we were at the Limelight he laughed about how Becky Bessard cut off his head in all the pictures in her scrapbook. How did he know that?"

"You probably told him."

"I don't think so. I've been thinking about it. I told him about the scrapbook, but I don't remember ever telling him about the heads. And I didn't mention that part of it on the air either. So the only way he could know is if he . . ."

"Was the one who went through her apartment," Clare said.

"Exactly."

"He was looking for something. Something that could tie him to Becky. Something a lot worse than the scrapbook. Pictures of the two of them together maybe."

"Or a tape recording. A video. Maybe even love letters. But it had to be him. Who else would have a motive for trashing the apartment?"

"That still doesn't prove anything though," Clare said. "You already know he had a relationship with the girl. This just takes you back to square one. It doesn't mean he murdered anyone."

"What if Becky did have some evidence of their relationship? And she took it to Eileen Clayton. She confronts Jerry, they fight, and he hits her over the head with the train engine. Then he has to make sure there's no copies of whatever it is Becky had. So he goes through her apartment."

"That's all speculation."

"It could have happened that way," I insisted.

Clare reached across the table and squeezed my hand. "The story's over, Jenny. There'll be other stories."

I shook my head. "It's not over."

"Jenny, what are you going to do?"

"What I should have done from the very beginning. I'm going to find out who really killed Eileen Clayton."

28
No Alibis

On the first night we slept together, Jerry Meredith told me he was in a singles bar on First Avenue near 77th Street when his wife was killed. He said he had picked up a redhead, in her twenties, who had a Southern accent and was dressed in punk clothing. She took him back to her place, which was just around the corner in a town house with a metal gate fence in front and a balcony overlooking the street, he said.

Jerry told me a lot of stuff that night. And I bought every bit of it.

There was no singles bar at the spot Jerry told me about. There was a dry cleaners, a grocery store, a bakery, and a sort of pizza parlor/café, which did sell drinks in the front.

I walked inside the pizza place. A heavyset man wearing an apron with tomato stains on the front was putting the finishing touches on a pizza. Cheese, tomato sauce, sausages, pepperoni. Then he slid it into a big oven. It looked like a labor of love. A middle-aged woman was chopping up lettuce a few feet away.

I told them who I was and asked, "Do you know Jerry Meredith?"

The man nodded. "Sure, the guy on TV. Everyone knows him."

"Does he ever come in here?"

"Absolutely."

I was stunned. "He does?"

"Jerry was just in here last night. He had Liz Taylor and Julia Roberts and Oprah Winfrey with him. Demi Moore was supposed to be here too, but she and Bruce Willis got tied up in traffic. Demi called and told me she'd probably drop in tonight." He turned around to the woman, who I guessed was his wife. "Isn't that right, Carol?"

Then he laughed uproariously. Carol laughed too.

Everyone I meet is a comedian.

"Jerry Meredith has never been here," I said.

He made a sweeping motion with his arm around the room. "Look at this place. What do you think Jerry Meredith would be doing here? We serve pizza, not escargot. You see what I mean?"

"Yeah, I guess so."

"It's good pizza. You want a slice?"

I said sure. I might as well get something out of this. A few minutes later, I was standing outside on the street again, nibbling on the pizza and going through my notebook to see what else Jerry had told me.

I was getting a sinking feeling in my stomach and it wasn't just from the pizza.

I walked around the block several times looking for the town house where the redhead lived. Nothing. Then I widened my area of search. Two blocks. Three. Finally five blocks in each direction. There was no building that looked like the one he'd described.

A refrain from an Eric Clapton song, "No Alibis," started running through my head. I wondered if anything Jerry had said was true.

The next thing I did was take a cab over to Jerry's apartment on Park Avenue. I walked up and down the neighborhood asking people if they remembered anything

THE MOURNING SHOW

from the day Eileen Clayton was murdered that could be a clue. No one did.

Until I got to the doorman of the building directly across the street.

"Wow, you're on the TV news, aren't you?" said the guy, who told me his name was Lester.

"Yep, Channel Six."

A fan. That always made it easier.

"I saw you with him too."

"Who?"

"Jerry. Jerry Meredith."

That one stunned me. "When?"

"Last Sunday. The two of you walked up the street here and then went into his building."

Lester was a very observant guy. I told him that.

He just shrugged. "Hey," he said, "in this job you've got a lot of time on your hands...."

I asked him about the day of the murder. He said he was on duty and saw the first police cars pull up across the street. Then everyone else showed up. And Jerry Meredith came home.

"Did Jerry know what had happened?"

"No way. He was looking around at all the police cars and the activity. He asked me what was going on, but I didn't know what to say. So I just told him I thought he better get upstairs right away. That's when they arrested him."

"How did he arrive at the building?"

"He was walking when I saw him."

Walking? From where? 77th Street? That didn't sound like Jerry. He was more of a cab and limo guy. I mentioned that to Lester.

He chuckled. "Yeah, I know. Actually he didn't walk too far that day. I happened to be out front hailing a cab for one of the tenants and saw him get out of a car down the block."

"What kind of car?"

I expected him to say he didn't know, but I was wrong. "It was a Lincoln. Brown. Probably 1992. Maybe '93."

"You saw all that from a block away?"

"The car came down the street and right by me after it let him off."

"Who was inside?"

"Two guys," Lester said. "One of them had a big, bushy hairdo. The other one looked like his was in a ponytail. They had the car window open, and they were playing some Sinatra music real loud. I didn't know who they were."

I did.

The Colony Café in Sheepshead Bay was just finishing up the lunch hour when I got there.

Kevin was sitting at the bar, reading a law book. He gave me a surprised look, but his greeting was friendly. I asked to see Vincent Guardere. A few minutes later, the boss man himself emerged from an office in the back.

"Miss McKay," he boomed. "This is a pleasant surprise."

"Let's you and me go for a walk."

"Where to?"

"Around the block," I said. "Where else?"

It was a scorching hot day outside. A new warm front had settled in on the city, and it didn't look as if it was going to move until December. Someone on the radio was screaming about a Con Edison power emergency and warning people not to turn up their air conditioners, which, of course, was totally ridiculous. Anyone who had an air conditioner was sucking every bit of life out of it. The ones who didn't sat out on the street or hung out of open windows. In front of us, a fire hydrant was open, and some of the neighborhood kids were running through the spraying water.

I didn't figure Guardere was going to shoot me on the street in broad daylight with all these people around.

"So tell me, Vincent," I said as we walked, "why did Jerry Meredith come to see you on the day his wife was found dead?"

"Did he?" Guardere asked casually.

Out of the corner of my eye, I could see Kevin and Doug quietly trailing behind us.

"Sure he did." I wiped some sweat from my forehead. "Let's not play games. It's too hot."

"Okay, Jerry came to see me. So what?"

"Did he tell you his wife was dead? Or maybe he didn't have to. Maybe you already knew that."

Guardere looked at me strangely. I thought for a second it might be like a scene out of *The Untouchables*. He'd make a gesture to Kevin and Doug, there'd be a burst of gunfire. But nothing like that happened. We just kept walking.

"What's that supposed to mean?" he asked.

"I have this theory. Becky Bessard didn't really kill Eileen Clayton. Becky killed Cox and Wolcott, but she went to Jerry's wife because she wanted to destroy his marriage. She probably had some sort of evidence—pictures, videotape, maybe love letters. Then Eileen Clayton threatened to divorce Jerry without a cent, so he had to do something. That something was to call his friend Vincent Guardere. You took care of Eileen Clayton for him. All of a sudden Jerry's worth a billion dollars—and he can pay you the $400,000 he owes. Plus a lot more probably, for services rendered. Only you have to make sure he doesn't get convicted for the crime."

"That's a helluva theory," Guardere said.

"Yeah, I know. I got an even better one too. Want to hear it?"

"Go ahead."

"Becky Bessard didn't kill anyone. Andrew Cox found out about Jerry's relationship with her and threatened to go to his wife. So you eliminated Cox and made it look like an accident. Then Cheryl Wolcott started asking questions, so you threw her out a window. Becky Bessard was a very confused young woman. It probably wasn't hard for you and Meredith to convince her she was somehow responsible for the deaths."

We were standing by the edge of Sheepshead Bay. We'd walked a couple of blocks now, and there weren't people around anymore. I looked down at the water. If anything was going to happen, this was where it was going to be.

"And you think all this was because of a love affair between Jerry and poor little Becky?"

"That's right."

Guardere shook his head. "You have a very romantic notion of the world, McKay. You think love makes it go round."

I didn't say anything.

"It's not love, you know," he said. "It's money. It's always money."

"What does that mean?"

He laughed. "I've been grilled by cops, prosecutors, and grand juries over the years. The best of them have all had a crack at Vincent Guardere. I never told anybody anything. Why should I suddenly start with you?"

"Look, Vincent," I said quietly, "the authorities are all over you. They're looking for anything to nail you—if you so much as cross the street against the 'Don't Walk' sign, you're going to wind up in jail. I can start doing stories about you and your whole operation. Stake you out everywhere you go. Follow you with hidden cameras. The cops and the feds would love that. Is that really what you want?"

I held my breath. This was going to be it. The end of Jenny McKay. Helluva reporter, that McKay. Of course, everyone always said her big mouth was going to be the death of her. They were right.

"I don't know what happened," Guardere said. Then he added, "I didn't kill anybody."

I let my breath out slowly. "Tell me what you know."

He looked out across the bay. "I think Meredith was skimming money out of his show's profits to pay for his gambling debts."

"He told you that?"

Guardere shook his head. "No, but it wasn't hard to figure out. He was desperate for money, and he couldn't get it from his wife. For a while, the payments on the gambling debts came in on time, but then they stopped. I guess his wife—or maybe even Cox and Wolcott—found out about it."

"So Eileen Clayton is royally pissed about that," I said. "Then Becky Bessard comes to the apartment, tells her about their affair, and Eileen decides to throw him out for good. Jerry can't let that happen, so he bashes her over the head with a model train. I don't think he planned it or anything. I mean, he didn't even have time to come up with a good alibi. But it all worked out, didn't it? He's free—and I helped him beat the charges. And there's no proof of any of it."

"Maybe."

"What do you mean?"

"It's like you said before—Becky Bessard probably had some sort of evidence when she went to Eileen Clayton. I'm not sure what it was, but I don't think Jerry's found it."

"Why?"

"On that day he came to see me he promised everything was okay now—that he'd have all the money soon. But he still seemed agitated about something. I don't think he was home free. The Bessard woman was still out there, plus he didn't know exactly what she had on him."

"What about Cheryl Wolcott, his producer?" I asked. "She came out here to see you too, didn't she?"

Guardere nodded.

"What did she want?"

"She was asking a lot of questions. Just like you."

"About what?"

"Jerry. His love life. His finances. I don't know how she made the connection."

I used to be an investigative reporter myself, Cheryl Wolcott had told me that day at "The Morning Show" studios. A pretty good one too.

That she was.

"What did you tell her?"

"Nothing."

"And then she just left?"

"That's right."

I thought about everything he'd said.

"Why should I believe any of this?" I asked. "How do I know you didn't kill Eileen Clayton and all the rest?"

Guardere smiled and nodded over toward Kevin and Doug. They were standing about ten feet behind, staring at us intently. They didn't look friendly anymore. Both of them were all business.

"You see, if I was really the cold-blooded killer you think I am, Miss McKay," Guardere said, "you would have been dead five minutes ago."

The Clayton Building was empty by the time I got there.

So was the street in front of it. That's a funny thing about New York City. There are spots like Park Avenue that are bustling with people during the day. But after five or six at night, when everyone's gone home, it's like a ghost town.

There was a pay phone on the corner, and I made a call from it. It was not an easy conversation. When I hung up, I made a second call. That one was even tougher.

Then I went inside.

The security guard in the lobby was even older and more tired-looking than the ones with Katherine Grieco. I waited until he settled down for a nap and then snuck past him through the empty lobby, onto the elevator and up to Eileen Clayton's office on the forty-fourth floor.

A long time ago I'd learned how to pick a lock, the results of a misspent youth. Actually I'd learned it from a professional burglar I was interviewing for a series on how to protect your home from theft. He showed me all the tricks of the trade, and I remembered a few of them. I figured they might come in handy someday for a reporter.

Like now.

Five minutes later, I was inside Eileen Clayton's office. I didn't know how much time I had, so I went right to work. I started going through everything on her desk, in her drawers, and in the file cabinets.

I wasn't sure exactly what I was looking for. But I'd know when I found it.

Something—like a picture or a love letter—that linked Becky Bessard to Jerry Meredith. If Jerry was still looking for it, that meant Eileen Clayton must have hidden it somewhere before she died. Why not here?

I'd been there for about twenty minutes without any success when I thought I heard a noise.

I looked around. Nothing there. Maybe it was a night watchman on the floor making his rounds. I froze for a few seconds, but I didn't hear anything else. So I went back to searching. Then I heard it again. This time it wasn't my imagination.

I whirled around and saw him standing by the door.

It was just like TV. All you needed was his theme music and an announcer booming: "Here's the host of 'The Morning Show,' Jerry Meredith!" Then the applause sign would flash on, and the audience would cheer wildly as America's favorite daytime TV personality flashed his famous smile.

Only this time Jerry Meredith wasn't smiling.

And he had a gun in his hand pointed at me.

"I'm really sorry, Jenny," he said. "I hoped it wasn't going to have to come to this."

29
A Picture Is Worth a Thousand Words

"You killed your wife, didn't you, Jerry?" I said.

"I had to. I had no choice."

"Sure you did. There's always a choice."

"And wind up broke? Or maybe even to go jail for embezzling corporate funds? I don't think so."

"The sentence for embezzlement is a lot shorter than the one for murder," I pointed out.

"But now I don't have to worry about either one. You cleared me, remember? You really are a terrific reporter, Jenny."

I shook my head sadly. "You used me. You wanted me on your side. That's why you went to bed with me."

"Hey, I wanted to go to bed with you too." He smiled. "Give yourself some credit."

Meredith moved toward me, the gun in his hand. I was standing behind Eileen Clayton's desk. He was almost in front of me now. He was going to kill me. We both knew that. But I still wanted some answers. I casually reached down underneath the desk.

"It probably didn't take much to convince Becky she was somehow responsible for your wife's death," I said. "She was very confused anyway, and she started out trying to destroy your life. Plus she'd told Eileen about your affair the day before Eileen died. So she blamed herself. Maybe someone even helped convince her of that. Someone who was very glib and sincere-sounding and convincing. That's you, big guy."

He didn't say anything.

"What about the other two? Andrew Cox and Cheryl Wolcott? Did Becky really kill them? Or was that you too?"

Still no answer.

"Jesus, Jerry," I said, "you had eight jillion dollars with Eileen Clayton as your wife. Why couldn't you just be satisfied with that?"

"Satisfied? You think it's easy to be satisfied when you're living with the rich bitch from hell? She treated me like I was some kind of goddamned trained seal. Showing me off for her friends and then practically making me perform before she'd dole out any of her money. Everybody thought I was rich. But they had no idea what I had to go through. It all belonged to her."

He couldn't see my hand below the desk. I fiddled with something down there. "What happened the night you killed her? " I asked.

Jerry shrugged. "Eileen told me Becky Bessard had given her evidence I was unfaithful. She went crazy, and we argued about it and about her money all night. Finally she stormed into the train room and told me she was getting a divorce. She laughed at me, called me a loser, and said her lawyers would make sure I didn't get a penny. I lost my head, I guess, and hit her with the first thing I could find."

Not the first thing, I thought to myself. You didn't use one of the expensive train engines.

"I was under a lot of pressure, Jenny," he said. "You know that. I owed big-time money to Vincent Guardere."

"Yeah, he says you're a lousy gambler."

"I've just had a streak of bad luck."

I looked down at the barrel of the gun. I needed to keep him talking.

"You know what's funny, Jerry? From the very beginning, I never really figured you for this murder. I didn't think you were the killer type. But I guess you could probably say that about most murderers. I mean, murderers don't wear signs on their chest saying, 'I'm a homicidal maniac.' They're just normal people. Store clerks, auto mechanics, housewives—sometimes even a famous TV host. Then one day they take a human life. And afterwards, everyone says how surprised they were because the murderer always seemed like such a nice guy." I shook my head sadly. "I never really knew you, Jerry."

He smiled. "Sure, you did. In the biblical sense."

"No. I slept with you. I spent a lot of time with you. I even loved you for a while. But I never knew you. And you want to know something? I don't think there really is a Jerry Meredith to know. That's not some phony act you put on when you're on TV. That's really you. And that's all there is. There's nothing underneath."

"Shut up!" he barked. "You always did talk too much."

"Didn't you know you'd be arrested for murder when you got back to your apartment?" I asked him.

"I figured I could beat it. Somehow I'd talk my way out of it. If not with the cops, then on the stand during the trial. I'm pretty good at that, you know."

"You took a helluva gamble."

"I like to gamble, Jenny. Remember? And this bet was for the ultimate payoff—a billion dollars."

"You still might not get the money. Don't forget about the prenup agreement you signed. Adultery was a no-no." I thought about LeBeau and the dancer from Cary's. "At least for you."

"No one has any proof I did anything. All they can do is talk."

"Becky had some kind of proof. She gave it to your wife."

"Which brings us to the reason we're here."

THE MOURNING SHOW

One of the calls I'd made before I came in the building was to Jerry Meredith. I'd told him I'd found out there were pictures and love letters about him and Becky in Eileen Clayton's office. I said I was going right over there to find them.

"I lied," I told him. "There is no evidence."

"I don't believe you."

"It's true."

"Why would you make up something like that?"

"It was all a trap. I wanted to lure you up here and get a confession. The cops are behind you right now."

I've seen people try that trick in the movies a million times. It never works. Usually the person with the gun just laughs and doesn't even bother to look around. Meredith laughed, but he did sneak a glance at the door.

There was no one there, of course.

But it gave me a chance to hit the light button on the control panel under Eileen Clayton's desk, plunging the room into darkness. I dived for the floor.

"Dammit!" Meredith shouted.

I saw a flash and heard a gunshot go off. Something splintered on the desk above me.

"Don't be stupid, Jenny!" he yelled.

"What's that supposed to mean?"

"There's no way out of here for you. Let's talk."

"Okay."

"Maybe we can make a deal. A billion dollars is a lot of money."

"You weren't talking about a deal a few minutes ago."

"I don't want to kill you, Jenny."

"Excuse me if I don't believe you."

There was a wastebasket on the floor next to me. I picked it up and threw it across the room. It hit the wall and made a loud clanging noise. Suddenly there was more gunfire as Jerry opened up on the spot where it landed.

So much for talking.

"You still there, Jen?" he called out.

I didn't answer.

"Why couldn't you just have left it alone after the girl confessed?" Meredith said. "I was cleared. I was home free. But you're like the goddamned Energizer Bunny or something. You just keep going."

I could tell from his voice that he was moving away from me. Back toward the door. He was probably going to look for a light switch there. When he found it, my life expectancy wasn't going to be very long. I needed to do something to delay him.

"The thing that amazes me," I yelled, "is how you could do that to your own daughter. Didn't you have any regrets at all once you found out who she was?"

"You worry too much about stuff like that. She was nothing to me. So I slept with her—big deal. I hadn't seen her in twenty years. And I never thought about her any of that time. She was just the result of some night of fun I had a long time ago in New Jersey. Hey, people always talk about doing a mother-daughter duo. I did a helluva one, huh?"

He laughed loudly.

"That's sad."

"Christ, you've got this damn code of ethics you pretend you like to live by, McKay. You think you're so righteous. So moral. It's all bullshit, you know."

"I try to do the right thing," I said.

"And look what it's gotten you. You're forty-one years old, and your career hasn't exactly been a rousing success."

"I think I like my life better than yours, Jerry."

"That's why you're stupid."

He found the switch. He hit it, and the room suddenly lit up. I could see him from where I was hiding underneath the desk. It was only a matter of time now. And not very much time.

"I did call the cops, you know," I said.

"Sure, you did."

"They're right behind you."

"Don't bullshit me, McKay. You can't pull the same trick twice."

"She's not bullshitting you," a woman's voice said.

Meredith whirled around. Katherine Grieco was standing there. So were a half dozen of New York City's finest, all with guns pointed right at him.

"Drop it!" one of them shouted. "And don't move!"

Meredith let the gun fall from his hand. It clattered loudly onto the floor. One of the cops picked it up. Two others grabbed Meredith and put a pair of handcuffs on him.

I leaned back against the leg of the desk and breathed a sigh of relief.

"Are you okay?" Grieco yelled.

I stood up from my hiding place and nodded.

Jerry Meredith wasn't totally beaten yet. He tried one more desperation tactic.

"I didn't know it was her," he told Grieco. "I thought it was a burglar. I mean, I came up here to get some of Eileen's papers and heard someone in here going through stuff. I guess I just panicked and then when you showed up..."

Grieco gave him an amused look.

"Give it a rest, huh, Jerry."

Then she said to me: "Did you get it all?"

"I think so."

I reached down and pressed one of the buttons underneath Eileen Clayton's desk. It was the master panel that controlled everything in the room. The lights, the doors, the air-conditioning.

And the hidden security cameras.

A color TV set next to me came on. Then I pressed the tape rewind button. A few seconds later I hit play.

Jerry Meredith's face appeared on the TV screen.

"She laughed at me," he was saying, " called me a loser, and said her lawyers would make sure I didn't get a penny. I lost my head, I guess, and hit her..."

Jerry stared at the TV with a dazed expression on his face.

Grieco walked over to where he was standing now, pointed her index finger and thumb at him and made a "gotcha" gesture.

"Smile," she said. "You're on candid camera."

He who lives by the tube dies by the tube.

30
. . . This Is Jenny McKay Reporting

ANNOUNCER: We interrupt our regularly scheduled programming to bring you this bulletin from the WTBK newsroom.

There was a shot of Conroy Jackson at the anchor desk.

JACKSON: Channel Six News has just learned there's been a major break in the Eileen Clayton murder case.

"Morning Show" star Jerry Meredith has been arrested—again—for killing his wife. He was taken into custody tonight following a shooting incident at the Clayton Building in midtown Manhattan.

We take you now to reporter Jenny McKay, who's at the scene and was involved in the shooting. Jenny, what's happening?

They cut to a shot of me inside the building, with a sign that said Clayton Enterprises behind me.

McKAY: Conroy, an incredible drama has been played out behind these doors.

THE MOURNING SHOW

TV star Jerry Meredith just confessed to the murder of his wife. He also is suspected of killing two other people—Andrew Cox, the director of "The Morning Show," and Cheryl Wolcott, the producer.

His confession was secretly videotaped during a tense standoff with this reporter, in which he fired several shots before being apprehended by Assistant District Attorney Katherine Grieco and a team of officers.

Assistant District Attorney Grieco is here with us now.

She appeared on the screen next to me.

GRIECO: Jerry Meredith is being charged with first-degree murder. We have an airtight case against him this time. He's going to jail for the rest of his life.

McKAY: Tell our viewers what happened in there.

GRIECO: Well, it was just a textbook example of the way our law enforcement agencies—including the District Attorney's office and the police—work together to crack a big case like this one. And it shows that no one—not even a big star like Jerry Meredith—is above the law. He'll get no special treatment from this office.

McKAY: (a bit flustered by her response) No, I meant I wanted you to tell everyone about him shooting at me and . . .

GRIECO: Look, I've got to run. I've got a lot of things to do here.

She left.

McKAY: That was Katherine Grieco, the Assistant District Attorney in charge of the Eileen Clayton murder case. Obviously, she's got a busy night ahead of her. So let me give you an update on what happened here.

Earlier this evening I let myself into the Clayton Building and then I . . .

After we went off the air, I tracked down Katherine Grieco.

"You could have been a little more forthcoming back there about my role in the case," I said.

"I'm not your PR agent," she snapped. "Any other complaints?"

"Yeah, now that you mention it. I was starting to get a little worried while Meredith was shooting at me that you weren't going to show up."

"What do you mean?"

"Well, you cut it a little close, didn't you?"

"We got here in time."

"Barely. Another minute and I would have been history."

"Gee," Grieco said with exaggerated concern in her voice, "that really would have been a shame."

"It's not funny. What took you so long? I called and told you what I was going to do."

"Who the hell do you think you are, McKay? You call me up five minutes before you pull off some wild, harebrained scheme and then get mad because I don't jump the minute you tell me. You're lucky I came at all. I couldn't believe you were serious."

"That wild, harebrained scheme was what caught Jerry Meredith," I pointed out.

"I could have done the same thing without you."

"Oh yeah? You weren't doing much that I saw."

"If you remember," she said, "I'd already arrested Jerry Meredith once. It was you that got him cleared. You told everyone that he was innocent. The way I see it, this case would have gone a lot smoother if you'd just kept your nose out of it. Then none of this would have had to happen."

She had a point. Sort of.

"But then we'd never have raised all these questions about the death of Andrew Cox," I said. "And Cheryl Wolcott. And Becky Bessard. And . . ."

Grieco held up her hand. "Enough. Okay, we both helped crack the case. Satisfied?"

I smiled.

"You know, Kathy . . ."

"My name's Katherine."

"Sure. You know, Katherine, I think we both learned something here. I mean, we're both very different, but in some ways we're alike. And we've learned to appreciate each other's good points. I feel like there's been some sort of bonding between us—a real woman-to-woman thing—that's come out of all this. Who knows? Maybe we can even be friends."

Grieco was looking at me in amazement.

"Sure, no problem. How about we meet tomorrow and go shopping together at Bloomingdale's? Then we can have lunch and maybe catch a movie."

She walked away and started talking to one of the cops with Meredith.

She was kidding, I guess.

But I think she is starting to like me a little bit.

Really.

They brought Jerry Meredith out of the building about thirty minutes later.

We were all outside now. Me, Sanders and Jacobson—along with the rest of the New York City press crew, which was just catching up with the story. I figured Grieco wanted to wait until everyone was there before she walked Meredith through and took him downtown for booking. She knew the kind of publicity she'd get:

TV STAR ARRESTED! FILM AT ELEVEN!

Jerry looked straight ahead this time as he walked past me. There was no plea that he was innocent, no panicky look, no emotion whatsoever. He looked like a beaten man.

I thought about that first time it had happened outside his apartment house. That was only days ago. But it seemed like a hundred years.

Just before he was about to leave, he turned around and looked at us all. His eyes settled on me. I stared back at him.

I was looking for something in them, I guess.

Some sign of remorse. Or regret. Or sadness. Or maybe even a flicker of love.

But I didn't see anything.

Then they put Jerry Meredith into a waiting police car, and he rode out of my life forever.

News Update

A funny thing happened to me on my way to becoming a star.

I got detoured by demographics.

You see, those ratings numbers that Pesin talked to me about at Elaine's when he got my hopes up for the anchor job weren't exactly accurate. Yeah, I did beat out Liz St. John in the across-the-board sweeps. But she wiped the floor with me in two crucial categories: men, aged eighteen to twenty-four, earning at least thirty thousand dollars a year; and working women with 2.1 or more children. Which—demographically speaking, according to Pesin—is all the advertisers really care about.

Got that? Well, if you do, explain it to me. Because I don't understand a word of it.

The bottom line is I'm still on the street and Liz St. John is at the anchor desk, a fact she points out to me with some glee on a regular basis.

Pesin's still at the station too.

He says the TV movie deal fell through because they wouldn't pay him the money he wanted. He says the same thing happened with offers to go to CBS and CNN. Pesin says a lot of things. I'm not sure I believe any of them.

When I see him now—bragging about himself and strutting around—I realize what a blowhard he is. I told him that the other day in front of a group of people at a party. I figured he'd blow up at me. Or fire me. Or maybe even hit me. But instead he just told everyone how he likes people who aren't afraid to tell him off to his face. Then he put his arm around me and said: "Don't you just love her?"

I still haven't figured him out.

"The Morning Show" has a new host these days.

He's some young, good-looking guy from Kansas or Wyoming or somewhere that *TV Guide* says "has captured the heart of America just like Oprah and Donahue and Jerry Meredith once did."

His big break came when the show somehow got ahold of Jerry's confession video from that night in the Clayton Building before anyone else. They ran it all—along with reenactments of the murders, and panel discussions by experts like Dr. Ruth. The ratings went through the roof. Since then, the show has become the hottest thing on TV.

Which just goes to prove Jerry Meredith's theory. You don't have to be a rocket scientist to put on a TV talk show. All you need is the right host and some guests. What he didn't realize is that the host didn't necessarily have to be him.

And Jerry? Well, he's doing twenty-five years to life at a prison in upstate New York, with no possibility of parole for a long time. He's become a big prison activist, I hear. Organizing inmates, fighting for longer library hours, giving interviews about overcrowding in the jails. "To Jerry Meredith's credit, he's used his incarceration to become an eloquent spokesman for prison reform," the *New York Times* said in an article about him the other day.

That's one thing about ol' Jerry. He always did have a gift of gab.

Every once in a while, I get an urge to write him a letter or even go visit him in prison. I mean, I've still got a lot of questions that were never answered. But I never do anything about it—and pretty soon the feeling passes.

It's the damnedest thing about Eileen Clayton's money.
Her will left a lot of it to the man she really loved. Or the men. Glen LeBeau. Bobby Santos. And a lot of others too.

We're not talking small change here either. LeBeau walked away with a cool ten million or so. I had lunch with him again at the Bull and Bear one day, and he showed off his Mercedes and told me about his new beach house in Southampton.

Boy, talk about easy money, I thought.

But then I remembered all the things he'd told me about Eileen Clayton. About the vasectomy she'd made him get. About the way she treated the people around her.

And I wondered if ten million dollars was really enough.

I never found out for sure who killed Andrew Cox and Cheryl Wolcott. I think Jerry did it—not Becky—because they found out he was embezzling funds from the show. But he never admitted it. And even though he got a life sentence for murdering his wife, the authorities never got anywhere with the other investigations.

They never found any pictures of him with Becky Bessard either. Maybe there never were any.

As for the bulk of Eileen Clayton's billion dollars, no one's gotten that yet. The money that was supposed to go to Jerry Meredith is tied up right now in some incredibly complicated estate case that experts say will take years to untangle.

They'll probably sort it out about the same time they figure out how to pay off the federal deficit.

Katherine Grieco got herself elected District Attorney.
Everyone says she's got a bright future ahead of her. The Governor's mansion. Or the Senate. Maybe even the White House. Hey, the country's got to elect a woman president someday.

I ran into her at a press conference one day and suggested that I should get some of the credit for her success.

"We made a helluva team," I pointed out.

"No, we didn't. You screwed up my case and almost got yourself killed."

I ignored that. "Maybe if you get to the White House, there'll be a place for me in your administration."

"As what? Secretary of the Department of Big Mouths?"

Now, I understand that kind of talk.

It's the same sort of thing I might say to her. That's the sign of a person who's afraid to express her true feelings of affection and gratitude. Someone who's gruff on the outside, but tender inside. Someone who deep down knows that the two of us are really a lot alike and would somehow, someday like to find a way to be friends.

I think.

Vincent Guardere I still see once in a while too.

A lot of people get upset when I tell them that. They say he's a gangster and a crook and probably a murderer too. Maybe he is. But he's always been a good guy to me. And that's the only way I know how to judge people.

A while back, the federal prosecutor launched this big legal offensive against him. He was indicted on about 112 charges of racketeering, money laundering, and in general being a nuisance to society. The trial took about four months, cost millions of dollars in taxpayer money, and consumed hundreds of man-hours by Justice Dept. workers.

In the end, Guardere was acquitted by a jury that deliberated for only thirty minutes.

Everyone figures he must have bought off the jurors.

Me, I say Kevin just did a good job studying those law books.

There's one other thing I probably should talk about here. Elaine Rivera.

That bothered me for a long time. I knew she was dead. And I realized her death wasn't my fault. But I still wanted to do something to make it right.

So one day I got the address from Clare and went to look up her husband. Ricky Rivera wasn't there, but his new girlfriend was. Her name was Connie. She was about thirty and pretty with dark hair, just like Elaine was. And, like Elaine, she had an ugly bruise on her—this one just above her eye. I guess Ricky wasn't as careful about staying away from her face as he was with Elaine.

"What happened?" I asked.

"I had an accident," she said. "I fell."

"There's a lot of that going around for people who live with Ricky," I said.

She didn't answer.

"Can we talk?" I asked.

Connie and I sat for a long time in her kitchen and drank coffee. She admitted to me that Ricky had a terrible temper and drank too much and sometimes beat her. Then the next day he would act as if nothing had happened.

I told her I wanted to do a series about battered women. I'd like to tell her story. We'd go to the authorities, get her some kind of protection, and then use her as an example of what happens to too many women all over the country. What did she think?

Connie shook her head.

"I won't do that."

"Why not?"

"Ricky really loves me," she insisted.

I looked at the bruise on her face. "And that's just a love tap?"

"He only does it when he's drunk or angry or upset about something. The rest of the time he's really very nice. He buys me things, he takes me places."

"That's a rough way to live your life," I said.

"It's the only way I know."

Finally I handed her a card with my name and the telephone number and address of Channel Six written on it. "Let me know if you're ever ready to try and change things," I said.

I forgot about her for a while after that. There were other big stories to worry about—a corruption scandal at City Hall, a juicy triple murder in Queens, a transit strike. There are always other stories.

But then one day I looked up and saw her standing in front of my desk in the newsroom.

"I'm ready now," Connie said.

We went to the cops first. They arrested Ricky Rivera on an assault and battery charge. Then I did a whole series of interviews with Connie about the hell she'd gone through being with him. The upshot is that the Mayor released more funds to set up shelters for battered women, a special prosecutor was named to look into the problem, and I'm up for a big award for the series.

Clare's never been prouder of me. She says I'm like a combination of Gloria Steinem, Hillary Clinton, and Joan of Arc—all rolled into one.

None of it will ever bring back Elaine Rivera.

But we do what we can do.

I'm sitting in my apartment with Hobo on my lap watching Mary Tyler Moore on late night cable TV.

It's the classic first episode again when Mary gets the job at WJM. Everyone has their favorite Mary moments. For some, it's the Chuckles the Clown funeral. Or the time Johnny Carson shows up to rescue one of Mary's god-awful parties. Or the final show when the whole gang sings "It's a Long Way to Tipperary" as they leave the newsroom for the last time.

But I like the first one the best because Mary looks so young and innocent and she still has all those wonderful friendships and adventures ahead of her.

I found a number on a piece of paper in my purse and dialed it. A sleepy voice answered on the other end.

"I'm thinking of reenacting the Lincoln-Douglas debates tonight," I said. "You can be Douglas and I'll be Lincoln."

THE MOURNING SHOW

"Huh?" Pete Rousch asked.

"After that we can analyze the military tactics at the Battle of Bull Run and then maybe share a plate of pasta."

"Jenny McKay? Is that you?"

"Yeah. Did I wake you?"

"Don't worry about it. My first class isn't until noon tomorrow."

"So what do you think about my plan?"

"Uh, there might be a problem. . . ."

"Okay, you can be Lincoln and I'll be Douglas."

He chuckled. "Do you always have this much interest in the Civil War, Jenny?"

"It's the passion of my life. That and chocolate marshmallow ice cream. Plus a few other things that usually require a member of the opposite sex to do properly."

There was a long silence on the other end. This was not good.

Then in the background I heard a woman's voice call out: "Pete, honey, who is that on the phone?"

"I sort of met somebody since we had dinner," he said to me.

"Right."

"I'm really sorry, Jenny. I mean, I wanted to go out with you, but you were still all tied up with that Jerry Meredith guy. And then I met Carol and . . ."

"Hey, these things happen. Is it serious with you and Carol?"

"I don't know. Maybe. I think so."

"Well, look—if it doesn't work out, you know my number. Right?"

"Maybe we could meet for coffee someday and talk."

"Coffee would be fine."

"I'll call you soon," he said.

He never did though. In fact, I never talked to him again.

But that's the way it is with people in my life. They drift in and out like tourists at a seaside resort.

Sometimes I still think about them all. Jerry Meredith. Becky Bessard. Cheryl Wolcott. Andrew Cox.

And Elaine Rivera.

Especially Elaine Rivera.

Mostly it's late at night like this when I'm home alone, which seems to be happening more and more as I get older.

"Just you and me, kid," I said to Hobo, giving him a big hug.

I stood up, got myself a beer, and carried it over to the window. Below there were the sounds of traffic and people on the street. Looking north, I could see the Empire State Building and the rest of the lights of the city. New York, New York, it's a wonderful town. The Bronx is up, and Jenny is feeling down.

I held up my beer and made a lonely toast.

"Here's to you, Elaine. Wherever you are. I hope it's better there."

Funny how attached you can get to someone you don't know. I only met her that one time. But I know she's going to be a part of me forever.

Maybe if I'd done things differently, she'd still be alive today. But I went after the big story. I went after the glory. I went after that anchor job. And Elaine Rivera wound up dead.

On the other hand, if I'd done things differently, maybe Jerry Meredith would have gotten away with murder.

That's the trouble with life. It always seems to be an endless series of compromises. You win a few, you lose a few. And you just hope that you come out ahead in the end.

Me, I want to win them all. I want everything to be perfect. It never works out that way, but I'm still trying.

Like I say, I'm always reaching for those stars.

I thought about that. I thought about a lot of things as I watched the lights of Manhattan twinkle below. Then, one by one, the lights began going off as the city that never sleeps finally went to sleep.

So did I.

"Fast, funny, and first-rate!"
—Associated Press

DICK BELSKY MYSTERIES

FEATURING

JENNY McKAY

"A more streetwise version of television's Murphy Brown." —Booklist

Television reporter Jenny McKay is in search of a break, a boyfriend, and a reason to feel good about turning forty. The big-time sleaze and bad ratings of New York's WTBK aren't exactly what she's aspired to—but it's a living. And when celebrity-tracking turns to crime-solving, she uncovers the city's deadliest secrets.

__BROADCAST CLUES 0-515-11153-8/$4.50
(published in hardcover as *South Street Confidential*)
__LIVE FROM NEW YORK 0-515-11265-8/$4.50
__THE MOURNING SHOW 0-425-14246-9/$4.50

Payable in U.S. funds. No cash orders accepted. Postage & handling: $1.75 for one book, 75¢ for each additional. Maximum postage $5.50. Prices, postage and handling charges may change without notice. Visa, Amex, MasterCard call 1-800-788-6262, ext. 1, refer to ad # 490

| Or, check above books and send this order form to: The Berkley Publishing Group 390 Murray Hill Pkwy., Dept. B East Rutherford, NJ 07073 | Bill my: ☐ Visa ☐ MasterCard ☐ Amex
Card#_____ (expires)
_____ ($15 minimum)
Signature_____ |
| --- | --- |
| Please allow 6 weeks for delivery. | Or enclosed is my: ☐ check ☐ money order |
| Name_____ | Book Total $_____ |
| Address_____ | Postage & Handling $_____ |
| City_____ | Applicable Sales Tax $_____ (NY, NJ, PA, CA, GST Can.) |
| State/ZIP_____ | Total Amount Due $_____ |

INTRODUCING...
Exciting New Mysteries Every Month

__THYME OF DEATH
SUSAN WITTIG ALBERT
0-425-14098-9/$4.50
"A wonderful character... smart, real and totally a woman of the 90's"—Mostly Murder
China Bayles left her law practice to open an herb shop in Pecan Springs, Texas. But tensions run high in small towns, too—and the results can be murder.

__HANGING VALLEY
0-425-14196-9/$4.99
PETER ROBINSON
"Emotionally rich."—The New York Times Book Review
The sleepy village of Swainshead is shocked when a neighbor's body is found in the woods. The murderer's trail leads Inspector Banks to Toronto, where he must uncover secret passions and family rivalries to get to the bottom of it all.

__A SHARE IN DEATH
0-425-14197-7/$4.50
DEBORAH CROMBIE
"Charming!"—The New York Times Book Review
Scotland Yard's Detective Superintendent Duncan Kincaid's holiday goes down the drain when a body washes up in the whirlpool bath.

__HEADHUNT
0-425-14125-X/$4.50
CAROL BRENNAN
"Enjoyable!"—Drood Review of Mystery
Public relations ace Liz Wareham begins her day finding a top headhunter murdered. Liz may be an expert at making her clients look killer...but she has no experience looking for her client's killer!

Payable in U.S. funds. No cash orders accepted. Postage & handling: $1.75 for one book, 75¢ for each additional. Maximum postage $5.50. Prices, postage and handling charges may change without notice. Visa, Amex, MasterCard call 1-800-788-6262, ext. 1, refer to ad # 478

Or, check above books and send this order form to: The Berkley Publishing Group 390 Murray Hill Pkwy., Dept. B East Rutherford, NJ 07073	Bill my: ☐ Visa ☐ MasterCard ☐ Amex _____ (expires) Card#_____ ($15 minimum) Signature_____
Please allow 6 weeks for delivery.	Or enclosed is my: ☐ check ☐ money order
Name_____	Book Total $_____
Address_____	Postage & Handling $_____
City_____	Applicable Sales Tax $_____ (NY, NJ, PA, CA, GST Can.)
State/ZIP_____	Total Amount Due $_____